I0640236

SCARECROWS
APPALACHIAN TALES

STEVE RASNIC TEM

Copyright © 2024 by Steve Rasnic Tem
ISBN 978-1-63789-171-1
Macabre Ink is an imprint of Crossroad Press Publishing
All rights reserved. No part of this book may be used or reproduced in any manner
whatsoever without written permission except in the case of
brief quotations embodied in critical articles and reviews
For information address Crossroad Press at 141 Brayden Dr., Hertford, NC 27944
www.crossroadpress.com

Cover art by David Dodd

First Edition - 2024

S leek and dark as the forest night, the crow glided over the Appalachian ridges corrugating southwest Virginia. Wallens, Powell, Cumberland. Those were their human names, but for Old Crow they were Home.

He flew early each morning, before the mountain witch got up, because he didn't want to remind her he had the freedom of the skies, and she did not. She'd tried when she was younger, but on her best days her long skirts barely cleared the ground. Now she'd lost even that. She couldn't keep the right words straight in her mind.

During the first hour after sunrise, the crow chased a rabbit and tormented a stray kitten. He meant them no real harm, and after a few minutes tired of the play. Having lived too long, over a hundred years now, games quickly bored him, as did most everything else. He still felt grateful and loyal because of the witch's gift, but he couldn't remember the last time his long life gave him pleasure.

During the second hour he paid his respects at a crow funeral, of which he'd seen many during his time in the world. They'd gathered around the body and in the surrounding trees, hundreds of them, because it was late summer and more than the usual few families were on the move, to gaze at the broken fledgling on the path. According to rumor a farmer's hunting dog was the cause. The alarm over the danger went out hours ago. But now they watched without noise, and after the appropriate time departed in silence but for the sound of all those flapping wings.

Contents

The Cabinet Child 1

Smoke in a Bottle 9

Willie the Philologist 19

The Bible Salesman 26

Old Men on Porches 36

Nightcrawlers..46

Sundown in Duffield...48

Saved 62

Scarecrows 73

Miranda Jo's Girl..86

Mr. Belano's Visit...94

The Passing 101

La Mariée 109

The Grave House 118

Diorama..128

Deep Fracture 138

Almost a Legend 153

Cattiwampus 161

Bingo Thompson's Flying Cat......................................168

Crawldaddies 176

Lookie Loo 188

Powell Mountain Cedar Grove 196

Redbud Winter 199

Old Crow 211

A Jack Tale 221

The Return 227

The Cabinet Child

Around the beginning of the last century, in a small southwest Virginia town which no longer exists, a childless woman named Alma lived with her gentleman farmer husband in a large house on a ridge on the outskirts of this soon-to-be-forgotten town. The woman was not childless because of any medical condition—her husband simply felt that children were "ill-advised" in their circumstances, that there was no space for children in the twenty-or-so rooms of what he called their modest home.

Not being of a demonstrative inclination, his wife kept her disappointment largely to herself, but it could not have been more obvious if she had screamed it from their many-gabled roof. Sometimes, in fact, she muttered it in dialog with whoever should pass, and when no one was looking, she pretended to scream. Over the years despair worked its way into her eyes and drifted down into her cheeks, and the weight of her grief kept her bent and shuffling.

Although her husband Jacob was an insensitive man he was not inobservant. After enduring a number of years of his wife's sad display he apparently decided it gave an inappropriate impression of his household's tenor to the outside world and became determined to do something about it. He did not share his thinking with her directly, of course, but after an equal number of years enduring his maddening obstinacy his wife was well acquainted with his opinions and attitudes. Without so much as a knock he came into her bedroom one afternoon as she sat staring out her window and said, "I have decided you need something to cheer yourself up, my dear. John Hand will be bringing his wagon around soon and you may choose anything on it. Let us call it an early Christmas present, why don't we?"

She looked up at him curiously. After having prayed aloud for some sign of his attention, for so many nights, she could scarcely believe her ears. Was this some trick? As little as it was, still he had never offered her such a prize before. She thought at first that somehow he had hurt his face, then realized what she had taken for a wound was simply a strained and unaccustomed smile. He carried that awkward smile out the door with him, thank God. She did not think she could bear it if such a thing were running around loose in her private quarters.

John Hand was known throughout the region as a fine furniture craftsman who hauled his pieces around in a large gray wagon as roughly made as his furniture was exquisitely constructed. And yet this wagon had not fallen apart in over twenty years of travels up and down wild hollows and over worn mountain ridges with no paved roads. She had not perused his inventory herself, but people both in town and on the outlying farms claimed he carried goods to suit every taste and had a knack for finding the very thing that would please you, that is, if you had any capacity for being pleased at all, which some folk clearly did not.

Alma had twenty rooms full of furniture, the vast majority of it handed down from various branches of Jacob's family. Alma had never known her husband to be very close to his relations, but any time one of them died and there were goods to be divided he was one of the first to call with his respects. And although he was hardly liked by any of those grieving relatives he always seemed able to talk them into letting him leave with some item he did not rightly deserve.

Sometimes at night she would catch him with his new acquisitions, stroking and talking to them as if they had replaced the family he no longer much cared for. She could not understand what had come over her that she would have married such a greedy man.

Although she needed no furniture, without question Alma was sorely in need of being pleased, which was why she was at the front gate with an apron pocket full of Jacob's money the next time John Hand came trundling down the road in that horse-drawn wagon full of his wares.

Even though she waved almost frantically Hand did not appear to acknowledge her, but then stopped abruptly in front of their grand gate. She had seen him in town before but never paid him much attention. When Hand suddenly jumped down and stood peering up at her she was somewhat alarmed by the smallness of the man—he was thin as a pin and painfully bent, the top of his head not even reaching to her shoulders, and she was not a particularly tall woman. The wagon loomed like a great ocean liner behind him, and she could not imagine how this crooked little man had filled it with all this furniture, pieces so jammed together it looked like a puzzle successfully completed.

Then Mr. Hand turned his head rather sideways and presented her with a beatific smile, and completely charmed she felt prepared to go with anything the little man cared to suggest.

"A present from the husband, no?"

"Well, yes, he said I could choose anything."

"But not the present madam most wished for." He said it as if it were undeniable fact, and she did not correct him. Surely he had simply guessed, based on some clues in her appearance?

He gazed at her well past the point of discomfort, then clambered up the side of the wagon, monkey-like and with surprising speed. The next thing she knew he had landed in front of her, holding a small, polished wood cabinet supported by his disproportionately large palm and the cabinet's four unusually long and thin, spider-ish legs. "I must confess it has had a previous owner," he said with a mock sad expression. "She was like you, wanting a child so very much. This was to be in the nursery, to hold its dainty little clothes."

Alma was alarmed for a number of reasons, not the least of which that she'd never told the little man that she had wanted a child. Then she quickly realized what a hurtful insult this was on his part—to give someone never to have children a cabinet to hold its clothes? She turned and made for the gate, averting her head so the vicious little man would not see her streaming tears.

"Wait! Please," he said, and a certain softness in his voice stopped her more firmly than a hand on her shoulder ever could. She turned just as he shoved the small cabinet into her open arms. "You will not be—unfulfilled by this gift, I assure you." And with a quick turn he had leapt back onto the seat and the tired-looking horses were pulling him away. She stood awkwardly, unable to speak, the cabinet clutched to her breast like a stricken child.

In her bedroom she carried the beautifully-polished cabinet with the long, delicate legs to a shadowed corner away from the window, the door, and any other furniture. She did not understand this impulse exactly; she just felt the need to isolate the cabinet, to protect it from any other element in her previous life in this house. Because somehow she already knew that her life after the arrival of this delicate assemblage of different shades of wood would be a very different affair.

Once she had the cabinet positioned as seemed appropriate—based on some criteria whose source was completely mysterious to her—she sat on the edge of her bed and watched it until it was time to go downstairs and prepare dinner for her husband. Afterwards she came back and sat in the same position, gazing, singing softly to herself for two, three, four hours at least. Until the sounds in the rest of the house had faded. Until the soft amber glow of the new day appeared in one corner of her window. And until the stirrings inside the cabinet became loud enough for her to hear.

She came unsteadily to her feet and walked across the rug with her heart racing, blood rushing loudly into her ears. She held her breath, and when the small voice flowered on the other side of the shiny cabinet wall, she opened its tiny door.

Twenty years after his wife's death Jacob entered her bedroom for the third and final time. The first time had been the afternoon he had strode in to announce his well-meant but inadequate gift to her. The second time had been to find her lifeless body sprawled on the rug when she had failed to come down for supper. And now this third visit, for reasons he did not fully understand, except that he had been overcome with a terrible sadness and sense of dislocation these past few weeks, and this dusty bed chamber was the one place he knew he needed to be.

He would have come before—he would have come a thousand times before—if he had not been so afraid he could never make himself leave.

He had left the room exactly as it had been on Alma's last day: the covers pulled back neatly, as if she planned an early return to bed, a robe draped across the back of a cream-upholstered settee, a vanity table bare of cosmetics but displaying an antique brush and comb, a half-dozen leather-bound books on a shelf mounted on the wall by her window. In her closet he knew he would find no more than a few changes of clothes. He didn't bother to look because he knew they betrayed nothing of who she had been. She had lived in this room as he imagined nuns must live, their spare possessions a few bare strokes to portray who they had been.

It pained him that it was with her as it had been with everyone else in his life—some scattered sticks of furniture all he had left to remember them by—where they had sat, what they had touched, what they had held and cared for. He had always made sure that when some member of the family died he got something, any small thing, they had handled and loved, to take back here to watch and listen to. And yet none was haunted, not even by a whisper. He knew—he had watched and listened for those departed loved ones most of his adult life.

His family hadn't wanted him to marry her. No good can come, they said, of a union with one so strange. And though he had loved his family he had separated from them, aligning himself with her in this grand house away from the staring eyes of the town. It had not been a conventional marriage—she could not abide being touched and permitted him to see her only at certain times of the day, and even then he might not even be present as far as she was concerned, so intent was she on her conversation with the people and things he could not see.

His family virtually abandoned him over his choice, but as a grown man it was his choice to make. He was never sure if his beloved Alma had such choices. Alma had been driven, apparently, by whatever stray winds entered her brain.

The gift she had chosen in lieu of a child (for how could he give his child such a mother, or give his wife such a tender thing to care for?) still sat in its corner in shadow, appearing to lean his way on its insubstantial legs. He perceived a narrow crack in the front surface of the small cabinet, which drew him closer to inspect the damage, but it was only that the small door was ajar, inviting him to secure it further, or to peek inside.

Jacob led himself into the corner with his lantern held before him, and grasping the miniature knob with two trembling fingers pulled it away from the frame, and seeing that the door had a twin, unclasped the other side and spread both doors like wings that might fly away with this beautiful box. He stepped closer then, moving the light across the cabinet's interior like a blazing eye.

The inside was furnished like some doll's house, and it saddened him to see this late evidence of the state of Alma's thinking. Here and there were actual pieces of doll furniture, perhaps kept from her girlhood or "borrowed" from some neighbor child. Then there were pieces—a settee very like the one in this room, a high-backed Queen Anne chair—carved, apparently, from soap, now discolored and furred by years of clinging dust and lint.

Other furniture had been assembled from spools and emery boards, clothespins, a small jewelry box, then what appeared to be half a broken drinking cup cleverly upholstered with a woman's faded black evening glove.

He was surprised to find in one corner a small portrait of himself, finely painted in delicate strokes, and one of Alma set beside it. And underneath, in tiny, almost unreadable script, two words, which he was sure he could not read correctly, but which might have said "Father," "Mother."

He decided he had been hearing the breathing for some time—he just hadn't been sure of its nature, or its source. The past few years he had suffered from a series of respiratory ailments, and had become accustomed to hearing a soft, secondary wheeze, or leak, with each inhalation and exhalation of breath. That could easily have been the origin of the sounds he was hearing.

But he suspected not. With shaking hand he reached into the far corner of the box, where a variety of handkerchiefs and lacy napkins lay piled. He peeled them off slowly, until finally he reached that faint outline beneath a swatch of dress lace, a short thing curled onto itself, faintly moving with a labored rasp.

He could have stopped then, and thought he should, but his hand was moving again with so little direction, and just nudged that bit of cloth, which dropped down a bare quarter inch.

Nothing there, really, except the tiny eyes. Tissue worn to transparency, flesh vanished into the dusty air, and the child's breathing so slight, a parenthesis, a comma. Jacob stared down solemnly at this kind afterthought, shadow of a shadow, a ghost of a chance. Those eyes so innocent, and yet so old, and desperately tired, an intelligence with no reason to be. Dissolving. The weary breathing stopped.

In the family plot, what little family there might be, there by Alma's grave he erected a small stone: "C. Child" in bold but fine lettering. There he buried the cabinet and all it had contained, because what else had there been to bury? Two years later he joined them there, on the other side.

Smoke in a Bottle

Daddy had the five beer bottles, their labels peeled off, lined up on the shelf. Then he puffed and puffed on his cigarette, packing the smoke into his mouth, making his eyes go funny because that was part of the show. Moving fast he put his mouth over each bottle, filled it with smoke, capped it with an old bottle cap, and moved to the next. When he was done he had five bottles full of smoke.

He held each one in front of the fire, turning it so that the smoke flowed, curled inside, made patterns, made faces, weird shapes dancing. Then he'd flip off the cap and the smoke escaped as fast as anything, leaving behind a little stink, that was all.

"Smoke in a bottle, kids," he'd say. "That's all it is. Just like people."

Then he'd sway like a ruined house in a hurricane wind, and sometimes he'd stagger around the room. We knew Christmas was over when Dad fell into the Christmas tree.

So maybe Dad didn't fall into the Christmas tree every year. Maybe it was only seven or eight years out of ten. But fall he did, and although it made our mother every way of being angry and frustrated, it made us kids laugh every time, even when he broke something. He was a man of simple entertainments, using the things he always had with him—cigarettes and beer bottles mostly, and a damaged sense of balance—but his act always worked with us.

I hadn't been back in St. Charles in twenty years. Not because I hated it. When you live in a place as poor as that people think you must hate it and you can't wait to leave. I knew I was poor, but I didn't know I was that poor. I got fed and I lived in the prettiest, greenest place I've ever known—southwest Virginia. Did you know the early Indians called Lee County "Paradise"?

As my cheap rental car rounded the bend I thought the town was on fire. Gray clouds drifted along the road, piled up in front of the car, broke apart and ran away. I rolled my window down and realized it was just morning mist, but there was this sharp scent that burned the nose, like cigarette smoke.

I drove slowly into town. The road had been patched so much it looked like an asphalt quilt. I'd kept a picture of the town in my memory but from the looks of things big chunks were missing, buildings cut out, blown away, replaced by weeds, worn out trailers, and a few hollow stores leaning like dozing drunks. No signs of Christmas, no lights, no street decorations.

In the Forties and Fifties St. Charles had thousands of people, with restaurants and stores and even a small movie theater. The valley's narrow there, so they built everything down close to the highway. A concrete sidewalk on each side didn't leave much room for road. On Saturday nights the road shrank down to one lane and you could barely get through. You could hear the party all through the valley, or so Daddy used to tell us. By my time in the late Sixties St. Charles was falling asleep.

Daddy drank a lot and worked only occasionally. These days you'd call him an alcoholic. I didn't know that word when I was a kid.

I knew there was still a lot good about the town, but it's not the kind of place you come back to. No jobs to speak of since the mines shut down. And part of getting older is looking back and understanding how much you didn't have.

The first Christmas I remember from elementary school we had to draw names and get a present for one of our classmates. The night before the party our mother sat the three of us down and handed us each a pack of chewing gum and helped us wrap them up fancy in a cloth package with dress ribbon and a quilting square. She showed us how to hold the scissors and where to cut the cloth and how to split and fold the ribbon until at the end we had three unique flowers attached to these beautiful little packages.

Because the girl I gave the gum to had been brought up right, she made herself smile when she thanked me politely. But I knew exactly what disappointment looked like. At the end of the day I saw her talking to her mom and showing the gum. Her mom looked at me then, not in a mean way but like she was measuring me for a suit. That was the first time I ever felt really poor.

Dad died from lung disease shortly after my freshman year in college and I went home for his funeral, then I came back again for my sister's wedding. And this last time for my mother's funeral while I was going through a divorce. That good woman never even met my kids. Three times in all those years. I'm not proud of that.

The house had been sold to an investor. When my brother and sister asked me if I could clean it out, I agreed, even though that was the last thing I wanted to do for Christmas. It was the least I could do. I wasn't going to see my kids until after the holiday anyway. You could say a lot bad about my dad, but at least he was there every Christmas.

Our old house had lost most of its yard and the sheltering trees, and a tangle of weeds and rusted metal hugged the foundation. I parked where my mother's flower beds used to be. Inside, the light was yellow from weak lamps and sun burning through brittle shades, furry dust over everything, as if some of that amber light had disintegrated into a thick layer of brown. I felt like holding my breath—it was like trying to breathe inside a grave. I wondered if this was anything like what my dad experienced all those years ago while his lungs were failing.

In one room I counted six cheap headboards, nine sets of bed-springs, a box full of wheels, two rotting pillows jammed into the corner, a dark, viscous stain on the top one. All would go in the trash.

The smallest bedroom was empty, except for some mud and grease on the floor. This had been Ann's. She was the youngest and always had the smallest room. My bedroom was a long, narrow room along the back of the house, like a closet. It still had a tiny little bookcase. I couldn't really find myself in that room, but I did remember that bookcase. It had never held more than a few books. One Christmas my mother gave me two—*The Adventures of Robin Hood* and *The Legends of King Arthur*. She couldn't have paid much, but she'd been so happy to give them to me. I'd read them over and over until they fell apart.

My brother's room was just an empty box. Mom and Daddy's room was on the other side of the house. This was where my mother died. It still had her bed, her dresser, her night table, a picture of an Indian in a canoe on the wall. It still looked like a real room, like she'd just stepped out to pick flowers for the dinner table.

I smelled cigarette smoke. I looked around and saw the brown silhouette on the shade, the figure outside swaying, probably drunk, struggling to hold onto his cigarette. By the time I got outside he was gone.

I looked across the yard at my neighbor's house: a man standing on the porch, smoking.

"Can I help you?" I could hear my voice shaking.

"Don't need no help."

"Were you just in my yard?"

"Nosir. Is that your yard?"

"My mother lived here."

"Hey! Hey, Willie? Is that you?"

I grabbed some chairs, and my old friend Eddie and I sat in the empty living room, mostly just staring at each other. We'd both changed a lot, Eddie more visibly. He weighed about half what he once had, and he had tattoos, and about half a goatee, as if something had eaten the right side of it. Eddie finally broke the silence with "So, you got any beers?"

I carried the six pack in from the car. I gave him the whole thing.

"You're not drinking?"

"Not tonight," I said. Actually I almost never drink. I had no idea why I'd bought the beer. "Just give me the empties."

He stared at the bottles dubiously. "What? They collectible?"

"No. I just thought I'd put them on that shelf over the fireplace, like Dad used to."

He squinted at the thin piece of wood. "I remember that. Hope they don't fall off—looks a little crooked." He started on the first one, then stopped, raising it in my direction. "Merry

Christmas." He drank a few swallows, then said, "Your dad fell into the Christmas tree one year, didn't he?"

"Six or seven years, actually."

"Yeah. I remember laughing about it. There were some years I wish my family had had something like that to laugh about. But six or seven times? Even if you're drinking heavy, that's kind of, unusual."

We didn't talk much after that—just the occasional burst of words, with long periods of silence in between. I didn't mind— that was what a conversation was in St. Charles. He'd tell me something about his life now, and he'd tell me about some classmate or other, who had died, divorced, or disappeared from that part of the country, never to be seen again. Periodically he'd hand me an empty beer bottle and I'd scrape the label off and balance it on the shelf.

As the night wore on I moved the old lamps from my mother's room in for more light, but the best I could accomplish was a few bright patches of brilliance and a great deal of dirty shadow that seemed to float along the walls and over the ceiling, making the house appear to sway, as if I were the one drinking. Eddie, on the other hand, seemed like the sober one, talking more as the hours passed of people and events I'd largely forgotten.

"You remember Jack Gilford, don't you?"

"Sure. Is he dead, too?"

"No, but he oughta be," Eddie said, giggling. "A mite cold in here, don't you think? Why don't you start something in that fireplace?"

I was surprised to find about an inch of snow on the ground. You got snow, you're a rich man, was something Daddy used to say. I'd understood that even as a kid. Snow was good for covering up shabbiness, and ugliness, and essentials missing. It even had a way of transforming those things into something quaint, suitable for a picture postcard.

I looked across the valley at the pinpricks of light floating down like slow-falling stars, and the steam from chimneys floating up, columns like vague figures standing on rooftops, watching. I couldn't see the main road from our old house, but I could hear the busy traffic and all those people.

I stopped moving. What was I thinking? Those noises were from another time, and I couldn't be hearing them now. It had to be some distortion in the air that had caused the effect, some echo off the stripped-to-rock hills. I heard coughing, a drawn-out wheeze. I went to the edge of the window and peeked inside. Eddie was peacefully drinking, head tilted back and lips around the bottle's mouth. And I heard the wheeze again, followed by the bone-rattling cough. I looked around. A few yards away a man stood with his back to me, wearing nothing out there in the cold but a T-shirt and boxer shorts. He coughed again, his whole body shaking, hunched shoulders seeming to broaden, as if in advance of some transformation. I ran a couple of feet to the wall and grabbed some wood stacked there, ran inside without looking back. I bumped against the wall in my haste and one of the beer bottles tumbled to the floor in an explosion of glass. "Sorry," I said.

"No biggie, bro. I'll have a replacement for you in just a sec."

I said nothing to Eddie about what I had seen and heard. I built a fire—it was a little smoky, there was probably debris blocking part of the chimney. But we tolerated it, even though it made us cry a little. After Eddie left there were scattered voices in the smoke, but I learned to tolerate them as well.

Early next morning Eddie showed up with a serious face, dragging a small white pine nailed to a crude base of crossed scrap wood. "Christmas Eve, Willie. I reckon you need a tree."

He grinned then, and in the burning glare off the snow I saw that he had numerous missing teeth. "Don't worry—I didn't steal it. It was in my back yard."

Eddie left to spend the next several days with family in Tennessee. I dragged the tree in and put it in the corner of the living room, sat down in a chair and spent some time staring at it. It leaned quite a bit, but still managed to stay up. I decided then to find something to put on it—I knew I'd feel even worse about the day if I left it bare.

I hadn't been down in the cellar since we found that rat the size of a beaver when I was nine years old. The rats used to scrabble out of the abandoned mines and sneak into town. About the only way to get rid of them was a shotgun. But that's where my mother always kept the tree decorations, and anything else she didn't want us kids to mess with.

The light fixture still worked, but it was like a candle at the opening of a mine. Inside it smelled like rotting vegetables and spoiled meat. The invisible walls were lined with mason jars whose dark contents absorbed just enough light to make me avoid them. I found the damp cardboard box with the decorations halfway in, pulling it close even as something scurried out of it. To my credit I didn't drop the box, but hurried upstairs and shoved it by the tree.

After a couple of years of Dad wiping out the Christmas tree, my mother had put her favorite decorations on the shelf by the beer bottles rather than risk them. There the glass angel and the ceramic deer and the little Santa Claus had had a perfect view of Dad's mysterious smoking bottles. I didn't need to be so cautious, and nestled them right into the front branches where I could see them. None of the colored lights lit reliably so I didn't bother with them. But I did discover that lighting a fire in the fireplace created interesting reflections in the shiny colored balls and fragments of icicle I scraped out of the bottom of the box. Shards of rainbow swam in the walls as an untraceable draft lightly stirred the branches. I wished my kids could see it.

I wasn't even sure what we'd gotten the kids for Christmas that year. Since they were all going to be at her parents' house she'd handled everything, and I hadn't even asked.

This tree had no presents under it, but there had never been many presents under the tree in this house.

I must have dozed off, and when I woke up I was sure I'd caught the house on fire—I smelled burning—wood and plastic, paper and cloth, a world of things turned to smoke and drifting into my nose and mouth. I gaped at the fireplace, my eyes blurry.

On the shelf smoke boiled in and out of the remaining bottles. I walked over for a better view: although smoke carved the air in all five, in the two on the end it swirled into miniature, fiery galaxies before floating up the necks and out into the room where they joined the shadows flowing across the ceiling.

I could hear a soft wheeze behind me but I could not bring myself to turn around. Instead I walked into my mother's old bedroom and went to sleep on her oval rug.

I found the Christmas tree lying on the floor the next morning, a great dent on the ceiling-facing side, branches pushed aside and broken as if from a great weight.

It's funny how sometimes you have all the evidence right in front of you, but yet it takes you years to give it the proper importance. A man doesn't accidentally fall into a Christmas tree seven out of ten years even if he is a drunk. And his wife doesn't just put up with that kind of behavior. It had all been an act for the benefit of my brother, my sister, and me. I remembered how in those years when we kids got practically nothing on Christmas morning Dad always told his best stories and did his best tricks to entertain us, to distract us. And we couldn't help but laugh when he swayed and stumbled and fell into that poor, blameless tree.

There on the shelf were the glass angel and the ceramic deer and the little Santa Claus, safe as houses.

Christmas was over. I spent the day cleaning and throwing the remaining pieces of that old life away (save three ornaments). The next day I would drive to the coast to see my kids.

Willie the Philologist

Words never came easily for Willie the child, named William then on his records, or Bill to teacher and the rest of that old town of Norton, first official city in southwest Virginia, named after the president of the Louisville and Nashville Railroad. "Willie" came much later, in that long, inarticulate tumble of years toward the end: a name he didn't care for, an insult, which stuck so easily to the lips of the town. But the words, they were hard-won, and prized. When he finally caught one he held onto it, squeezed it as if his life depended on it, until all its juice was gone. Then he saved the empties as if he might turn them in someday for pocket change.

Bill's passion lay undiscovered and unrecognized, except by his grandfather, who didn't care that Bill was shy, or verging on the slow, with hands and feet a disappointment to his brain. He only cared that it caused him pain.

"Fill your wagon full of words," his grandfather would say, "and drag that wagon with you on your journeys. When you need a proper word, you'll find you have just the one."

Bill knew his grandfather didn't mean a real wagon, but the old man loved to explain.

"I speak in metaphor, of course. Metaphors are strong language, stronger than curses, Bill, carrying as they do their own meaning as well as that of another. You understand that, don't you? About metaphor?"

Bill had been slow to nod. Although he usually managed to catch most of the words thrown at him, it was always a struggle pushing them out to his tongue. "Pa told me, yesterday? He said grab the bull? By the horns?"

"Good boy! You're a regular philologist, Billy!"

Bill blinked slowly. Twice. He'd never heard such a word. His tongue wrestled with it in silence. His panicked brain told him to spit it out—as beautiful as it was, he might choke.

"That means you're a lover of words, Bill! A bona fide lexical romancer!"

Bill smiled. His mother had always said it didn't really matter what Bill couldn't do—the most important thing was to love something. She told him, "That's the one true thing separating us from the lower animals."

Bill wasn't sure which animals were the lower ones. But sometimes she called them "beasts," like in that story she loved about Beauty and the Beast. That was one of the best things about words—they let you love them. You could still love them, even when you didn't understand them. People ought to be like that with each other, but too often were not.

"Metaphor, Bill!" And Bill blinked again, trying to concentrate on the wagons full of words tumbling out of his grandfather's mouth. "About what your father said. Because, you know, there really isn't a bull."

Bill nodded. "No bull. No horns. Nothing I can grab on to."

"Exactly."

"Pa got so, excited. When he talked, about the bull horn. It was important for me to understand! Like he wanted-he could make a pretty song! Blowing on that horn! He was enthuse … elastic."

"Enthusiastic."

Bill nodded. "It was like, his arms stretched out, and his hands got all, wobbly, and his eyes got so big. He was all, bent, out of shape."

His grandfather looked sad. "He just wants you to do well."

"I'm okay," Bill said. "I was never sick, except the one time."

When his grandfather died, his mother and his father told him he could have anything he wanted out of the old house up on the ridge. Bill knew what he wanted, but gave up trying to put the words together in the right order so that they could understand. He wandered around his grandfather's house for days, just like he was sightseeing, taste-tasting, smell-smelling, searching until he found it: a wagon that once was red but now was brown, with a bent axle and a bent handle.

When Bill was little, sometimes his father would say, "You don't stop that, I'm going to fix your wagon, young man." The memory made him smile so big, like his teeth grew until you couldn't see his lips anymore. His father had said he would fix his wagon, when it was his grandfather who had the wagon in need of fixing.

But he was glad his father never fixed this wagon. When Bill dragged it around the block like a flat dog on a leash it made a sound like a sad flute-player who loves a woman so much but he can't find the right words. The wagon never traveled straight down the sidewalk, but wandered side to side smelling the grass.

A great wagon like that needed important things to carry so Bill took some of his grandfather's biggest books with hides thick and tough from crawling back and forth across that oak desk.

His father couldn't stop saying why. "Why, Bill, you can't even read those books. Why do you want them? Why, you have no clue what they're saying."

He wanted to tell his father he understood that was just metaphor. The books weren't saying anything, they were just lying now in his wagon asleep, dreaming their own dreams of being carried around fancy libraries in the arms of smiling lady librarians.

And maybe true Bill had no clue but those tough old books had big bellies full of words. He loved each word for itself and didn't care what it said. He didn't say much either but that didn't mean … just because he didn't say much didn't mean people didn't have to listen!

Bill was no good at stringing the words together, "making a sentence," which, as his grandfather explained, was like being a painter, or a sculptor. But sentences also made Bill think of judges—they made sentences, too, didn't they? Sentences could be sad stories that told you something nice or important happened, and then ended, period. Not being able to make sentences did give him time to admire the different words— they had their own lives, and a music, and a history, even if they weren't connected.

Now sixty years later and the few calling him by name call him Willie, but his Brown Bomber wagon is still that same vehicle of dreams. Its voice is rustier but so is his. It still carries those same big books plus a few passengers: a restaurant menu from where his Pa took him on his birthday the month before he died, a Christmas card with nine rhymes for "day" saved from a trash can, a newspaper telling a lie about someone he used to know, with eight ads for furniture stores, two of them Everything Must Go sales, and a clipped-out magazine story about an actress who died too young. It seemed like actresses were always dying too young and Willie had saved the story of the one to honor them all. A small box in one corner of the wagon holds everything else he owns: changes of socks and underwear, nice pants, toothbrush and soap, cup and plate, knife and spoon, assorted stale bites of food.

Still following his grandfather's words, Willie drags this wagon behind him everywhere he goes, but mainly up and down Park Avenue, Route 58, from the Dairy Queen to the steakhouse and back. Norton is a small place, or so everybody tells him, but it doesn't feel so small when you're on foot dragging your whole life. He has a sister in Atlanta, and visited her once, where the people live in houses folded over the top of each other, and the land's shrunk up to gardens and medians and yards. Here they've let the town relax out a little in a wide place in the road, but the mountains on each side show who's boss. It's a fine place to pull a wagon, and no one bothers him — he's never had one book stole. Over the years he has managed to learn to read a little, very little, but he is thankful for even that. He loves just saying the words.

He knows he isn't much more than a bump on the sometimes smiling, sometimes crying face of the earth, and not even as important as the words he loves. Still, he won't allow meanness to go unanswered. He knows what rude means, and he never lets it pass without repeating his grandfather's most important advice, "You can't tell a book, Bill, by its cover."

These days he has books to sell, assorted volumes from different sets of encyclopedias he's been letting go a dollar apiece. Mostly they go to teenagers who want to use the pictures, or need to write a quick report, and can't get to the computer up at the library. But last week a fine-looking lady bought the J volume, because she liked junipers, and jellyfish, and agreed with Willie that Jupiter was the most interesting planet by far.

When people point out that the encyclopedias are old, and out of date, and can't be of much use in the time of the internet, Willie just tells them how those books hold the history of what our best minds thought, even though they might have got it just a bit wrong, and what a great thing it was, what a marvelous thing, that the thinking of all those historians, all those scientists and philosophers, those philologists, could wind up in a rusty old wagon in the little city of Norton.

Sometimes Willie likes to think of himself as a single word, his favorite being gregarious—he learned it back when he was still Bill. His grandfather told him it meant he was still one of the flock. He thought it sounded like he was happy about it, too.

Rue was always another word that said loud and clear things he felt every day, sounding like something to eat, whether you wanted to or not, something you could fill your wagon with, a spoon full of sorrow, a cup of remorse, bowls overflowing with regret.

He also likes slapstick, and pell-mell, because of their sound. He isn't sure if he understands what either of them means, but he's pretty sure it's the same gang involved.

Most words are like that for Willie: he repeats them over and over for a time, but then their meanings always creep away, as if ashamed of themselves, and all he has left are their carcasses. But like most people, he thinks, it is hard for him to let go of dead things, and in his old age he sings their names aloud over and over in the town with no understanding: inculcate, belated, ex cathedra, down one street, then Parthian, capitulate, cajole down another, the people staring at him, or walking the other way, some of them laughing, with their own absence of understanding. They can't see that he just loves the words, and with his head back, mouth open, eyes streaming, singing, he has only followed his grandfather's advice, and hitched his wagon to a star.

The Bible Salesman

Jimmy bragged he saw the little brown man first. But Sam was looking out the living room window when the fellow showed up at the end of their road, dressed in gray slacks, a short-sleeved white shirt, striped tie, and carrying a shiny leather suitcase. Everything about him said he weren't local, though he did look like one of them Collinses up on the ridge, the ones Daddy said had Indian blood.

When the man got to their front porch he stopped and stared a minute, like maybe he didn't want to knock on their door after all. Their steps needed painting. Sam knew how wobbly them steps were, chipped and crooked and some of the naked gray wood showing through. The whole house needed painting, and Daddy said he would do the damn painting when he had time and not before. They weren't to bring it up again, and they didn't, not after Mama said it made them look poor and careless and she got slapped for it.

It was hotter than a blister bug, but the little man looked cool as could be, even wearing that tie. He didn't have a car, or maybe he parked it somewhere else. If not, how did he get to their town? Thinking about it hurt Sam's head. He held his breath. Something different was happening. Maybe he'd learn something new today.

Jimmy was getting excited. "Molly, come look at this little feller! I seen him first!" It wasn't worth arguing over. Jimmy made a big deal out of most everything. Now that the man was standing on the porch Sam could see he weren't that small, just short, and Sam knew a lot of short men. Grandpa Taylor, for one. Maybe this fellow was as nice as Grandpa.

The man was knocking on the door now. It made a rattly sound because their door was loose on its hinges and like most of their house not quality. Mama came running in from the kitchen with Molly close behind. Molly hid behind Mama whenever company came.

"It's a brown man, Mama," Jimmy said. "I reckon he's an A-rab. He's knocking on the door. What you think he wants?"

"Now how would I know, Child? Shoot. Shoot! Do you think he saw our ditch?" She didn't mean shoot, but Mama never cursed. The ditch was what she decided to focus on of all things. Mama was embarrassed about their ditch. It was full of tall weeds and sometimes it got standing water after a rain and then it stank like a sewer which it wasn't. Unlike the people up on the ridge they were lucky enough to have a septic. "Has it been smelly today? Oh, shoot."

"No, Mama. It's good today," Jimmy replied, but they'd been watching cartoons all day and hadn't been outside.

Another couple of knocks and more rattling while Mama patted her hair and smoothed her dress. She opened the door. "Hello," she said with her sweet company voice. "May I help you?"

Sam and Jimmy stayed on the couch while Mama talked to the man. Sam could hardly contain himself; he wanted a good look at this person so bad, but when push came to shove, he was shy around strangers. They all were. From the couch Sam could see Molly peeking out from behind Mama's dress and smiling up at the man.

"I'm terribly sorry to interrupt your day, Madam, but do you believe in the bible?" He had a nice voice, and some kind of accent. Soft and musical.

"Why of course I do! You won't find anyone around here who don't."

"You are all good people, I know. You and your neighbors love the bible, cherish the word of God, and understand the value of his teachings as laid out in the good book, a bible your family has passed down for generations, a valued family heirloom. Do you own such a bible?"

"Well, I'm afraid not. My daddy's bible, he had one like that, but my eldest sister took it with her after he died. That was years ago, and I haven't laid eyes on it since."

"I am so sorry to hear that. Right here in this case I have such a bible, Madam. A brand-new edition, and I would venture one of the finest specimens of biblical artisanship you will ever see. May I come in and show it to you? I would love to share this beautiful object with your family, and all I ask in return is a few minutes of your valuable time."

He was a salesman, and like most salesmen Sam had ever heard he spoke well, better than any of the teachers at school. Sam remembered the encyclopedia guy from last year, and he used beautiful words too, spun out of his mouth like cotton candy at the county fair. Sam had so wanted the encyclopedia, and the set of children's classics that came with it—maybe those more than the encyclopedia—but of course they couldn't afford it. Folks like them didn't have things like that in their houses.

Mama laughed that scared laugh she had when she was worried or embarrassed or ashamed or afraid. Sam hated hearing that laugh. "Well, it's time for me to start supper. It needs to be ready by the time my husband gets home." She stopped, and Sam could feel himself getting scared, too, and angry that he was scared. Send him packing Mama. He didn't say it, but he thought it hard. "But I suppose I could at least look at what you have. Just for a minute. Please come in."

As much as Sam wanted to see the man and hear him talk some more in that nice voice he knew no good could come from inviting him in. He didn't understand why Mama didn't know that by now.

Mama stepped back, Molly still clinging to her dress. The salesman stepped in quickly, like maybe he was afraid she'd change her mind.

"I'm sorry things are such a mess. I haven't cleaned." Sam snickered, because she'd cleaned house that very morning.

"You have a lovely home, lovely home," the man said. Sam didn't know what the fellow was used to, but he could tell from the man's face he was being polite. The salesman's eyes were big and chocolatey. They glanced at the dirty walls and the ragged furniture before taking in Sam and Jimmy on the couch. "Hello young gentlemen." Jimmy brayed like a donkey.

"Clear off the couch, boys. Let this nice man sit."

Sam and Jimmy scrambled off the worn cushions and stood to the side. When the salesman passed Sam was impressed by how good he smelled, like all the spices in Mama's spice rack mixed together.

Molly surprised them all by plopping herself down on the couch right beside the man, a grin splitting her face in two.

"Look she's in love," Jimmy said, chuckling. Sam punched him on the shoulder. They tussled a few seconds then squeezed into the old rocker together, each struggling for more space. Sam didn't like doing that in front of company, but he couldn't help himself. Mama sat in Daddy's chair across the coffee table from the couch. She put her hands on her knees and leaned forward.

"Thank you for letting me share this with you," the brown man said, opening the case and lifting out a silky red bag with golden tassels. He set the bag on the coffee table and slipped on a pair of skinny white gloves. Sam couldn't help but smile because the salesman's hands were small, and the gloves looked like the kind ladies wear. He lifted the heavy bible out of the bag, spreading out the bag to protect the bible from the crappy coffee table.

Sam didn't have much interest in bibles, but it was the most beautiful book he'd ever seen. White leather with a fancy HOLY BIBLE in gold letters pressed into the cover, and more gold on the edges of the pages. Red and blue jewels were laid into the H of Holy and the first B of Bible. It looked like the book cover version of one of Elvis's fancy concert jackets.

"My my that is so pretty," Mana said.

"The inside is even more breathtaking," the salesman replied. "Not just the words, but the care with which they are laid out and printed. And the ornamentation is exquisite." Sam didn't exactly understand what the man was saying but he liked the way he was saying it.

The salesman lifted the cover and the bible fell open to a gold ribbon about halfway through the book. He turned the pages like this maybe was the very first bible and worth a fortune. On some pages the first letter on the page was bigger than the others and colored bright red as if it had been painted by hand. There were "color plates" at the start of every book of the bible, with illustrations of all those pretty people who lived back then, one each for the books of Samuel and Kings and Acts and Luke and John and all them others Sam remembered from vacation bible school.

"Did your family bible have a place for entering your family history, births, marriages, deaths, all that?"

"Why it did," Mama said. "Daddy had all kinds of things stuffed into that bible. Maybe that was why it was falling apart. Hair braids and leaves and pressed flowers and photos and some letters my grandaddy sent Grandma during the war. It was a bible and a scrapbook."

"At the back of this volume there is a convenient place for all that, including a static-free folder for important papers and photos. All the important records a family wants to preserve. Every family should have one, wouldn't you agree?"

"Well, yes." Mama let go of another strained laugh. "If they can afford it."

Jimmy interrupted. "Are you from Arabia? Like where Aladdin comes from?" Sam felt his face burn red.

"Jimmy!" Mama yelled. "Oh, I'm so sorry."

The salesman looked surprised, then smiled. Made himself smile, Sam thought. "That's fine. The young man is curious. I grew up in New York state. But my parents are from Pakistan. Have you heard of it?" Jimmy shook his head.

"It's a country. In the … East Asia," Sam said. "I don't remember where exactly."

"Very good. My parents came to this country a long time ago. Maybe one day one of you children may want to visit."

Sam saw Jimmy nod. It was crazy. Might as well say some day they might visit the moon.

"I really must get supper going," Mama said in her scared voice. "A bible like this. It must cost a fortune."

The salesman smiled. He looked like he'd never been afraid of anything his whole life. "My company does payments. We do this so Christians of modest means can afford something so important to your family. Four easy payments of fifty dollars each. If you give me a check for fifty dollars today we will have your bible shipped to you in two weeks."

"Why that's, that's …"

"Two hundred dollars total, but the shipping is free."

Sam looked at his mother. Don't, he said hard in his head. Just don't.

"I know that's reasonable for a bible this beautiful."

"A beautiful bible with beautiful words, full of moral knowledge and the answers for every difficult life situation. Grief, marital discord, illness, spiritual doubt. All the answers are there. Not just for you, but for your children and your children's children. A legacy of holy wisdom for generations. And if you order today, my company will emboss your family's name on the cover. In gold."

"Gold," Mama repeated.

"Your family name. A unique *objet d'art*. Only fifty dollars and you will have it in less than a month."

Sam was thinking harder now. Fifty times four, Mama. Two hundred dollars. What's Daddy going to do to you if you spend two hundred dollars? But still, he loved the way this man talked.

Mama was already pulling the checkbook out of her purse. She filled out the check so slowly Sam thought he was going to scream, but it really only took a few minutes, and the salesman was taking the check and putting the receipt down on the coffee table along with the bright four-color brochure they could look at until their fancy bible arrived.

He was fitting the bible back into its red bag and slipping off the gloves when they heard the car pull into the gravel drive behind the house.

"Oh lord that's my husband!" Mama said. "You have to get out of here!"

Hearing his mother's voice like that made Sam want to throw up. He jumped out of the chair and looked through the dining room and out the kitchen door to the porch and the screen door where he could see the bright blue of Daddy's patrol car and the red taillights blinking off.

"I don't un—understand," the little brown man said, but he was already standing, fumbling with the red bag and getting it back into the suitcase.

"Please! My husband can't see you here. He gets so mad." Mama's cheeks were red and her forehead white as a dead fish belly. Sam thought she was going to pass out. Molly was bawling and even Jimmy looked scared.

"Mister, you gotta get out of here!"

He staggered off the couch, juggling the suitcase with both hands. Jimmy opened the door before the poor fellow could crash into it. Then he was out on the porch and stumbling onto the steps. There was a loud crack and the bible salesman made a terrified cry as the first step splintered. He tumbled onto the patch of dirt they called a yard, the case buckling under him.

Sam and Jimmy watched as he struggled to his feet, one pants leg stained and the other split to the knee. He scooped up the parts of the case, clutching them to his chest as he limped into the road.

"Shut the door!" Mama yelled behind them. They did as they were told and ran over to the couch and slid in next to Molly, who was still sobbing uncontrollably.

Daddy came in carrying his leather uniform jacket over his shoulder. He wrapped it across the back of a dining room chair and dropped his Smokey the Bear hat on the table. It was the kind state troopers wore but the sheriff allowed his deputies to have them if that's what they wanted. Where the hat covered his head was pale as Mama's face right then, but everywhere else his face was raw and red. Daddy always looked angry as hell even in his sleep.

The lower back of Daddy's uniform shirt and under the arms were soaking wet. He stared at them all sitting there not saying nothing. He didn't say a word either. Sam knew somebody had to say something, but he wasn't about to be the first one.

"What did you boys do to your sister?"

Sam looked at Molly who had her eyes closed, still red-faced, still crying.

Jimmy started crying too. "We didn't do anything! Tell him Mama, we didn't do anything bad."

Daddy stepped forward and Sam pressed himself into the back of the couch. "What's this?" Daddy reached down and snatched the receipt and the brochure. He turned to Mama. "What did you do, Janet?"

"Frank, it's a bible. Look at the pictures. See how beautiful it is. Every family needs a bible, and you know my sister took the one Papa …"

Daddy walked to the front door and jerked it open. He looked down the road. "Hey you! Little fucker! Come back here!" He turned around and pounded through the house and jumped into his patrol car. A second later they heard it rumbling around the side of the house.

Jimmy and Sam went out on the porch and watched as their father drove down the street, siren on and lights flashing, tires spitting gravel. The little brown man hadn't gotten far. Daddy pulled his patrol car crossways over the road in front of him, slammed on the brakes, and jumped out.

"You boys come back inside!" Mama shouted, but Sam and Jimmy weren't about to turn away. Sam couldn't hear what was being said, but he saw the man drop the case and stretch out his arms and hands like he was trying to push whatever was about to happen away. Daddy had his right hand resting on top of his gun holster.

Sam closed his eyes. He knew Daddy had killed people. It was something else they weren't allowed to talk about, but Sam knew it had happened and more than once.

He waited for something terrible. But when he opened his eyes he saw the little man with his knees in the gravel, his head bowed, trying to hand Daddy a piece of paper. Even this far away Sam could see how much the little man shook.

Daddy grabbed the check out of the fellow's hand, spit on the road, got back into his car, and headed back toward the house.

Jimmy went inside, but Sam stayed there watching. He watched the fellow pick up his broken case and dust himself off, tuck his shirt back in, and limp toward the end of the street. Even after Sam couldn't see the salesman no more, he kept watching.

So, something different happened that day. Something new, but maybe not so new. Maybe not so big even. Sam would never forget how that fellow changed from being one person, with the lovely voice and them nice clothes, and then became another, out there on the road, scared shitless, begging for his life in front of that big, tall man. It hurt Sam so much to see. He knew he needed to learn something from that day, something more than how ashamed he was of all of them, including himself for being there and seeing. But he didn't know what it would be.

Old Men on Porches

She remembered riding around Mooney Holler in Daddy's clanky pickup, tires dropping into ruts shaking her bones, Daddy's singing making her giggle, even back before she understood the words. For the longest time she was too short to see out the windows, except for the gray wood shacks up on both sides of the road, where skinny old men peered down from their porches and waved.

It seemed like evening crept down into the holler before anyplace else in the world. Then she couldn't wait to get home. Even Daddy grew quiet when the trees started losing color and the shadows seeped and spread. There weren't no street lights back in the holler, and it would be awful easy to lose yourself, or get found by something you didn't want.

Around the dinner table Claire had asked the question she'd been chewing on for weeks. "Daddy, whose them old men up on them porches? They're just about everwhere, ain't they? They wave to us ever time we pass. Do they know you? Do they know me? Are they like the fairies?"

Billy laughed until the mashed taters fell out of his mouth. Momma shushed him.

"Retired miners, Honey," Daddy said. "Most of the men up in the holler these days is miners and the sons of miners. They wave 'cause everbody up here's friendly, or mostly. We know most of 'em. The old ones sit out where they can breathe better, because it's like to wear your lungs out breathing in them mines."

"I thought they was fairies, Pa," Billy laughed until Momma slapped his arm.

"Well, I don't know if they is or they ain't," Daddy said. "I'm no expert in fairies. But if you ever have yourself some trouble, and Momma and I ain't around, you can go to one of them old men. They'll help you out I reckon, day or night."

All that was a couple of lifetimes ago, and Claire's daddy was long gone with the miner's asthma. Before he passed he became one of those old men waving from their porches, coughing and struggling to breathe. Billy was gone too, killed over in Vietnam. The grieving had looked like it might take Momma as well. Claire sat with her in the back room for days, feeling guilty that she never got over being mad at Billy, because he was always doing things to aggravate her up until the day he enlisted.

But now Momma was dying for real, and as Claire sat with her in a hospital room down in Big Stone, she kept thinking about what a fine thing it had been for her daddy to tell her about those old men.

Of course Daddy eventually wore out the story like he wore out most things, and Momma got fed up one night. "Those old fools wave at everbody what come by, friend or stranger. If the Russians was to march up this holler those old men would just be grinnin' and a wavin' them on!"

Imagining the Russians messing with a place like Mooney Holler had made teenaged Claire laugh. Later, she was sorry about the laughter, because Daddy never talked about those old men ever again.

Momma had been murmuring from the bed nonstop most of the day. "There was Stonega, and Kimmerjim. Always liked that name, like in a fairytale, but it weren't no fairytale working there. Nosir. All the mines he worked, it were a hard life. And I weren't always good enough to him, sometimes I made him wrong depending on how I got up that morning. But we had us three stillborn right out the gate, so I just knowed I'd be an old woman with no children to watch over her." Claire had seldom visited the past few years, and now she was hearing things she was never meant to hear. She'd never heard of her stillborn siblings before. "Then we was blessed with our Billy. But he died. Never came back from that awful place, and Claire, a tiny thing, but how she loved her Boo-Daddy. Boo-Daddy this and Boo-Daddy that, following him all over that ridge 'til she was nine."

Claire went shaky, and walked over to stand by the open window. Aunt Jean took Claire's place, and held her big sister's hand. "Jellybean, oh Jellybean!" So Momma recognized her little sister. Did she know Claire had been sitting there the whole time?

The wet wind reached in and touched her face, pulling on her skin like she could just float out the window. Even here in town the light was spare—just enough to shine the streets and illuminate the hunched crippled shapes of the ridges—a few scattered lamp poles with dim globes to draw the Miller moths that crashed over and over into the glass with no more sense than the folk who stayed here long after the jobs were gone.

But that was just mean thinking, and Claire had never been a mean person, even though she'd been the one who came up with that "Boo-Daddy" thing. She'd never meant to hurt him.

The family legend was that she'd been two, two and a half, and one afternoon she was playing outside when Daddy came home from his shift at the Stonega mine. Billy was the one watching her, and he'd told how she'd started grinning 'cause she'd recognized Daddy's old rust pickup pulling into the cinder driveway. And then how she'd stopped grinning when he came into the yard.

Back then miners had to pay for pretty much everything— explosives, smithing, even use of the bath-house. Finally Daddy figured he could just as well take a bath at home.

So when he came into the yard that day he was smeared head to toe in coal dust, his face so black his eyes popped out, huge and bright as headlights. That was the first time Claire had seen him like that, and she started hollering like pigs were eating her, screaming "Boo-Daddy! Boo-Daddy!"

Daddy waved his arms but that only made it worse. Then Momma came out the door yelling. "John, wash yourself down at the barn before you come into this yard!"

And that was the start of Momma's new rule—Daddy had to make himself "presentable" before he could rejoin the family. Claire's tantrum had been just the excuse Momma had been looking for—she'd been brought up a town girl and didn't have much taste for dirt.

Daddy never complained, not once, and came smiling into the house well-scrubbed every evening. But after a few years Claire could tell it wasn't quite a real smile—it was a sad and hard one—and if she looked close she could tell where he'd scrubbed too hard—there'd be scratches under his chin, and angry red places behind his ears, and sometimes little drops of blood, because they'd made him feel ashamed to come into his own house.

Finally Momma stopped murmuring, her lips smacking drily. The nurses drifted in and out all night, sometimes to check the monitor, sometimes because Claire was worried they weren't doing enough to make her mother comfortable.

Every few minutes Claire went to look out the window. Maybe because it was so quiet out there, nothing like Richmond at all, except now and then there'd be people walking—you couldn't see them, just their dark shapes. Meeting, maybe sharing a cigarette, then going their separate ways. It wasn't like country people to be up so late.

Around five a.m. Aunt Jean came in and sat with her, holding her hand sometimes, sometimes going over to touch Momma, look into her face.

Then as the sun was coming up, the walls warming to gold, her mother began to speak again. "Take the family albums, Claire. Will you? They're yers now. I hid 'em under them loose boards." On the other side of the bed Aunt Jean looked at Claire and shook her head. Momma died that afternoon without saying another word, like she'd been pushing to get out her allotted amount of speech and then she was done.

The next day Claire asked to borrow Aunt Jean's car. "I want to be holding those albums in my lap at the funeral. That's what she would have wanted."

"Claire, Honey, she's been down here in the hospital for months. I sent Jim up the holler to check on the place and he says there's hardly nothing left—just a couple of beds, maybe a table and a few chairs. They tore up everything, even stripped out that copper wire and them pipes your dad put in. It's them druggies—they take everything they can carry. They wander around in the night and they do their business up these hollers where nobody can see them, and some of them cook that meth, and some of them deal them cancer drugs, that Oxycontin and such. You don't dare go up some of them old roads after dark. The good people, they just keep themselves inside with their doors locked. We never locked our doors when I was growing up."

"But she said she hid them."

"Honey, it's dangerous. And I'm afraid you won't find nothing anyway."

It took a lot of talking, and Claire had to insist Jim wasn't to come, because this was hers to do. So by the time she took the old Ford up the holler it was late afternoon, and the trees that grew ever thicker the further you went in were going into that deep shadow green.

The car whined and wheezed and struggled on the steep parts, and the tires looked a few miles away from treadless. She was beginning to wish she'd allowed Jim to come.

The wheezing became an irregular rhythm, a harsh and unhappy struggle. She needed to grip the wheel as tightly as she could, and she needed to keep her eyes locked on that ancient winding road. But she found herself glancing up on each side, until she found one of those old gray shacks, the roof fallen down into the porch, the walls collapsed like a bony chest caved in, no more than a pile of ancient sticks, and then she knew she'd been looking for those old miners, gasping for breath and looking down from their porches.

An explosive horn made her jerk the car to the right. She fish-tailed trying to keep the Ford out of the ditch. A new pickup pulled up on the left, staying even with her. Two skinny, shirtless young men stared in. Their faces appeared slightly frayed, as if losing threads of skin. The one on the passenger side had a dark red bug covering half his lower lip, then Claire realized it was a burn.

She smiled and waved, as folks around here would do. They just continued staring, until they snapped their heads forward, and took off with a shower of gravel.

She mostly watched the road after that, and her rear-view mirror. When she did look for more of those old shacks she found most of them gone to ruins or nothing at all. Only occasionally would there be one she remembered, fixed up and painted, owned by some new family. Of course those miners would be gone—they'd been dying when she was young.

The home place looked pretty much the same when she pulled in front. But when she came closer she noticed how impossibly far the barn leaned. There were damp clumps of old clothes in the yard, and both front windows of the house broken. The door was a few inches open, the frame at the latch shattered into a fan of long splinters. Inside most of the furniture was missing or broken. Bits of wire and lathe hung from gaping holes in walls and ceiling. Papers and trash littered the floor, and it looked like someone had once had a fire in the middle of the living room.

Funny how she didn't notice the sprayed graffiti at first. There was so much of it on the flowery wallpaper, and so completely indecipherable to her, that it seemed just another layer of design, but some design ordinary folk couldn't appreciate.

A lot of the floor boards had been pried up, probably to get access to some of the pipes and wiring. She'd probably come all this way for nothing.

It took about three hours, and after a while she had to go back to the car for the lantern Aunt Jean had given her, and it meant getting down on her knees and prying up every likely board with the car jack, then lying flat on that filthy floor with a flashlight to peer between the floor joists. Maybe it was all that dust or the awkward position that made her breathless and disoriented. The floor beneath her appeared to shift back and forth arrhythmically and it felt as if the entire weight of the mountain was coming down on her chest. She began choking and dark mucous sprayed the floor. Once she'd finished checking the bedroom she determined that would be the end of her search.

The flashlight caught a few squares of red and white shoved back away from one of the vandalized openings in the floor. Claire reached in and snagged it with a few fingers, pulled, got a better grip on the package and pulled. When she got it to the opening she pulled it out with both hands: a squarish bundle wrapped in one of Momma's tablecloths.

Inside were several wrappings of stiff Piggly Wiggly paper grocery bags, crackling as she opened them, then a flowery pillowcase, and two photo albums of black leather worn almost through from constant handling.

Standing up, dizzy from the effort, was when she heard the vehicles outside. She walked unsteadily to the front room and peered out the door.

They'd driven them right up into the yard and in front of the porch—two shiny cars and the pickup truck she'd seen earlier. The two shirtless young men and a lady with a plainly unwashed face had gotten out of their vehicles and were staring right at her so it was too late to hide. She went to the door thinking if she were Momma or Daddy she'd step right out on the porch to greet them with a smile and a howdy no matter how unwelcome they actually were, but that wasn't going to happen. She waited. A forth figure climbed out of the biggest car, an older, fat man with greasy hair and a shotgun.

No one said anything. Claire looked down at the albums, opened one on top the other, and looked at the yellowing photos of grandparents and great grandparents, cousins near and distant, promising herself she would not look up again until the people outside had left.

She didn't know the names of the people in at least half the pictures, but she recognized herself in some of their faces, and the rest of the family, so she knew them to be kin.

She heard one of the car doors close, then the engine revving like some kind of animal ready to leap up on the porch, but she still refused to look up from the album. She turned the page and there was Momma and Daddy in their wedding clothes, and Billy as a baby, and Claire herself standing in the yard with Daddy when she was a little girl.

A distant gleam caught the corner of her eye, the wrong angle for one of those headlights, probably just a star, but it made her raise her head.

A short distance away, on what used to be the Toliver place, the front of an old house was lit up like a stage, a bent figure standing on the porch there, looking her way. But the Tolivers had been gone a generation. That land had been an empty field since she graduated high school.

Then behind the trees across the road, another house lit up, where one of those old men used to live, always smiling and waving from his porch when she and Daddy rattled by.

Then there was another. And another. And again, maybe a dozen more, all lit up like some museum displays. The people in her yard were looking around now, and looking less calm, or less dumb, or less stoned.

Then in the trees on the mountain-side of the property, she could hear a breeze picking up, but after only a few seconds she knew it wasn't wind at all, but breathing, difficult breathing, from lungs that never could get enough air. Dark figures appeared in the spaces between scattered trees, carrying lanterns that did nothing to illuminate them.

When the figure walked out of the old barn and into the yard, striding purposely, the intruders got into their vehicles and pulled away, disappearing down the windy road into the bottom of the holler.

The figure halted a few feet from the edge of the porch. Claire stepped through the open door, the albums clutched to her chest. But even from the porch she couldn't make out a face, or even the reflection off a hand, or any bit of skin. It was like blackness hanging there, woven into a mobile shape for convenience.

Finally she said, "Daddy. Oh Boo-Daddy, please come inside. It's almost time, you know. You don't want to be late."

Slowly the darkness began to move again, and she really couldn't see much even as it passed her, just the slightest thickening of the night air, until it crossed the threshold, and in the front room she could see all that coal dust just hanging there in the lantern light, in the vaguest form of a man, until it fell, and disappeared into the cracks between the boards.

Nightcrawlers

"Go down, you'll find them
under the rocks," Daddy whispered,
and motioned with a pale, bloated hand.
I nodded solemnly
and followed his crouched form
as he paced the path raccoon-like,
twitching his head, snarling
when I stumbled and made noise.
He upended a stone
and the worms danced there
just like he said, their questing
front and back ends pointing, then
waving in distress.
Under another stone they sang
for us a tune so quiet the dark
carried most of it away.
I wanted to go
into the darkest woods
where the worm songs go.

But to Daddy,
they were bait.

Sundown in Duffield

John convinced his grandson to take him on this trip even though Franklin had his doubts. John felt apologetic. He knew he was asking a lot. Franklin was a fine young man, and had always been a loyal and dutiful grandson, but clearly John's progressive disease frightened him. John persuaded him this was his final opportunity to see the house where he'd lived as a child—"before my mind goes"—and so reluctantly Franklin agreed. It was a shameful manipulation. John felt embarrassed for the man he once was.

The old homeplace was near Duffield, Virginia off Pattonsville Road. Scott County, deep into the southwest corner of the state. The population had always been small, and now was down to a tiny community of seventy-three, according to Franklin. He'd looked it up on wiki-something. John had lost the ability to use the computer. He didn't miss it.

John couldn't remember how old he was when his family left the house, fleeing in the middle of the night with time only to throw a few things into the car. But it had been at least sixty years. He'd been nine or ten. Maybe eleven. He'd never gone back, not until today.

His sister died a few months ago, and much to his surprise he discovered she still owned the place, and now it was his. How did that happen? He couldn't follow the legalities involved. He hadn't seen his sister in years. Were they estranged? Certainly, they'd been strangers. Was he being unkind? In any case the state was about to take the property for unpaid taxes. Let them have it—he certainly had no use for it. John just wanted one final look.

They had a map from his sister's lawyer. They couldn't have found the house otherwise. The road was gravel, dirt, and weeds. Franklin kept saying, "It's a jungle in here," and each time he said it John felt guiltier. Franklin's vehicle had a high ground clearance, but it wasn't designed for off-road travel. John lost his license some time ago and couldn't share the driving. Although it was for the best he supposed he still resented it.

John was about to suggest they give up when Frankin cried, "There it is!" and stopped. "It's only a few yards. We can walk the rest of the way. You can hold onto me just in case."

Despite his misgivings, John could tell his grandson was enjoying himself. He was still at an age when inconvenience felt like an adventure. Franklin unloaded a backpack, snacks, and a powerful battery-operated lantern he bought especially for this expedition. He reserved a yurt for the night at the Natural Tunnel Park a few miles away. John was confused at first—he thought the word referred to a kind of drink. Then Franklin explained it was like a tent. He seemed quite excited about it. John didn't want to sleep in a tent. Camping had never appealed to him, not even when he was a boy.

No doubt Franklin would want to see the Natural Tunnel itself, which William Jennings Bryan once called the eighth wonder of the world. Of course, Bryan had been a bit of a blowhard. Hundreds of thousands of years of a stream running through the limestone carved it out, and like every other natural tourist attraction in the U.S. it had its own Lover's Leap, and a tragic story of star-crossed Indian lovers to go with it. Or he'd want to hike up to the Devil's Bathtub, a natural depression in the bedrock full of water. Nature took multiple millennia creating these wonders and human beings spent fifteen minutes manufacturing semi-appropriate metaphors. John would remain back in the yurt during any such sightseeing if Franklin let him.

The land here was rampant with porous limestone, sinkholes, and caves, many of them hidden or undiscovered. You never knew when you might step off the trail and into a hole. John had no intention of risking any broken bones, certainly not at his age.

"Damn! No reception." Franklin kept pushing buttons on his cell phone.

"Do we really need that thing?" Franklin gave John a cell phone for Christmas. It was still in its box in a drawer somewhere.

"If there's an emergency, yes."

"I guess we'll have to avoid emergencies."

John couldn't see the house, but he couldn't see a lot of things if there were trees or other distractions around whatever he was looking for. He counted on his grandson to lead the way. Instead, Franklin had John grab his left arm and they walked together. John wanted to say he wasn't blind, at least not yet, but it seemed silly to fuss.

They kept away from the road's deep ruts and pushed through thick growths of chickweed and bull thistle, button weed and spotted spurge. How come he could remember the names of all these weeds and yet so little of anything important?

A patch of gray ahead of them evolved into the side of a house with all the paint worn away, the structure difficult to distinguish at first from the overgrowth and the shadows among the trees. John couldn't remember the original color, white or a light blue, but even back then the paint hadn't been kept up.

So many places to hide, whether you were a victim or someone intent on doing harm. The leafy trees smothered the light. He imagined it always felt after sunset here. He didn't know if his grandson kept a gun in his car—most of the locals did. John should have asked.

Like many older homes in the area the house dated from the Civil War. The house still wore the remains of the fancy gingerbread fretwork and medallions and eave brackets of that era, split and half-rotted. The brick and stone foundation was losing its integrity, splitting into its component blocks in parts. The ancient shutters were shredded or missing. The windows were all broken, reduced to black rectangles of rotted screen. The porch roof sagged several feet on one end and the porch floor itself had fallen onto the ground. Pieces of a shattered swing hung from rusty chains. The fence in front of the house was missing its rails, leaving a few posts covered in thick layers of vine.

John knew time had been the chief perpetrator here, but his eyes kept searching the greenery for evidence of others.

"Was that your family's car?" Franklin pointed to the corroded skeleton of an automobile beneath a collapsed shed.

"No. Daddy drove us away in his Bel Air. That was Grandaddy's. Daddy always said he'd get it running someday."

The warped metal roof of the house was rusted brown and there were large holes where sections had fallen in. The old cook stove sat in the side yard. John supposed someone had tried to steal it for scrap but given up because of its weight. Nearby the balcony which once hung from the second story lay spilled through the weeds.

"We only have a few hours before losing light. You're not sundowning are you, Grandad?"

John knew the term well but refused to acknowledge it in relation to himself. "I'm just fine."

"Okay, I'm going to check inside and see if it's stable enough to be in there. If we go in we should be quick about it, though. Think about what you want to see, if there's anything you want to get, whatever you want to accomplish here. That'll make things go faster. But don't go wandering around."

"Whatever you say." John tried to keep the irritation out of his voice but didn't think he succeeded, given the way his grandson was looking at him. He could feel his annoyance rising like a fever he could not control. Along with it was a rise in paranoia. He didn't want to be left out here alone.

"I'll be quick." Franklin tested the boards of the porch before putting his full weight on them, then stepped side to side as if looking for soft spots. The front door stuck for a moment, but then he put his shoulder into it and disappeared inside.

John meant to ask his grandson if it was spring or summer. For the life of him he couldn't remember. But asking such a question would have been a big mistake.

He was of two minds. His grandmother used to say that. But in his case one mind was sharp and clear and the other overflowing with bewilderment. John never knew at any given moment which one was going to show up.

With Franklin gone John could listen to his surroundings. The wind through the trees. The songs of small birds. He used to know his birdsongs. Not anymore. If there were larger animals around they were holding their peace.

Then the distinctive trickles and burbles of running water became evident. Of course. A branch of the Clinch River ran behind the house. He and his dad used to go fishing there. He was suddenly thrilled, and took a few steps in that direction before stopping himself. If he weren't here when his grandson came out of the house the child would have a fit.

The river flooded a few times while they lived here, bringing water, and whatever was in the water, almost to the edge of the house. John remembered he and his sister being so excited to see fish splashing in their backyard, but Mother wouldn't let them go near the flooded stream. He wondered if there had been worse flooding since then.

But they didn't leave because of the flooding. They fled the house in the middle of the night because of something far, far worse. If John could only remember what it was.

"Okay, I think it's safe enough," Franklin said. "It's more stable inside than it looks. We can't take the staircase to the second floor—we'd fall right through—but the main floor should be okay."

The interior looked nothing like the pictures in John's memory. Stain patterns on the walls and ceiling resembled badly healed wounds. The checkered kitchen linoleum floor appeared vaguely familiar, like a kitchen he'd once encountered, but not lived with. The kitchen chair seats were caked in layers of fallen plaster. Vines grew down the kitchen walls from a rent in the ceiling.

For a moment he thought he saw his mother standing there, staring at a pot on the stove with a blank look on her face. It happened more than a few times. She'd forgotten what she was doing. After a while Daddy took over the cooking. Both would be dead less than ten years later.

The walls were much closer than he remembered, and there was a bush growing in one corner of the living room. Spicebush, he thought. They used to grow outside the house and the berries tasted peppery.

A collapsed couch near the flaking brick fireplace appeared too filthy to touch. If it once belonged to his family John didn't recognize it. Some sort of abandoned animal den was evident inside the fireplace, scattered small bones left behind. Either the animal itself or what it ate.

We shouldn't be here. John was suddenly convinced.

Franklin was in another room, poking at things, looking for heirlooms John might want to retrieve. He was going to tell Franklin this might not be the right house, even though he was sure it was, when he saw the mirror standing in one corner of a shallow alcove off the living room.

His mother's old dressing mirror leaned against a background of split and moldy wallpaper. He recognized the scrollwork around the bottom edge. When he was small he'd held onto that edge while his mother modeled some new dress she'd made. This might have been her sewing space, although his fragile memory told him the sewing room had been upstairs. Moisture had gotten into the silver backing creating mirror rot. He could see parts of himself, but the rest was shadow and distortion. From certain angles the mirror cast bad reflections across the room. Out of the corner of one eye he glimpsed things creeping from the walls.

He caught a peek of his head in an unspoiled spot in the glass. His hair looked crazy, and he hadn't buttoned his sweater right. Usually, Franklin fixed those things for him. He hastily moved his palm across his hair and fumbled with the top of his sweater. Another hand came up behind him and brushed the hair off his right ear. He twisted around. There was no one there.

"So, did your family grab the important stuff when they left?" Franklin stood a few feet away.

"Pictures mostly, some jewelry and a few changes of clothes, whatever money was in my dad's wallet. My sister and I each grabbed a favorite toy. I can't remember what I took. By the time we reached my uncle's house upstate I know I didn't have it whatever it was."

"Why did you guys leave exactly?"

How many times was his grandson going to ask him this question? "I don't remember. But I know my folks had their reasons."

There was soiled and sour-smelling clothing scattered throughout the downstairs. John didn't think they belonged to his family. They looked a little too new. Some had gray and fading reddish-brown stains on them. There were numerous signs of squatters: candy wrappers and food packages, indications of a fire along one wall, women's undergarments, pornographic magazines. There were long rips in the walls where scavengers had removed copper wiring or pipe. John started to pick up a plastic bag off the floor when his grandson told him to stop. "It might have had drugs in it, Oxycontin, or something worse." John couldn't remember what Oxycontin was but heeded the warning nevertheless. All this evidence looked several years old. The squatters were long gone.

"Just let me know when you're ready to leave."

John knew that meant his grandson was eager to abandon this pile of wreckage. "I won't be long. I promise."

Despite his grandson's warning he wanted to go upstairs where his and his sister's rooms had been. A taste of his childhood. A reminder of the rare things which brought him joy. But he didn't dare try the mossy stairs.

In a back corner of the first floor, he discovered a sagging armchair in the middle of a vacant room, a place to sit and watch the house disintegrate at one's leisure. A rotting pile of lovely old books made a smelly mound by the chair. He remembered his father had a small study where he liked to hide. Was this it? He would have liked to sort through these books to see what his father liked to read, but he was afraid to touch them.

John knew his father had stopped reading sometime before the family ran away from here. The reason he remembered was because it was such a dramatic change. Used to, John's mother had to drag Daddy out of that chair for dinner or for most family activities. But after he stopped Daddy looked so sad. John overheard Daddy telling Mother he still liked looking at these old books and turning the pages, but he could no longer follow the sentences.

The bedroom by the kitchen had been his parents'. He was eager to see it. After the family left this house things were never the same. They'd moved around the South, losing much of what they owned along the way. He didn't even have photographs of them.

The air in the room was dusty, the room dark, and it was difficult to tell which details were actual objects, and which the random effect of overlapping shadow. Jagged timbers poked down from the broken ceiling.

A portrait hung on the wall by the door. A woman's body, but she had lost her face. Something had scrubbed at the paint until all her features were erased. He thought she might have been his mother, or his grandmother, but thanks to his failing memory she'd been demoted to the anonymous dead.

He often had trouble determining distances in the dark but today seemed worse than usual. Was that a wall or a shadow? As he stepped further into the room he was assaulted by an awful stench. The drapes sagged with mold. Corrupted bedding hung off the side of the blackened mattress like ruined folds of skin.

John took another step, and the floor sank an inch or so. He was suddenly having balance issues. This sometimes occurred, but usually in a safer setting. Everything felt soft underfoot. He looked down and was alarmed by the amount of seepage from the cellar underneath. The floor swayed as if floating. Things began to fall off the walls and slide toward him. He didn't dare move because of the mess and the peril. He wanted to call for his grandson but at that moment he could not remember his grandson's name.

Layers of wall began to fall, revealing the naked lathing beneath. The shadows painting the walls began to drip.

"Grandad, I don't think it's safe for you to be in here." Franklin, of course. His name was Franklin. His grandson grabbed his hand and pulled him from the room. Glancing back, John saw the room was a terrible mess, but nothing extraordinary. Light was bleeding through tears in the window shades.

"Is it morning yet?"

"No, Grandad. It's late afternoon. Sometimes the late afternoon light and the morning light look the same. I know that must confuse you, but it's okay, really."

They were about to pass the cellar door when Franklin grabbed the knob and tried to pull it open. John barely suppressed a warning scream. But the door was either locked or swollen shut. Good, he thought. Let it be.

He watched a memory leak out of the cellar door: his father shouting at him to run away, something tall coming up the cellar stairs behind his dad. But his dad kept blocking whatever it was so John couldn't see. Then his dad shook his head back and forth until his dad's face went away.

But Franklin wouldn't give up. He kept twisting and yanking on the knob. John, anxious the door not be breached, though he couldn't have explained to his grandson why, grabbed that sweet child's arm and began to screech "no no no!" until his voice went thin.

"Please step back, Grandad."

"Don't tell me what to do boy!" John could feel the anger rising from his chest into his head. He wanted to stop it but could not. Franklin squirmed out of his grip and John almost fell. He stared at this young man. "Is it morning yet?"

"No, Grandad. It's almost sundown. I think we should get you to the campsite."

"What's wrong?"

"Nothing's wrong, but you're getting tired. We'll check into our yurt, get something to eat, and then a good night's sleep. We can still come back here tomorrow if you feel you need to."

"I sleep too much during the day. That's why I get confused. That's the problem."

"Maybe. Maybe it is. We should go now."

Franklin hurried John along the dirt road and into the car, but he couldn't get the engine to turn over. He tried and tried, but all he got out of the vehicle was a rapid clicking sound. John sat quietly, afraid he might say the wrong thing.

"I always keep blankets in the car. You taught me that, remember?"

John did not. "I did? I'm glad I at least taught you something."

"You taught me lots of things, Grandad. You've always been … so wise. I've also got two air mattresses. We'll camp out in the house where there's more room. Maybe the car will start in the morning. If not, we'll figure something else out. Everything will be okay."

John smiled and nodded but knew better. In his experience when someone says "everything will be okay" it usually won't be.

Franklin found a broom in a debris-filled closet and used it to sweep out the living room. John kept getting up and pawing through the more interesting bits discovered by the broom until his grandson persuaded him to sit in the kitchen. It was embarrassing, but John had just enough sense of himself to know it was necessary. His brain was filling up with wreckage, and sometimes he couldn't find the right memories, or the thoughts he needed, because all that wreckage was in the way.

Every few minutes John stared at the cellar door. He kept seeing his father running up those steps, something tall and borderless following him from below. Unfortunately, it was the clearest picture he had of his father. It was a memory which threatened to erase everything else the man ever did.

Both his parents died when John and his sister were teenagers—first his mother and then his father. The disappearance of his mother's mind had already begun in this house. In retrospect the evidence was clear. The same was true of his father, although his father was at least able to hang on until he got them out of the house.

They died hooked up to machines, having forgotten how to swallow or breathe. John didn't really know how his sister died. He should have stayed in touch, but that was as much her fault as his.

They made their beds on the floor with the lantern between them. The dark came quickly, rushing up to the very edges of the lantern light. In recent years it had become increasingly difficult for John to perceive objects in the dark. In his eyes, things were either visible in his world or they were lost to the shadows. But he understood the shadows were still there, waiting.

Either because he was nervous himself or because he wanted to distract John from the demons which came to him most afternoons as the sun went down, Franklin began a seemingly endless monologue about his work at the bank, the young woman he was dating, possible plans and their alternatives, what he remembered about his grandmother (John's wife, who had been fading so quickly from his own memories he barely remembered being married), and much more.

John interrupted. "It's okay, Franklin. I'm feeling relatively calm."

"Are you? I'm glad. We're both okay then, aren't we?"

"Yes we are," John said, although he'd suddenly forgotten why they were here. His grandson had obviously wanted to go camping, but why? John was always losing the thread of things. It was becoming tiresome.

"Was it always this damp?" his grandson asked.

"Damp? What do you mean? Is it raining? I don't hear any rain."

"This house. It smells of damp. I know there's a river nearby. But this floor? Doesn't it feel—I don't know—wet?"

John felt cold and tried to shake it off. "I remember the cellar always flooded. There were cracks at one end, and a cavity that went, well, who knows where it went? Did I tell you there were caves all around here?"

"You did. Water carves its way through limestone. Hundreds of thousands of years."

"That's right! They call that kind of landscape karst. That's a new word for you, child! Sinkholes, caves, all kinds of cavities in the rock, and under your feet. Daddy said we got water in the cellar because of that, and rats too, all sorts of creatures living inside those caves.

"I used to hate that damp smell! It got into your head, and it made it hard to think straight. You had to make an effort to push your thoughts through. I'd walk around the house numb and not feeling much of anything. I felt rubbed out."

Franklin stopped responding, and soon John could hear the boy snoring. But John kept talking. It comforted him to hear a voice, even if it was just his own.

John opened his eyes in the middle of the night and thought himself outside the house. The roof over his head was full of holes, and full of stars. Everything was creeping toward him. Everything his grandson had swept to the side was now sliding in John's direction.

He twisted around and found Franklin sitting up on his air mattress, staring at the cellar door. "Franklin, are you okay?"

"Grandad, is that you?"

"Of course it is, son. What's wrong? What's bothering you?"

"Where are we? I have no idea where we are."

"We're. We're." But John could not speak because of the cellar door. Which was open. He hadn't noticed it at first, but the door was now wide open, showing them the way into the emptiness beyond.

Saved

Because of his job and the pandemic and several other less valid excuses Walt hadn't visited his mother in the nursing home in two years. He tried to call, but phone calls confused her. Either she didn't recognize his voice, or she thought he was standing outside her door. Sometimes she picked up the phone but wouldn't talk. The nurses tried to help, but his mother was stubborn. No one could make Doris Russell speak if she didn't want to.

He left Richmond early. He was already tired by the time he got to Charlottesville, ate and drank coffee, then headed down I-81. He considered it strange he had to leave Virginia and go to Tennessee before he could get to Virginia's poorer parts. The drive was beautiful, the hills drowning in trees turning orange and red. As he headed north out of Tennessee back into Southwest Virginia it struck him how the towns got smaller, the roads narrower, with increasing evidence of the abandoned coal operations which once fueled the local economy. Both the houses and the land resembled the landscapes in his dreams. He hadn't lived here in over fifty years. It felt like a house he still owned but never slept in.

On the outskirts of Big Stone Gap someone had put up a hand-lettered sign, GOD SAVE WISE COUNTY. Was that a prayer? The road was nicer than he remembered, maybe wider, the trees, weeds, and vines still close to the pavement. He passed under several railroad bridges on the way into town. The beauty of the Alleghenies was undeniable. The mountains dominated the town. Walt had always felt small living here. But he'd loved it until he understood he couldn't stay.

The Gap was where the Powell River Valley widened between Stone Mountain, Little Stone Mountain, and Wallens Ridge. They'd built a supermax penitentiary up on the Ridge since Walt lived here. With no attempt at rehabilitation, the inmates often several states away from any family, and almost a third of them in solitary confinement, the prison wasn't a nice place, but as his brother Frank, a corrections officer there, would say, "it's not meant to be a nice place."

His brother had a tidy, newly painted house, much nicer than Walt's. They spent a few minutes talking sound systems. Walt envied Frank's big screen TV. They'd always been competitive over property.

"You sold Mom's house?" Seeing Frank's expression, Walt corrected his tone. "I mean, I trust your decision, but why?"

"Had to. Cost too much to keep it up. It needed repairs, and I couldn't find reliable renters. I should have told you sooner. I have a small check for your share."

"I do appreciate you handling things. You've always been good at that stuff." There was a lot more to say, but Walt didn't need the bother. "How's she doing?"

"She's ninety-three years old. How do you think she's doing?" Frank stopped and forced out a grin. "Better than Dad, maybe. But I'm not sure. There's nothing anybody could have done to rescue that old man, and Mom, well, I don't know why she's hanging on. Maybe just waiting for you to visit, brother."

Their father died in the same nursing home ten years before. He had half a dozen terminal illnesses at the time, exacerbated by alcoholism. Frank's house was only a few blocks from the old homeplace, and he got along okay with their dad in his later years. Out of respect for Frank Walt never talked about their old man. "When was the last time you saw her?"

Frank turned away and began setting the dinner table. Peggy would be home from her realtor's office soon. Walt couldn't imagine who was buying houses here, but Frank said she kept busy. "A week ago Sunday I reckon. I drop by for fifteen minutes at a time, you know? No point in staying longer—she hardly talks, and if she's interested in my news she don't show it."

"The last time I was here she talked about the old days, things that happened to her when she was a girl. I'd ask her questions and she'd answer, stories I'd never heard before."

"And you believed her? She was probably making it all up. They do that you know, after a certain age. Not Dad though. His mind was sharp, even after all his drinking. She's not who you remember, Walt. A lot can happen in five years."

"It's only been a little over two."

"Is that right? I lose track it's been so long. You know, I was saying to Peggy the other day it would be great to see you with a wife, or at least someone special. A man our age shouldn't be living alone. A good woman can make a real difference for fellows like us. Or do you reckon that's sexist? I don't know if it is or isn't, all I know is Peggy rescued me from a pretty empty life."

"You don't deserve her, Frank. That's the truth." He could have said it better. "I've never been able to close the deal. Attraction is a mystery and when it's not returned, maybe it doesn't mean a thing about you, but damn it sure feels like it does."

"At least having Peggy I know what I'm doing with the rest of my life. I pray to God I don't outlive her."

"Don't tell me you're religious now."

"When you got limited time you have to wonder how you're going to spend it. What you reckon our mother has to look forward to? If you visit her tomorrow you can sit with her through one of them nursing home church services. I took her out a few Sundays back to the Pentecostal church up on the Ridge. I won't be doing that again. Count your blessings."

"Mama, are you liking it here in the nursing home? Are they treating you well?"

Walt wasn't sure she heard him. Her eyes looked milky and wandered. She had *Gunsmoke* playing on the little TV on top of her dresser. He didn't know they still ran those old reruns. He wished they could watch it together instead of having this awkward conversation. She wasn't watching the screen, but it had to be distracting. Finally, she turned her head in his direction looking surprised to see him. "Nursing home? Walter, what are you talking about?"

He saw the worried look in her eyes, and he thought he'd made a terrible mistake. It had been a vague, but mostly normal conversation up until then.

"This nursing home, Mama. Are they nice to you here?"

"Honey, this ain't a nursing home."

"What is it then?"

"It's my daddy's house. We've always called it the farmhouse, but it's a grand old house. You've been here before haven't you?"

Walt had no idea what to say, but he didn't think he should contradict her. He was curious how detailed her delusion was. An old man was creeping by with a walker in the hall. "So that out there, on the other side of the door, is that the road in front of Grandad's house?"

"Oh, I don't know. Walter, you don't think I've lost my mind do you?"

"No, no. Of course not. I was wondering how you're seeing things is all."

"I see fine, but I can't read with these glasses. Maybe I need new ones. Could you take me to get new ones, dear?"

She didn't own a pair of glasses as far as he knew. "Of course, Mama. I'll get you anything you need."

One of the nurse's aides came to the door. "Doris, church is about to start. Did you want to come today?"

His mother turned her head and whispered. "I shouldn't miss church."

"That's okay, Mama. I'll take you down." He'd never pushed someone in a wheelchair before and feared dumping her. The chair had a belt and he kept trying to secure her and she kept complaining it was too tight. Finally, he gave up and tried pushing her down the hall with one hand on the grip, the other holding her shoulder. She shrugged it off and he had to trust she'd keep herself upright.

He thought to ask her if they were going down the street in front of the old farmhouse now, her wheelchair out in the middle of traffic. He was genuinely curious about her sense of location, but that seemed cruel. The walls were decorated from Halloween, the last holiday, mostly with drawings of pumpkins and haystacks, but nothing scary or supernatural looking. There was a photograph of several of the residents, including his mother, by some haystacks. She looked stiff and wide-eyed, as if awakened from a nap.

A dozen or so residents were gathered in the cafeteria for church. None looked particularly alert, and several appeared unhappy to be there. At the front of the room next to an upright piano stood an alarmingly pale young man too thin for his jet-black suit and wrinkled white shirt. His yellow hair was cut close on the sides with short bangs in front. In his left hand he held a battered bible—strings and ribbons hanging from between the pages—so tightly his arm shook. Beside him an elderly couple were fiddling with a tape player and speaker.

The woman of the couple looked up and waved in his direction and Walt, puzzled, waved back. Then he realized she was waving at his mother. The woman came up to them and put her arm around her.

"Hello, Doris. How are you this blessed Sunday?"

"Oh, I'm fine. This is Walter. My son. I haven't seen him in many years."

"Well, Mama, not many years." Embarrassed, he tried to smile at the lady.

"He's here now. That's good isn't it?"

"It's wonderful," Mama said, grinning. Walt noticed for the first time she wasn't wearing her dentures. He wondered if she still had them.

"Would you like to play piano for us today, Doris? You played so beautifully last Sunday."

"Did I? I don't know, I didn't practice. Do I have to?"

"Oh no. Maybe you'd just like to sit with your son today?"

"Yes. Yes. I haven't seen him in years."

The church lady offered Walt a faint smile as she left. He pulled up a cafeteria chair next to his mother's wheelchair. He didn't want to be there, and he wasn't used to doing things he didn't want to do. He hadn't been to a church service since childhood.

He glanced around at the rest of the congregation. Although most were seated in twos or threes at the various tables none were engaged in conversation. They either looked down or they watched the preacher curiously, as if ready to be entertained.

He noticed an old man near the front, incompletely shaved, his eyes pink and wet as if he'd been weeping. Four elderly ladies were seated behind him, their hands folded identically in their laps, their necks stretched as if to see better. About half the room were in wheelchairs like his mother. Several were slumped and sleeping. One man kept clasping his hands together, nodding furiously.

The service began with the elderly couple singing old gospel tunes, "Peace in the Valley," "I Saw the Light," "The Old Rugged Cross," accompanied by tinny-sounding music from the tape player. They encouraged the residents to sing along with them, but no one did. Walt saw his mother tapping her foot in time, and he was unexpectedly pleased.

The tape started giving the couple trouble, sticking, then speeding up with a distorted whine. The elderly man stopped the machine, apologized, and tried again. "I reckon we need new equipment," he said. The church lady attempted to smile and failed. They barely made it through "The Church in the Wildwood," started another Walt didn't recognize, when the song ended in noise. The man leaned over and stopped the player. "I reckon that's all the music we have for you today." The woman glanced over at Walt's mother, as if hoping for a volunteer. Mama was staring at her feet. Walt saw she was wearing one pink slipper and one blue one. He was embarrassed he missed that.

Walt saw the church lady lay her hand on the elderly man's arm, linger, then pull it away as she stepped to the back.

The man stepped forward and straightened himself, smiled. "A blessed morning to you all. I am so glad you could join us here today. May the power and glory of the Holy Spirit be with you always amen."

The woman and the young man in the black suit replied, "Amen!"

"Janet and I are so pleased to bring you a new preacher this Sunday. He hails from Harlan County, Kentucky, and I do believe he has a special gift. Please welcome Reverend Parkey as he delivers his wonderful message for all of us."

Walt didn't know if he was supposed to clap or not. No one else did so he let his hands rub his knees.

"Thank you, Brother Carl. My name is Reverend Bill Parkey and I'm here to save you today." Despite his callow appearance the preacher possessed a strong speaking voice. Walt didn't know if any of these folks were hard of hearing—there were probably a few—but he figured most could understand the preacher's words. "As Brother Carl told you I come from Harlan, Kentucky, and Lord if that ain't a sinful place. Oh yes, Harlan is drowning in sin! I'm doing my best to change it folks, but don't you know a job like that can wear a feller out! I'm out on a street corner every day preaching the Lord's truth and most days I don't know if them sinners is hearing a single word coming out of my mouth!

"Yes, I said street corner. I don't have a church. I don't need one. Didn't they say in Matthew 18:20, 'For where two or three gather together in My name, there am I with them.'? That's what they said, them prophets of old, and that is what is writ down in this precious book."

The preacher held his bible high over his head. Walt saw his mother and some of the others follow it with their eyes. "Ever thing you ever need to know about life and death is written down in this here book. Have you read it? Tell me if you've read it."

No one said anything. After an uncomfortable pause Brother Carl and Sister Janet called out "I have," their voices overlapping. Then Carl interjected, "I love my bible!"

"Well, I can tell this is a righteous crowd so I know most of you've read it, even if it were a long time ago. Not like them folks in Harlan, no sir! I bet most of them folk ain't read nary a word!

"Now Jesus wants to heal you. He wants to purify you with his precious blood. If any of you was still young, I would pray to Jesus to cure you, but you know there is no cure for old age. My father knew that when it come his time, as did my grandfather, and all the fathers in my family afore that. A time to every purpose under heaven, that's what the good Lord tells us in chapter three of Ecclesiastes. We got to respect that. There is a reason we pass on when we do, and that exact time is writ in a special book only God knows about.

"But even if I can't heal you, I can sure as heck save you, because it's never too late to be saved. Blessed are the meek, and I can't say I've seen a meeker bunch than our congregation here today.

"But it don't matter if you got the rheumatiz, or your back is broke, or your arms and legs is twisted. Jesus don't care about none of that. Whatever you got wrong with you Jesus has a place for you in Heaven.

"It's never too late to repent your sins. If you repent, the gifts of Heaven shall be yours. If you repent He will set you free of your sins. Jesus died to redeem you. What a gift it was!"

The preacher began moving among the residents, speaking the whole time, praying, and asking for amens. But the only ones answering were the elderly couple who'd brought him here.

"I believe in a Lord of compassion, a Lord of forgiveness, and a Lord of vengeance when necessary. May He watch over you and yours when you reach those golden fields of paradise."

Now and then the preacher would touch someone on the shoulder, sometimes waking them up from a nap, sometimes confusing them with his proximity. One lady started laughing and the preacher moved away from her.

"I'm so ready to go to heaven, aren't you? Won't that be a wonderful day?"

One of the old men was crying. The preacher laid his hand on the man's head, then moved on.

"I can feel it just beyond the golden rays of the sun, that beautiful ridge, the trees flooding them hills in paradise, the mountains of paradise hanging over us all, and that sky! Let me go Lord! I can't hardly wait. I want to be there! Any day now! It's just waiting for me! It's waiting for you!"

The preacher approached his mother, but Walt stared at the young man sternly and waved him away. It made Walt angry to hear this youngster speak to them that way, of heaven and paradise and the beautiful world to come, when this fellow knew so little of growing old, when death for them was so close. Walt believed in being respectful. He bowed his head when everybody else bowed their heads. But this preacher was a young man who didn't know what he was talking about.

Walt wished he had a partner he could tell about the things he'd heard and thought today. He didn't know if it would help, but it sure would be nice to be heard.

By the time they got back to her room his mother was sagging in the wheelchair. The TV was still on, an old episode of *The Rifleman* playing. Walt and Frank used to watch that one with their dad. Lucas McCain was a great father.

"The chair," his mother said.

"Something wrong with the wheelchair?"

"Big chair."

"Oh, you want to sit over there." Her head jerked forward in a nod. He put his hand on her shoulder to stop her from falling. He moved the wheelchair to the wingback in the corner and locked the wheels. He'd seen the way the aides transferred people. He wasn't sure he could do it. But he bent down and hugged her to him and stood her up. She weighed next to nothing. All he felt was her dress and some bones inside. He gently put her down in the high-backed chair. She sighed and settled in. There wasn't another chair, so Walt sat in the wheelchair, pulling it in front of her.

He watched her a minute and smiled. She smiled back. "Mama, do you miss Dad?"

Her eyes went lazy for a moment, then she beamed. "My father was a great man. I miss him every day. Do you know he built this house by himself? He had a couple of helpers was all."

"You told me. I wish I'd known him better."

Her smile grew wider. It was almost—what was the word— beatific? "Walter, Honey, I look forward to meeting your wife. I can't hardly wait. Won't that be a wonderful day?"

"It will, Mama. It will."

Scarecrows

Gibson stumbled out of the woods with his orange jumpsuit covered in beggar-ticks and burrs. Maybe walking away from the county road crew wasn't the smartest thing he'd ever done—he only had a couple of months left on his shoplifting sentence—but as his mama used to say her son wasn't known for his smart decisions.

"You got no self-control." Mama was right. But Gibson believed in grabbing opportunities when they came, and their guard was young and not much good at guarding. The kid spent most of his time on his cell phone sitting in the truck. Gibson and another convict named Frank Moore were working in a ditch not more than thirty feet from the woods. It took them less than five minutes to get gone. Moore wanted to split up—Gibson had an unlucky reputation—and so they did.

But Gibson had at least one good reason to take off. Two years ago, he killed a man in Memphis with a lug wrench after a quarrel in a parking lot—another lapse in self-control—and the police hadn't figured it out yet. But when they did, and they most always did, he'd never see the outside of a jail again.

Once clear of the woods he looked for a way off the mountain. The road they'd been repaving cut across the top of the ridge. He worked his way down the slope through the firs and the pines and the worse undergrowth he'd ever seen. Apparently these folks never heard of forest fires. But he still had a lot more mountain to go. He was looking for a cabin or a farm, some place where he could get out of this jumpsuit and into some regular clothes, and maybe steal a vehicle.

He saw the barn first, its dark gray boards warped and the building on the verge of collapse, and then a stretch of plowed ground, a good sign the land here was still being worked. Then that field full of crosses, like in the bible, a fellow hanging from each one.

Gibson thought about turning around and running right then, but he was pretty much out of run. He raised his hand to shield his eyes from the sun. Those weren't men. They were scarecrows. A collection of thirty, maybe forty of them. His mama used to have one in her garden at home, said it was pretty much useless. The birds perched on the silly thing and squawked at her. Crows and blackbirds especially figured the scarecrow out awfully quick. But every year she put new clothes on it, shirts, and overalls his daddy wore out. When Gibson asked her why she said, "I don't know son. But folks been putting these up for thousands of years. Wouldn't feel like a garden without a scarecrow."

Staggered like a platoon of dying soldiers, struggling to make their way out of the field, these many scarecrows were overkill on a patch of garden this size. Like most fields on mountain farms, it was relatively small. The farmers had to remove a ton of rock and cut down a lot of trees to prepare an area big enough to warrant planting. This little garden had tomato plants, cabbage, and a couple of rows of potatoes was all. Whoever bothered to put all these up must have really liked scarecrows.

He kind of identified with these raggedy looking things. He'd lost a lot of weight in jail, and after running through those woods his jumpsuit was dirty and torn, and his hair felt like straw. But the scarecrows themselves were kind of pretty, in their way. Ingenious. As Gibson walked between the furrows he saw heads made from bleach jugs, buckets, baskets, flowerpots, and burlap bags full of rags. Sometimes the faces were missing and sometimes they were painted or drawn on with black marker or lipstick. Some of the figures were just old rakes and shovels with wigs stuck on top. One had six arms, and another had eight. One held an umbrella over his head to keep out the sun.

Some of the cleverer ones were made from car parts, or bicycle parts, metal pots and coat hangers and pieces from an old wringer washing machine, and one had bells and clacky wooden bits and shiny clangy pans attached all over like some kind of one-man band.

There were two brides with their less-than-handsome husbands. Most were clean shaven, but a few had rope or bead or straw beards. Several old women scarecrows with large breasts and big fannies made a circle around a withered old scarecrow who didn't look like he'd eaten in a year.

Whoever did this put an awful lot of time and effort into it. He didn't know if these things scared the crows, but they sure made him feel more than a little edgy.

Most of the clothes were old and faded, ripped up, and liable to draw attention if he were to walk around in them. But near the end of one row, he came across a scarecrow that looked freshly dressed, a rickety wooden ladder still leaning against the upright pole. It even wore a nice straw hat on top of its big fat mixing bowl of a head. It looked like it was smiling at him. Gibson felt practically chosen.

The old ladder creaked and shook like crazy with each step of his climb. He wondered how long it had been left out in the weather. Once he got near the top he grabbed onto the pole to steady himself. The clothing had been stuffed with straw and rags, the arms and legs tied with twine to the crosspiece and upright. It didn't take much effort to set them free. The strawman had boots attached to a small crosspiece at the bottom of the legs. That made him grin. Gibson had never seen a scarecrow with boots before. If they happened to fit him they were now his.

The mixing bowl was attached somehow to the top of the pole, the straw hat glued on. Gibson reckoned he'd have to do without that hat. Without a body the head at the top of the pole still grinned, which made the dismembered scarecrow that more gruesome.

He'd undressed the downed scarecrow and stripped to his skivvies when he heard the distinctive sound of someone pumping a shotgun behind him. "Freeze, jailbird!"

Gibson could feel his lungs seize. "I mean you no harm. I just needed some clothes."

"Them's Hector's clothes!"

"Hector?"

"That scarecrow you done slaughtered and robbed."

"You name these things?"

"They needed names. Hector was my second cousin, died last year. I named all these folks after my kin."

"Can I at least turn around?"

"Long as you're buttoned up down front. But take it slow."

Gibson turned around. The woman holding the shotgun was short and skinny, in her sixties, maybe older, maybe younger. Appalachian people generally looked older than they were. "I'm harmless, really. Let me go and you'll never see me again."

"You're a jasper, ain't you?"

"What's that?"

"Outsider."

"I grew up in Maryland, the southern part. And I've lived, well, all over the South."

She spat in his direction. "You killed my Hector. He done nothing to you. These are peaceful folk, unlike some I could name."

A crazy woman with a shotgun. Gibson's luck was at least consistent. "I'm really sorry about that. I guess I was desperate. I meant no disrespect to you, or to Hector. Look, I can put him back together for you. Good as new."

"Keep your thieving hands off my cousin! You can't bring back the dead."

"There must be something."

"Cover yourself! Put Hector's clothes on."

The shotgun was shaking, either from her anger or her infirmity. Gibson dressed as quickly as he could. The clothing smelled like sunshine, although the shirt felt a little damp. The boots fit him, so at least there was that. "I guess you really must like scarecrows." He made a weak smile. He hoped it was okay to call them scarecrows and not people.

"They keep me company."

He needed to keep her talking. Keep her mind on something besides shooting him. "You've been using the same ones year after year?"

"No, I burn 'em after harvest time. Early each spring I make new uns. Birds is smarter than folks think, so I have to keep switching them out and changing their outfits. I'll put a necklace of fishbones around some. Sometimes I'll stuff spoiled meat into their shirt pockets. You gotta get up early to outsmart them birds."

"They look lonesome out here."

"Oh, you'll keep them company."

"What, what do you do with them exactly?"

"What a question! Anything I have a mind to. I made them, didn't I, like a ma makes her babies? I like looking out at them at sunrise, and some evenings I sit on the porch and talk to them."

"Do they talk back?"

"No, they don't talk back! I ain't crazy! Now get back up on that there ladder."

"Pardon?"

"You heard me. Climb up the ladder." The shotgun continued to waver. Gibson did as he was told. "Now lift that old mixing bowl. It's on a hook. Lift it off real careful and hand it down to me. My good'un broke and I need it."

He handed it to her, the straw hat still attached. "Can I get down now? I can do some work for you, pay you back for Hector. Not that he's replaceable. At least I could pay you for the clothes."

"Oh, you're going to do some work for me I reckon. Grab onto the pole and step up on that little piece at the bottom. Then turn around careful so's you don't fall off, holding on to that cross piece. Break a leg and you're no use to me at all. Then stay like that, all Christ-like, iffen you even know who that man was, until I get up there." Gibson hesitated, staring at the open ends of the shotgun as she gestured up with it. "Go on. Git up there!"

Gibson was convinced the old bat was going to go all New Testament on him and perform a crucifixion right there in her piddly garden. But she didn't have a hammer on her as far as he could see. Maybe she had some long nails in the pocket of her faded apron. Then he noticed the loops of rope around one scrawny shoulder. She'd come prepared after all.

He thought about jumping her then. There wasn't much to her. She was just a withered old lady. His mama would have been much more of a challenge than her. But the shot gun, and the way it wandered around in the air in front of her, terrified him. He was barely able to hold onto the cross piece with his fingers as he turned around, hugging the pole as closely as possible. Once turned, he hung onto the cross piece for dear life with his sweaty hands. She began wrapping the rope around him, pulling it snug around his arms and chest and making the knots behind his back. She acted like she'd done this before.

"I could die up here, you know."

"I'll feed you. I got some long poles for that, and a water bottle."

"What if it rains?"

"Maybe Uncle Clarence over there will let you borrow his umbrella." She made a dry coughing noise which might have been a chuckle.

"How will I use the bathroom?"

"Do what the beasts of the field do. You're no better than them. I reckon after a while you'll stink bad enough you'll scare the birds better that way. Squirrels and raccoons too if you're lucky."

Gibson wasn't feeling all that lucky. "These ropes are too tight. Could you loosen them just a little?"

She cackled at that and climbed back down. She took the ladder away and headed toward the barn.

After suffering through two days and nights Gibson was more than ready to quit his role as replacement scarecrow, but he could find no way to do that. The old woman tied him up so tightly he could barely breathe, much less wiggle free from his bonds. He had rope burns around his wrists and armpits and severely strained leg and arm muscles from the attempt. Now and then he would get these awful leg cramps, and all he could do was moan his way through them.

He really could have used some kind of head covering. Every time she brought him water or food he begged her for a hat or a cap, but she feigned deafness, didn't even acknowledge he was speaking. So, he guessed that was a No.

The sun was merciless, and the occasional rain brought only temporary relief, quickly turning into a downpour of misery. When the sun came out again he could see the steam rising off his arms, as if his spirit were escaping the prison his body had become.

She did keep her promise and fed him: sausage off a nail at the end of a long pole, whatever bread he could eat before the main part of it crumbled to the ground. He had no way of holding the food but had to gobble it down like a dog. More than once he choked on what he was trying to eat. She'd wait until he was done making noises before offering him more. Water was plentiful, sucked through a plastic straw from a bottle tied to another pole. Sometimes she dumped it on his head "to cool you off some." Most of the time he didn't want that, but she did it anyway just for spite.

She called him "Hector," and talked to him all the time as if they were having this friendly one-sided chat on her front porch. Mostly gossip about other members of the family, Mary Sue's marriage, Cousin Carl's divorce, the ailments which were killing Mildred, Phyllis, and Amelia. There were lots of "You'll remember" and "I reckon you know," about people and things he absolutely had no knowledge of, and sometimes she'd blame him for inconsiderate things he'd supposedly done in their shared past.

Hector had apparently been a bit of a rascal, always in trouble with the law. The connection wasn't lost on Gibson.

At some point she took down the scarecrow next to him, a zombie-looking thing with two eye holes cut into an old pillow, and another bigger hole suggesting a howling mouth. All these holes leaked damp, rotted stuffing that stank when the sun was at its hottest.

He didn't watch her closely. He was feeling particularly bad that day and kept his head turned away, eyes closed. When he could pay attention again he saw that she'd taken his orange prisoner jumpsuit, stuffed it with whatever, and turned it into a scarecrow. For a head she'd taken a partially deflated basketball and drawn a frowny face on it with red marker. She'd written JAILBIRD in large, crude letters across the front of the suit.

With Jailbird's round orangish face and unhappy expression, Gibson thought the resemblance wasn't that bad. The scarecrow didn't have any shoes, just an old pair of men's white socks. For some reason this annoyed him.

For the next few days, his keeper came down to visit the new scarecrow, calling it "Jailbird" and offering it food and water which of course it ignored. Each time she said, "Not good enough for you Jailbird? I'm sure Cousin Hector over there will eat it—he ain't picky at all. Why I believe if I offered him some roadkill he'd gobble that mess right up." Then she'd offer the food to Gibson, who yes, would gobble it right up, whatever it was. But sometimes she'd drop it, pretending Jailbird knocked it out of her hand, in which case Gibson got nothing.

He couldn't last much longer like this. She obviously meant for him to die. His hands had gone numb. He could see blisters on the backs of his fingers from the intense sun. His face felt sore, his forehead tight. He imagined blisters were there as well. Pain had been such a constant companion he'd barely noticed.

He hadn't handled this situation right. His mama used to tell him to make friends with people. Make allies. Wherever you go make friends with people. People wouldn't hurt you if they thought you were their friend, if they saw your humanity. It was the first rule of avoiding becoming a victim, but also the first rule of the con.

The next time the old lady visited he said, through lips cracked and bleeding, "These your late husband's clothes?"

That got her attention. She stared at him. "He ain't late, far as I know. He just run off. Ten year ago, maybe more."

"I'm sorry."

"He was like you. An Es-cape-ee. A jailbird. A convict. A good-for-nothing. But Lord, he could sweet talk. The sweetest words a gal ever heard. Trouble is, they was all lies."

"My mama always told me, you should never lie to a woman, especially after she's given you her heart. That's about the worst thing a man can do."

He could tell, even through his pain, that he'd sparked her interest. "Your mama a good woman?"

"Oh, my mama is the best. I just wish I could see her one more time before … it's all over." He might have rushed and laid it on too thick. But he didn't have a lot of time left.

"You shoulda thought of that earlier … convict." She turned to go.

"My name's Frank. Frank Moore. I should have introduced myself a long time ago."

She tilted her head back, shielded her eyes from the sun. For good or bad, she gave him a long, hard look, then she walked away.

Gibson woke up to something dripping over his right hand. He didn't have a lot of sensation left in that hand, but he could feel the stickiness. He opened his eyes. The old lady had a pole with a rag attached, and something yellowy brown slathering his blisters. "What?"

"It's honey, Frank. Good for the burns. Can't put any on your head though, might drip into your eyes. Sorry about that."

"This works?"

"Grandma swore by it, and she knowed a thing or two. Got some tasty grub for you too."

Bacon speared on a nail. Fresh orange juice sipped from the bottle. It wasn't much, but Gibson relished it. "Are you still going to let me die up here? Burn my body with the others after harvest?"

"Don't be talking about dying now. Got to keep your spirits up." Her voice had softened considerably. Gibson didn't want to get too encouraged, but it was amazing the magic a few kind words could work on a lonely old woman.

After he'd eaten what he could, instead of going back into her house she sat on the ground and watched him. "So, what did you do?" she asked, "that they had to lock you up?"

"Shoplifting, I'm afraid. I knew it was wrong, but Ma'am, I was so hungry. I shoplifted some fruit." At least the shoplifting part was true. That's what they caught him for. She didn't need to know what else he'd done. But it wasn't fruit. A camera, an expensive watch, some earrings, a fancy cell phone. He'd had his pockets full when they stopped him outside.

"They put you on a road crew doing hard labor for a little bit of fruit?"

"Yes, Ma'am. The government, they've got no pity for the little guy, for poor folks."

"My ex done way more than that! Your mama, was she at least able to visit you in that jail?"

"My mama's been sick, unable to travel. I just hope I can see her before, well, you know. But 'blessed are those who mourn, for they will be comforted,' as it says in Matthew." Gibson had a half-dozen bible verses memorized, which he used on an as-needed basis.

"Have faith, son. You're a young man still."

"Not so young, really. Not much younger than yourself, I reckon. I just wish I'd spent my time better, you know? Been a better son. Contributed more. I could have been a real help to someone like you, trying to run this place all by your lonesome. It must be an awful burden."

She stood up. "For true. Most years I hardly manage." She was looking at him intently again. "You in much pain?"

"Quite a bit, I'm afraid. Quite a bit." It almost pleased him not to have to lie.

She walked over to the Jailbird scarecrow, where the weathered ladder still leaned against the pole from when she hung the faux-Gibson up. She dragged it over to Gibson, the top of it level with his thighs. He still didn't want to get his hopes up, but he could feel the tears rolling down his cheeks.

She climbed the ladder slowly. He couldn't tell if it was her shaking or the ladder. Maybe both. She smelled like flour and honey, and a sweet touch of cinnamon. He saw the glint of the knife in her hand, and for a second he thought she was there to do him harm. Maybe she felt sorry for him and intended it to be a mercy killing, so what he'd said to her hadn't landed as he'd hoped.

But then she used the knife to cut the rope around his legs. He felt immediate relief now that he was able to at least flex his knees. She climbed further, reaching around him. He felt her hand on his butt. She may have rested it there longer than she needed to. She hugged him tightly as she sawed at the knots in the rope behind his back. They were both shaking.

Once loose, he would take the knife and kill her with it. It couldn't be helped. A crazy lady like this, she could change her mind at any time, and Gibson couldn't take that chance. He could feel the rope around his back loosen slightly, but it was still tight across his chest and under his neck.

He felt her shift suddenly. She gave a little cry, and then she dropped. Out of the corner of his eye he saw the fallen ladder, the broken rungs.

But she still held on to him. She was strong for a woman her age. She hugged him around the knees, her face buried between his legs, her full weight dragging him down.

He heard a crack, and the little bit of wood he was standing on broke away. She fell all the way then. He heard her moaning on the ground.

But he couldn't see her. He had his eyes closed from the pain. Their combined weight had pulled him down, the rope around his chest slipping higher, and now it was pressed against his neck.

She was saying something. He couldn't quite hear her. It sounded like "Frank," but maybe not. He thought about correcting her, giving her his real name, but the rope against his neck was too tight, and at least for now, Gibson was going to sleep.

Miranda Jo's Girl

The car in the Willisville Store parking lot—"lot" meaning a wide patch of rough gravel by the road—was a new one, from Japan. It was smaller than what Betty liked, but she figured the fellow in the driver's seat was getting good gas mileage. No small thing, the way they robbed you at the pump. Betty's store had two pumps, and she hated how much she charged, but she just provided what folks needed—she didn't always set the price. She couldn't help how much things cost people—she just hoped it wasn't more than they could afford.

A lot of the local people just walked to the store, and only drove to get to their jobs down in Big Stone or Wise. Obviously this blond-headed fellow wasn't local, and when he got out of the car his colorful tie confirmed it. At least he wasn't wearing a suit. But he was carrying a clipboard, and in Betty's experience men carrying clipboards were usually bad news.

She worried it over as he walked toward the store. Willisville wasn't actually a town anymore. If it weren't for the store providing a few convenient necessities to the locals it would just be a ghost town like Ender's Ivy or Castle's Wood or

Drunkard Bottom. Just a weedy spot on the mountain where something used to be. Betty wasn't ready to be a ghost, not just yet. But all it would take was some fellow from the county seat at Wise carrying a shiny metal clipboard.

Not that a young man like this could be charmed by an old gal, but Betty smiled when she gave the fellow a biscuit, another cup of coffee, and a little jar of homemade apple butter as they sat at the small table usually reserved for visiting with friends. "Pretty car you got there," she said, trying to catch him with her eyes. "Bet you get good gas mileage." Her daddy used to say a plain-looking woman like herself had no business flirting with people, but she always had. She guessed it just came natural to her.

He nodded back kind of perfunctory, started thumbing through those clipboard pages like he was going to ignore her pitiful little charms, then spared a second glance for the biscuit, and she knew she'd hooked him. He put down the clipboard, picked up the biscuit, and started spreading on the butter.

"Ma'am," he raised the biscuit to his mouth. "Do you know a Miranda Jo Wheeler? Her, and her daughter Charlene?" He slowly pushed the doughy bread smeared a greasy cinnamon-color into his mouth like that would give her time to consider her answer.

"Mister, I've known all the Wheelers. Known them all my life. Had Miranda Jo in my Sunday school class when she was just a slip of a thing. But Charlene, she's—" Betty stopped then, poking around her head for the words.

The clipboard man dabbed at his mouth, the biscuit gone. A man could choke to death, eating so quick like that. "Troubled? Hard to discipline?" he supplied. "Constantly running away— it's all in here." He tapped the paper. "But Ms. Wheeler's ex-husband Randall is the custodial parent. You knew that, didn't you? Whatever reason the girl gave for running away, she'll need to go back to him. Unless—" He leaned closer. "She is truly missing, and something has happened to the child. Or maybe—" He stopped, looked down at his papers without really looking at them. "She has accused him of abuse."

Betty felt befuddled, not sure how the conversation had gotten where it did. "That would be terrible" was the first thing she thought of.

"Terrible things happen to children, Ma'am." He didn't finish with "in these hills" but Betty was pretty sure that was what he thought. "So you've seen her, then?"

Betty didn't want to lie to this clipboard man. She didn't like lying, nor was she good at it. "Mister," she said. "Did you know that when Charlene left this mountain her mama said she was sure she'd never see her little girl alive again? That's a terrible thing for a mother to feel. Randall—he's a rough character—everybody around here knows that. Miranda doesn't have much money, and she was never very bright, but she tried to do right by that girl. They should have never taken Charlene away. A child belongs with its momma."

"Well, Ma'am, I'm not the judge. It wasn't my decision. I'm just here to determine the child's whereabouts and check on her welfare. Once I turn in my report the higher-ups will finally determine how to proceed."

If Betty had been her father, she would have told him that God was the only "higher up" capable of final determination. But she wasn't her father. She was more like her mother, who had her own ways of doing things, and more interested in helping people than judging them. "I'm not blaming you, Sir," she said. "It's a hard business. I'm sure we all want what's best for the child."

"Well, apparently someone has fallen down on the job, Ma'am. Because I've had a phone call from a Mrs. Presley—"

"Mrs. Presley? The school teacher?"

"She identified herself as a local grade school teacher, yes. She called to tell us she was driving home from a movie in Big Stone Gap Wednesday night when she saw Charlene walking in the middle of the foggy road by herself. She states here." He went thumbing through pages again. "The child's clothes were torn and stained, and there appeared to be blood on her face. Mrs. Presley avoided hitting the child by inches, she says, almost running off the road. When she went back for the child there was no sign of her." He looked at Betty, grim-faced.

Betty thought to say that that was terrible—so much in this world was terrible—it was a word that said what she felt about many, many things. But she figured you could only use the word "terrible" so often in the same conversation before you lost credibility. "Was she sure it was Charlene?" she asked instead. And maybe just asking that question was perilously close to a lie, because of course she was sure. Alma Presley had taught Charlene math for practically all of grade school.

"Sure enough that she has agreed to make a sworn statement. Now Ma'am, I really just have one question for you. Have you seen this child alive?"

"No, I have not," Betty replied without hesitation.

Betty closed the store early. She didn't like to do it—people in their small community depended on her when they had some immediate need. Of course the fact was people on the mountain had all kinds of needs, and if a need was years, even decades old could you still call it "immediate"?

If Betty had been another person in a better life she would have gone home to her family, spent time with her special someone, hugged her own children and breathed in the sweet perfume of their hair. Worried about her own for a while, instead of someone else's.

But she had this life, not some other, so instead of going home to an empty house she pushed her old pickup at a stately creep over to another part of the mountain, into a remote hollow where the fog settled into the rippled ground like clots of milk, and the rough slabs of dark wood cabins gleamed like damp stone. Here the people watched you from empty windows and shadowed porches, but didn't wave like they did in the more sociable parts of the county. Most of these folks never left the sorry protection of their falling down shacks. Most couldn't, and sat still and quiet like moldering pieces of furniture.

The Wheeler house sat by itself below the grade of the road, looking like it had sunk, or been pushed off the edge. Betty eased herself down the path, thinking that if she broke her hip now, and here, she might never open the store again. The bare dirt yard was unsettlingly quiet, without the usual scatter of half-starved chickens and even worse-off cats.

When Miranda came to the door half-dressed and stinking of whisky Betty wasn't at all surprised, except at how disappointed she was still able to feel. Miranda looked at her blearily. "Mizz Betty," she slurred.

Betty pushed past her, looking warily into doorways and behind furniture. She registered the piece of bloody fur by one chair leg, the little bit of throw-up under the TV stand. The screen flickered and rolled, showing people with their cut-off heads nodding below their feet. "Miranda, I told you to watch her, to keep her close."

"She's a handful. You don't know—"

"Of course I know. I told you the way it would be, remember? Remember how we talked about the price you'd have to pay? Something like this, there's always a cost."

Miranda laughed then. It was high-pitched and fading, like someone falling off a cliff. "I said I'd do anything," she said. "Anything."

"So has she left? Miranda, when was the last time you saw her? Because other people, they've seen her, I can tell you that."

"She's there, in the back. I heard her come in a bit ago."

Betty went a little cold hearing that, but she tried to make that chill over into something hard that would allow her to do what was necessary. "How does she look?"

"I ain't checked on her yet."

"Oh, Miranda. They need—well, they're like any other child—"

Miranda howled at that, a laugh so ugly Betty couldn't be in the same room with it. So she let it drive her toward the back of the house.

The rooms stank of filth, and blood, but not Charlene's own blood. Charlene was long past bleeding. Betty found her lying on some faded potato sacks and a spread of old newspapers like you would leave out for a new puppy. Her eyes were white and big as hen's eggs, her mouth like a split in the rough bark of her face. She tilted her head up, but Betty couldn't tell if the child actually saw her. She made a sound, which might have been a hungry sound, and the tongue came out like a worm peeking out of an infected wound. Betty would have left then, if the child hadn't reached out that dirty little hand with the soft, puffy fingers.

Betty's mother used to say the best thing you could do for a child was talk to it. It didn't matter if you were trying to teach the child, or comfort it through some sickness, or just keep it occupied so it would stay out of trouble. "Words is magic," her mother would say. "You'll see soon enough, when you have some of your own."

Of course Betty never had any of her own, and seeing what some of these folk went through, what with the sicknesses and the delinquency and all the things in the world that could take a cherished child away from you she was just as glad, for the most part. And how could she know she'd be any good at it anyway, how could anybody, until it happened, until you raised your child, or until you killed it?

When Miranda Jo had called her that night, crying and carrying on and so worked up she sounded more like some animal in distress than a normal human being, and asked her to come out to the road and bring her truck, that's exactly what she did, because Betty always tried to do what people asked of her. It wasn't any of her business if they could afford the cost or not—they had to decide that.

It was hard to say if Charlene had run away from Randall and been hit by something—something with someone driving it who didn't care enough or was too scared to stop—or if Randall had just driven along and pushed the girl out— certainly he was capable of that kind of meanness. At the time it didn't matter to Miranda Jo—she just wanted her baby girl back. Maybe if Betty hadn't agreed to do what she did with the knowledge her mother had taught her Miranda Jo would have cared who did what. But that bridge had been crossed and the bridge had fallen into the water.

Betty hadn't been able to bring herself to hold the child, or touch her more than absolutely necessary. She had Miranda Jo rub in the salve she made out of certain herbs and certain weeds and mayonnaise and licorice—you'd think they were preparing to roast a pig if you didn't know otherwise. Betty had just said the words, a lot of words, all the words her mother had taught her to make an arsenal against death.

And then she had set that cocoon down the girl's throat, that cocoon for a moth no one had ever had a name for, that cocoon you had to harvest in moonlight and under the weather of despair.

But now that the deed was done, and the child had asked in her way, Betty sat down with her to do what she asked, holding the girl as the mother came into the room to watch. She sat down with the stench of her, down with the death of her, and it wasn't much different than with any afflicted child, she guessed, any child that made you uncomfortable with its differences, with its spasms and jerks and mysterious behaviors. All you could do was hold it, and use your words on it, speaking of the wooden children of the world, the stone children, the empty and the cold, and hoping that someday out of the darkness it would find its way back.

Mr. Belano's Visit

October, a sleepless fog rolls off the Ohio River, inciting hunger in those with no more bellies to feel it, for all that was lost, and all that remained …

Carla, the new girl at the front desk, shook herself awake. The owners of the Lowe had left her alone that slow afternoon with all the old hotel's sighs, creaks, and groans.

Under her elbows the tattered brown envelope stuffed with photos had burst its seams, spilling images of fading forms, startled out-of-focus faces, all over the desk's surface, cascading onto the lobby floor. People were always sending them pictures—old snapshots of the lobby and the front of the building, somebody's granny or Uncle Bob or Cousin Joseph standing at attention in the rooms, long-dead guests sitting on beds and around tables on the mezzanine, with nary a smile in sight.

And of course the crazy pictures. People sent them photographs of the famous ghosts they'd encountered during their stay. Some came in the mail months or even years after the photographer had actually stayed here. You couldn't tell much from most, lots of over-exposed film and mysterious lights, odd reflections, obscuring shadows, sometimes a shot of someone in a Halloween costume. A few might actually be of something, but what exactly that something might be she couldn't say.

Carla didn't know if she believed in any of that stuff. Maybe, but she wasn't sure. So far she didn't think she'd seen anything, except maybe that time by the front windows, a kind of empty form, an absence, filling with light so soft and gauzy it might have been fog. Then again it might have been anything. Or once early in the morning, a maybe-whisper floating through the halls like static bleeding out of a radio. She'd wanted to go searching, but it had only been her first week, and she'd felt too self-conscious.

She actually liked all the old timey pictures of past guests sitting in the lobby in their antique clothes, but it puzzled her that everyone looked so glum, like no one was having fun. A vacation should be a happy thing, or what was the point?

One photograph kept rising to the top of the pile—a dozen or so sepia-tinted grainy shapes looking at the camera as if the photographer had suddenly burst through the door—when a sliver of bright light cut across her eyes. She looked up and saw the old fellow coming through the door, his head tilted to the side as if listening to somebody. She thought he might be a bit confused, or maybe he had some kind of phobia, the way he gave all the lobby furniture such a wide berth as he walked to the desk, his head still cocked, as if attentive to some inner instructions.

She gazed at him directly and smiled broadly—it was the first thing they'd taught her in training. "May I help you?"

He kept glancing to the side as if to catch someone's eye. Carla didn't think she'd ever seen anyone so pale, and as short as he was, and the way his skin blended into his white hair, he appeared more a soft reflection of a real person than true flesh and blood. Then he began looking around the lobby—floors, ceilings—squinting, making soft sounds that might have been appreciation, or distress, or half a dozen other small emotions Carla might imagine. "Sir—are you all right?"

He snapped his head around. "Oh, I'm okay. It was my wife who died. You probably have our reservations as Belano, Mr. And Mrs.? She made the reservations—she always did. We'd always planned this trip, driving up from Charlotte, going to some of the old towns, just to see it all before it disappears. It's all disappearing, did you know that?"

"Well, I guess I never thought about it."

"You should. Because it is, old buildings, even entire small towns, even ways of life. Like fog burning off a windshield, which I've seen a lot of, by the way, since I entered West Virginia."

"We certainly have our foggy days."

"We always planned to do this together. It was to be our big—what do you call it?—road voyage."

"You mean 'road trip'?"

He blinked at her. "Could you show me around? I know she made the reservation, but I'd like to look around first."

"Certainly. Let me grab some keys." She was used to this, having to show people around before they'd check in. Actually, she preferred it—it usually avoided problems later. People didn't always understand what "an authentic, historic hotel" actually meant. To her, and to the people who liked staying here, it meant quaint and colorful, a step back in time. To others it might just mean unimproved.

She noticed as they climbed the stairs to the mezzanine that Mr. Belano held tight to the left railing, his other arm crooked out and stiff as if paralyzed. It made her nervous—what if he was about to have a stroke? She didn't really know how to deal with old people—all her grandparents had died before she was born. "The original kitchen and dining room were here. Now we rent it out for parties, teas, that kind of thing." She didn't know if he was listening, he seemed more interested in the long curtains now billowing out from the windows. She launched into the prepared part of her tour. She could feel her face going red as she made the little speech. "They say that sometimes you can see a beautiful, but disheveled young woman, barefoot wearing a nightgown, dancing to music only she can hear."

He interrupted. "I wouldn't call it dancing, more like swaying."

She stared at him, unable to continue with what the owners had taught her. Up on the second floor she was guiding him down the hall when he turned to the wall and said, "if we had had children, I would have bought them a tricycle just like this one."

"You can see it?" Carla asked. But it was obvious he hadn't been speaking to her.

After a moment he turned and said, "Heard it mostly. My eyes aren't what they used to be, and this hall is a bit dim."

Up in 316 he sat on the side of the antique bed with the ornate metal headboard, stroking the covers softly. "I love this old furniture, don't you?" Carla said. "But people don't always like it."

"My grandmother had rooms just like this. It's wonderful!" Then he swung his legs up and stretched out on the bed and closed his eyes. Carla stepped to the bed in alarm, then stopped. He had moved over to the side. She hoped he didn't expect her to lie down, too! Then it occurred to her that maybe he was just finding his side. Anybody who'd been married a while had their own side of the bed – she'd seen that in her own parents. But still, he shouldn't be on the bed, unless he was renting this entire suite. She started to say something when he opened his eyes and squinted at the window, then jumped up and walked toward the door, stopping once to make a deliberate nod to the window.

He sees Captain Jim! she thought, and hurried out into the hall to catch up with him.

Downstairs he beamed and said, "This is definitely the place!" and she signed him into a room she'd shown him with a nice fireplace and mantle. She helped him bring his bag in—his old dusty station wagon looked like he had been driving thousands of miles, and the back of it was so full of books and clothes and a chair, a lamp, a couple of stuffed trash bags, she wondered how he could possibly see out his rear-view. He must have been buying things in every town he'd stopped.

A few minutes later she was behind the front desk tidying up when she heard the irregular creaking on the stairs. "Mr. Belano?" The only reply was an increase in the ferocity of the creaking. "Mr. Belano?" Carla started around the front desk when the old man swept by in a wind of excited whispering without bothering to answer. "Mr. Belano!"

He stopped and jerked his arm down from its awkward position. He appeared to be arguing with himself then twisted his head around with a huge forced grin. "Yes, dear?"

"If you're going out, I have some brochures you can look at. And I can recommend some places for dinner. There's always the Red Parrot, of course—"

"Why, thank you, but I'm really not all that hungry. I'd love to look at your brochures later, certainly, but this first time out, I believe I'd like to poke around town on my own."

"Sure, I understand—" But he was already at the door, pushing his way through to the outside. For such a frail-looking man he was suddenly moving with surprising energy, his head held sideways, his mouth moving as if speaking over his shoulder. She stepped a few feet outside onto the walk and continued to watch him as he came up to the gleaming stainless steel sculpture of the Mothman, smiled as he actually stroked the thing, chattering away rapidly to himself. After she came back inside she wondered if she should have mentioned their eleven p.m. curfew—she had to lock the front doors when she left—but she couldn't imagine a fellow that age would be gone so long.

When eleven p.m. came and went and there was no sign of him she couldn't bring herself to leave, to lock that poor old man out in the cold. It must have been freezing outside, and he hadn't even been wearing a jacket! At midnight she called the Point Pleasant police. Around one in the morning a patrol car rolled up to the curb with only an officer inside. She watched impatiently as he got out, strolled over to the old station wagon, and opened the door with a set of keys. He spent a long time inside the vehicle poking around, rifling through stacks of papers, taking notes.

"We found him down at the amphitheater. Looked like he'd been watching the river. Went quick, I reckon. Peaceful, I'd say, by that big smile on his face. You say he was just visiting?"

"It was a trip he'd planned with his wife. She died, but he decided to make the trip anyway. I think it was his way of honoring her."

"Or maybe he had nothing better to do. I found a bill of sale for his house in the car. And the back there is full of random personal items—I reckon he just took whatever he could get his hands on, no rhyme or reason to it."

Over the next few weeks Carla spent hours going through that big pile of pictures over and over again. She'd added a few of her own: Polaroids of a smiling elderly couple strolling the hotel arm in arm. Maybe. They were both so pale, and their hair so white, they could have been anything: light from a passing car, a particular pattern of wear or fade in the wallpaper. They were almost transparent, a trick of the light, a flaw in the film, visiting.

The Passing

Some mornings on Little Stone Mountain, Wise County, in the heart of the world, the air was like cold milk, and regular folk couldn't see much past a front porch or their mail box. But Granny Gibson could see, all the way to where the sun waited to burn down the day, and down below her feet, deep into the wells beneath the sacred places, where the energies of the earth coiled.

Granny could do lots of things, but seeing was her special talent. Even with cataracts like two chips of melting ice on her eyeballs. Fact is, she wouldn't let them doctors fix them, lest they interfere with her seeing.

About the only ones up this morning were farmers with cows bawling to be milked, or parents up with a sick child. For Granny Gibson it was a time for gathering roots and herbs, for ferreting out old animal bone, for reading messages from Spider Grandmother in the webs, and for visiting graveyards with packages to deliver.

She gathered up some buckeye and pokeberry roots for Rose who was dying in that hospital down in the Gap. Rose's son told her how they couldn't control Rose's pain and Granny had her own recipe. She'd have to sneak it in, and Granny didn't like to sneak, but Rose was her oldest friend so it couldn't be helped.

Granny had her own pain in her right side, which made her use her dogwood rod for walking, instead of for finding well water or drawing the sickness out of anything from a field to a newborn baby. Until the pain traveled down her leg, and she had to sit, and make herself breathe. Every night she made a poultice for the pain, and drank three different kinds of teas, but the best she could do was make it almost bearable.

Cancer was a word the educated doctors used, but she never, because it scared folk, and because it was too inexact. Cancer was the magic word they used for all the different ways a body would turn against itself. And when she got sick last month, and could hardly sit up or speak, her daughter and granddaughter had hauled her off to that doctor in Kingsport and "cancer" was the word he had used.

So the word was out there and couldn't be taken back, and she had to live with the consequences. For Granny Gibson, the worst thing about having the cancer was the embarrassment that she hadn't cured herself. When folk depended on you for birthing and healing and reading omens and just generally fixing what needed to be fixed it didn't look none too good when you couldn't fix your own self.

But no cure was a hundred percent—she knew that—and all the mountain magic in the world ain't going to save you if your time has come. She'd built her life around reading signs and listening to her body and listening to the world through her body. She wasn't about to deny what it told her. Folk weren't built to last forever, and she'd grown content to take her turn on life's big wheel. Fact was, she was looking forward to doing something she'd never done before. She'd made a drawing of how she wanted them to build her grave house: four windows with bright yellow curtains, because that was the color that gave her power.

She was hiking back up the path toward home, the milky air turning clear as the sun set fire to the trees, when she heard the crying, and that's what set her on edge. Any time she heard crying in the woods she paid close attention. It just might be a lost child needing help, or the ghost of a dead child wanting comfort. It might even be a creature no folk had ever seen before, and it was waiting on Granny Gibson to come over and introduce herself.

Granny Gibson didn't hurry. She never hurried as a rule. Things would most likely still be there when she arrived.

Closer to home she was still hearing the crying, and figured it had to be coming from her place. When she reached the yard, her left hip throbbing because she had hurried a little despite her rule, there was her granddaughter Betty sitting on the edge of the porch, her face in her lap. She wasn't making any sounds now, but her shoulders were heaving like a little bird who'd gotten too wet.

She came up to Betty slow, put her basket down, and used her rod to help lower herself beside the girl. "I reckon your mother found out you was pregnant," she said, stroking the child's hair.

Betty turned her head around, black mascara drips plowing twin tracks down her cream-colored skin. "How did you … Grandma, do you see everything?"

"Not 'tall. I been a midwife since before your mama was born. Not too hard to tell—you about two months out?" Betty nodded with her face in her hands. "I reckon it were that boy from down in the Gap, and I know he ain't involved no more since he moved up to Cincinnati." Betty turned her head again and tried to speak, couldn't. "No offense, sweetheart, but I could smell him."

Betty threw her head down and wailed. "What am I going to do, Grandma?"

"Since you're here on my porch I reckon your mama threw you out and you'll be staying with me. Your mama's a good church goer, but sometimes that confuses a body from doing the right thing. I'd say you already know what you're going to do. You're going to have that baby and get on with your life like the rest of us have to."

"I want you to be there, Grandma, when the baby's born."

"Well, I reckon I'll be nearby sure enough. That much I will promise. But by that time your mama's going to want to be involved and she don't care much for what I do. She'll set you up with a medical doctor and that doctor will do fine by you. Until then I'll do all I know to keep you and the baby healthy."

And quick as that everything changed. Granny Gibson had to ignore what all the signs were telling her. She couldn't just relax and let the cancer take its intended course. Both her daughter and granddaughter were going to need her for some time to come. She had no choice but to heal herself, but even as the intent was writing itself into her heart she saw a black bird drop down from a hickory on the edge of the yard and fly right through her open window, where it would wait, she knew, until it had a human soul in its claws to fly away with.

That night before crawling into bed Granny Gibson stood before her mirror, dogwood rod in hand, passing it over her body, eyes half-closed as she scryed the extent of her disease, mapping its nodes of greatest influence, looking for some place to attack its dark disorder.

Through the haze of her seeing its presence was clear and strong, making a softly glowing shadow just under the bottom of her ribcage, and prob'ly already too big to pass into some stranger's grave, which was the way Granny got rid of warts. But she had promised the girl, and would find a way to keep her word.

There were practices long tested for curing blood poisons and shrinking tumors, and over the next months Granny tried them all. She stopped using sugar except for an occasional shot of corn whiskey, and every day she drank cup after cup of chickweed and nettle tea. She mixed squaw root in with her taters, saving out some in case Betty needed it for labor.

When she thought she'd gotten as much benefit out of those remedies as she could Granny turned to her substitutions, wrapping her skin scrapings and nail clippings in a scrap of yellow apron, adding a few drops of blood and burying the whole package in the cemetery. She sat there all night singing and whispering, trying to make the cancer believe that was her buried there, so maybe it would pass into the ground to join her corpse. The next day she didn't even bother to check herself—she could feel the disorder swelling with pride against her lungs, huge with the pleasure of her defeat, so well-fed she wouldn't at all be surprised if it started speaking.

As the weeks wore down toward Betty's delivery day Granny's pain grew much worse. She let out her dress to hide her belly, which looked like she'd swallowed an eight pound melon whole. But she kept herself busy searching the house for knots to remove in order to protect the baby's umbilical cord, driving nails into Betty's bedposts to deflect the evil influences that drifted over the mountains seeking pregnant women, and preparing the proper salves and herbs to ease the pain of contractions or speed or retard delivery as necessary. She grew tired of scowling at that black bird perched on top her big dresser and invited him down for some raw dough and corn. Soon enough he was eating right out of her hand and she almost forgot why he was there.

Every week Granny caught a ride down to the Gap, no matter how bad she was feeling, and visited Rose in that hospital. She sat with her and talked to her and every now and then gave her friend some root paste to chew on. She was sure Rose knew she was there, but her friend had a hard time showing it. She lay wrapped tight in her sheets, her eyes closed and her breath ragged and gaspy and hard to listen to.

As her time approached Betty grew whiny and lazy and Granny Gibson had to stop herself a dozen times a day from snapping at the child. Granny was afraid she was going to be breaking that promise she made, because she honestly couldn't see herself there on Betty's delivery day.

One morning Betty was sitting at Granny's kitchen table, her head resting on the oil cloth as she sang one scrap of riddle or song after another, her belly as big as it could possibly be. "Snips and snails and puppy dogs tails—that's what little boys are made of. Sugar and spice and all things nice—that's what little girls—Granny? That ain't true, is it?"

"Not exactly, but sometimes it seems that way."

"So what are babies made of?"

"Blood mostly, I reckon. Mother's blood. And the mother's flesh, and the flesh that grows out of mystery, all weaved together."

"Gross."

"Why, Betty Gibson, don't you be disrespectful in my kitchen!"

"Sorry, Grandma," Betty said, and closed her eyes.

Granny gazed at her granddaughter, no more than a child, with her belly so round and tight against her dress, until the idea came, and once it came, it had to be delivered quick, because time was running away from them both.

"Betty, child, I have to go out, but I'll be back soon as I can. There's stew on the stove—can you manage?" Betty mumbled something, and Granny filled her basket with what she needed, grabbed her rod and headed out the door.

She asked one of the Carter brothers to give her a ride down the mountain and into town. He plainly didn't want to, but she knew he wouldn't tell her no. He dropped her off at the hospital, just like she asked.

Rose's chest rose up jerkily with each harsh breath, like she was being punched in the back. The sound was like air blown through water, bubbling, rattling, as her old lungs drowned.

"Rose, Honey, I'm sorry, but I know you'd understand." Granny's work never hurt nobody, not even if hurting was what they deserved, which certainly didn't describe Rose, the kindest person Granny had ever known. But Rose was past hurting, and passing her way out of the world, and wouldn't mind at all, Granny knew, this one last favor for an old friend.

In the bathroom Granny slashed her hand deep with her paring knife, let the blood drip into the stuff already gathered onto a piece of tin foil—dough and select pieces of squirrel meat, some saffron root left over from a cure for gout, a black feather clipped from her newest friend—and then she molded her poppet with skinny legs and swollen arms and a twisted little head, and a hard round belly where the cancer was, rough-made because she was in so much pain, both hands trembling and clumsy. But it didn't need to be pretty, and the foil helped hold the shape.

She wrapped it in a towel and hid it under the lower mattress, because that was the one they never moved when they changed the sheets. She had no idea how long that awful transfer would take, but imagined it would be hours. Of course if Rose died before the thing were done it would all be for nothing—there had to be a container for the tumor to pass into. She couldn't even look at Rose again, tried to make it out to the street, but ended up lying behind a bush, imagining the cancer out of her as she fell asleep.

The next morning Granny went inside to use the bathroom, but passing by reception saw her daughter sitting there, who came over and made her sit down. "Mother! Where have you been—you've got dirt all over you, and weeds sticking out of your hair!"

Granny stared at her. "I slept in the bushes. What are you doing here?"

"I got a call from your neighbor's house last night. Betty was having contractions, and had no idea where you were. You know I was going to pick her up anyway. I was just mad about her being an unwed mother like me—"

"Is she alright?"

"Delivering her any second. At first there weren't no beds, but then your friend Rose—oh, Mama, you knew about Rose didn't you? She died last night."

Granny felt her belly, which was flat, and empty.

Granny Gibson used to see—that had been her talent. Seeing what other folks couldn't, or didn't want to. Country folk see a lot—they see calves born bad, and they see kin dead in all kinds of ways—life is hard, but country folk usually aren't shy about telling what they've seen.

Except for the Gibson baby. All the nurses would ever say was it looked like it had a mouth. Just that one thing. It looked like it had a mouth.

Granny Gibson could have seen more, but chose not to.

La Mariée

Jan couldn't remember exactly when he'd acquired the print. Sometime early in his college years, certainly, not long after he'd first discovered Chagall. Then he'd seen it hanging on the dusty back wall of some bookstore, priced at more than he could afford—he couldn't afford anything in those days. But he'd wanted a Chagall on the wall, even though he didn't understand much of what he saw in Chagall's paintings. He just admired the way they made him feel, and it didn't really matter which Chagall, so he'd bought the first one he saw.

He didn't grow up with nice things. They didn't have art in that three-room cabin high in the Tennessee hills. But he still thought of that region as one of the most beautiful places on earth. It just didn't offer everything he needed.

Despite his affection he didn't look at the print very much in those days—he didn't really know how to look at art. The pieces he really liked always filled him with an indefinable sense of longing. And although "longing" was an emotion he did not want to feel, or even to think about, he fully understood its importance.

The painting appeared to portray a world much better than the world he'd grown up in. Not necessarily safer, or more luxurious, but certainly more interesting than his world, and furnished with the things he cared most about. It was all too much, in the end. Jan could not think about these things and still have a normal day. So although he did not consciously intend to, he hung the picture too low on the wall, and very quickly there were pieces of furniture in front of it. He always remembered it was there, and now and then would catch a glimpse of the beautiful bride's face when he moved things around in the room, or he would see the fish with arms holding the candle on some shadowed part of his wall where it could not possibly be.

The young bride in the painting wears a red dress. She stares forward, doll-like. Her eyes are wide and her mouth is so small perhaps her lips are pursed in amusement or for a kiss. Perhaps she simply has an extremely small mouth, and that, coupled with her incredibly long neck, more horse's neck than woman's, makes him think she is no ordinary bride but someone magical—if you married her your life could never be ordinary again.

The way she stares, the stillness of her, might lead you to think she's not a real woman but a mannequin the dressmaker has outfitted for a wedding shop window. See, there he is fussing around her head, positioning the bridal veil so it looks perfect on her.

But then you look at her hands, and they are so expressive, the fingers of the right spread in order to delicately hold the bouquet of white flowers, the left slightly open to hold the fold of the long veil back so that she can see more of the dress, so you know that she is a living, breathing bride, staring at herself in the mirror, and she is still because she is overcome with emotion—never in her life had she imagined she could look this good.

But Jan kept her in the shadows behind the furniture in his crowded little apartment in Bristol Tennessee, his little secret. Over the years he brought many women to this apartment, some he thought he loved and some he knew he did not, and he never told any of them about the painting. And if they noticed a dusty edge of the frame and wondered what the rest of it looked like they said nothing about it to him.

Perhaps he never mentioned La Mariée because he knew none of these women loved him. Or because he suspected that once he exposed this young bride in the red dress she would never mean the same to him again.

Although he went north for college, and lived there for a time, the southern Appalachians kept calling him back for funerals and reunions and long visits. He eventually came back to teach, now and then full time, but mostly as a fill-in, a substitute, going where he was needed. Mostly poor schools in the mountains. History, English, and Social Studies were his specialties, but he led gym classes when necessary, or managed study halls, or hired out for private tutoring.

But he didn't want to live in those little mountain towns. Bristol wasn't a big city, but it had a library system and some culture. At least it didn't feel poor to him. He paid for the privilege of living there with lengthy commutes.

Of course, he was poor. He could only afford this small apartment, and the few things necessary to fill it. He always told his students they could be anything. They just needed to aim high. It was advice he did not take himself.

When Jan was in his fifties a woman moved into the apartment next door. He supposed she wasn't a very attractive woman, and the fact that he should care to think such a thing filled him with shame, particularly since he avoided looking at his own body. He had two mirrors in the apartment, one above the bathroom sink and one mounted on the wall between his bathroom and his bed, tall enough that he could use it to judge his outfit before going out for the day. He used the one in the bathroom for shaving, for cleaning his face, a broad pale face which seemed to have little to do with him. He barely recognized its rounded square shape, the wrinkles around the eyes, the hesitant mouth and weak chin. When he took a shower he moved swiftly through his bedroom to his dresser, the blur in the mirror nothing more than a wraith, an approximation, a pale memory of who he used to be.

He'd never married, not by choice but because he'd never been able to make the proper connection. He supposed some people had a talent for making such connections, although he couldn't be sure, because he had no knowledge of how such a talent might work. He'd lost touch with the basics of dating—it had become a foreign land he no longer had a visa for.

He'd listened to the woman as she'd moved in, two men in blue coveralls hoisting the large items up the stairs—the dry steps popped and cracked so loudly under their weight he almost expected some catastrophic collapse. She handled the rest of it herself, puffing and groaning and cursing under her breath as she struggled up the stairs. Unlike in a Chagall painting, objects did not float around until they found their perfect placement. He knew he should have gone out and helped her, but he didn't know exactly how to begin such a transaction.

In his agitation he got up out of his chair and started to rearrange his own furniture. He wasn't exactly sure why he decided to do such a thing, except if he were asked later (and who would ask?) why he hadn't helped her move he might say he'd been so busy moving his own belongings he hadn't been aware of her struggle. To make this anticipated lie more plausible, he moved rapidly around the small apartment with his arms full of his displaced possessions to make as much noise as possible. He pushed and pulled chairs and tables and bookcases and cabinets around the rooms, leaving them at barely-considered locations, going completely on instincts he knew he did not have. And in the process brought La Mariée out of the shadows for the first time in years.

He stopped then, exhausted and a little dizzy. Sweat trickled down his body in discrete tracks, like tears. It was a ridiculous thought, the body crying, not out of sadness and not out of joy, but out of the relief of purposeful movement.

Jan stared at the print mounted in the same spot for all these years, the painting he'd loved but had never felt comfortable looking at and had never been able to stop thinking about.

She was younger than he remembered her, her face less defined, but still as beautiful as ever. The man floating above her—whether a dressmaker or impending husband— seemed overjoyed just to be able to look at her.

The flowers she carried had not wilted, and the goat-headed man beside her still played a lively cello, but much of the original blue background was laden with dust.

Jan found a rag and began to wipe the dark away, the dust smearing where it mixed with his sweat. He tried to touch the surface as gently as possible, afraid that age and rough handling might deform her. He still felt slightly light-headed, which resulted in small, barely discernible movements, or transformations, in the figures. An enraptured fish appeared suddenly out of the darkness holding a candle aloft, slowly blinked his eyes, moving his tail fin ever so slightly in order to remain in the same position. It felt almost as if he'd been resting deep in some other place until Jan rediscovered him. And was that red-topped table behind the fish just beginning to dance?

As the dark night began to seep out of the painting, and the deep Chagall blue—the color of oceans, or the color of dreams—began to appear, the houses of the painter's lost village became visible, and the figure of a man Jan had not remembered began to play the flute, his energized limbs seeming to fade in and out of abstraction. This flute player didn't even look at the beautiful bride. He was so intent with his performance it was obvious he was in love with something else.

Jan understood the painting no more than he did decades before. Apparently the years had taught him little which would illuminate the mysteries of La Mariée. But still he understood there was something vital about these two-dimensional images which generated longings he could not quite understand.

Some time that afternoon music began to drift out of the woman's apartment. He was not well-versed in classical music, could not have provided the names for more than three composers, the names of any of their compositions, certainly couldn't have matched a composer to a specific song, but he was able to distinguish the separate voices of their instruments, sometimes even when they were part of a swelling wall of sound. Out through the woman's door, down the short hall and into his rooms floated violins and cellos, flutes and oboes, and drums soft as distant cannon.

He took off his shoes and walked to his door in his stocking feet, turned the knob slowly and pulled the door open an inch or so. His new neighbor was just coming up the stairs: a vintage floral scarf over her head made her look old-fashioned with her wide face, reddened cheeks and nose. As she trudged higher up the staircase he saw that she carried a bag of groceries in one arm, and a bouquet of white flowers in the other hand. She was old enough to be someone's grandparent, but then again so was he.

She turned her head and their eyes met. There was no way he could pretend—she knew he was watching her. He closed the door softly, quickly. No doubt she thought him some sort of pervert, or at least someone closeted and eccentric, someone who did not know how to behave normally in the presence of other people. He walked away, putting some distance between himself and the door as if that would protect him.

A few minutes later there was a knock. Of course, it had to be her seeking some sort of accounting. He could simply not answer, but she certainly knew he was there. And if he didn't answer now, what was he supposed to do in the future, hide in his apartment as long as she lived next door?

He eased the door open. She stood there, the music sweeping out behind her from her open apartment door. She smiled (she did have a wide face), and examined him up and down. She still wore the floral scarf over her head, and she still carried the bouquet of white flowers.

"May I help you?" he asked hesitantly.

"We're neighbors now, did you see?"

What did she mean by that? "I heard the movers earlier."

"Correct. An arm and a leg, I tell you. I decided to handle a lot of it myself." Was she about to accuse him? "But it's done. Do you have a vase I can borrow, for these?" She shook the bouquet.

"I've—I think I have a jar."

"That's great, I'll give you some." She walked past him before he could catch his breath.

He practically ran to get the jar from the kitchen. When he got back with it half filled with water she was close to La Mariée, examining her. "Beautiful print," she murmured. "I just love Chagall. I take it you do as well?"

"I like the picture." He thought about it. "I don't understand it very well."

"Let me take that before you spill it." She eased the jar out of his trembling hands. "Why don't we sit down? I'll take care of this." She put the flowers in the water and placed the arrangement in the center of the coffee table. She glanced around. "Oh, did you just move in as well?"

Embarrassed by the mess, he wondered why he had allowed her to—guide him like this. Then he replied, "Just rearranging things."

"Feng shui! Absolutely." She sat down near him on the couch, looking not at him but at La Mariée. Her forwardness intimidated him, but there was an awkward quality about her that reminded him of himself and put him at ease. "You have a lot of Chagall's standard imagery here. The goat-headed man, the musicians, so much music, the language of love, you know?" Amazingly, she winked at him.

He again became aware of the music pouring out of her open door. Should he remind her it was still open, anybody could walk in? He didn't think it was his place.

"His main subject was love. The musicians play at births, deaths, weddings? Every time you're at a crossroads, but these are also important events in your love calendar." Love calendar? Was she talking astrology here? "There are tons of fish in his paintings—his father worked in a fish factory. All the houses are from Vitebsk, his hometown. He must have missed it terribly. They signify memory, and dream, as does all the blue."

"I thought the blue might be dream," Jan said, surprising himself.

"There you go! See, you may understand this painting better than you know. His use of space, the arrangement of the objects, I think he's suggesting that memory, dream, the past and the present, they all exist at the same time for us because of love."

"What about the bride?"

"Well, it is called La Mariée. Maybe she thinks it's the most important day of her life. Everything's floating around her, including that happy gentleman fixing her veil. They thought that way about marriage back then. I wouldn't know, never having been married myself."

So they sat there, both of them propped awkwardly on the couch, staring at this painting, neither of them young, or good-looking in any conventional way. She talked some more about the picture, but he had stopped listening. He was listening only to the music from the other room. He gazed at the way the man adjusted the bride's veil, and totally unexpectedly, reached over to touch this woman's scarf where it lay against her head, and immediately felt he might float away.

The Grave House

Your head was like a house, Annie thought. Livin' inside was your teeth and tongue, your eyeballs and a whole lot of foolishness. Like in any other house, what lived inside could ruin it. And what died inside, stayed.

Back when Annie's grandma was still alive, between the two big wars and before all those little uns, if you built a house in the hills you built it fast and you built it simple: four walls, floor, and ceilin' all pretty much the same, a roof with some tin on it, and a good size sittin' porch. How you divided it up inside was up to you: most went with a kitchen in back and a front room married to it with a hall (that's where the family pictures went). Bedrooms come in between, two to each side if the house was deep, sometimes two on one side and one on t'other (the big one for the parents and maybe the baby). If you wasn't too lazy you built yourself a big back porch. The outhouse was outside ("whar hit belongs," accordin' to Grandma). Most houses was pretty much the same when you first built them — they kept your head dry.

If you started doin' good you might do a fix-up, add on a parlor and a dinin' room, or maybe even go with an inside toilet off that kitchen. Maybe you'd replace the newspaper on the walls with somethin' better. Like everythin' else, some did and some didn't. But most folk back in the hills was stuck their whole lives in whatever they built that first time out. "So best build it right," was what Grandma told her sons and daughters. Which they pretty much did, except Annie's own pa. Every time in her memory, at least, when her grandma came to visit, at some point she'd hear her say, "Well, Jake's no carpenter." Annie didn't like that—it made her feel unlucky. But she guessed it was true.

Another thing she'd hear her grandma say, especially when she drank too much to be polite, was "Remember I want me a nice grave house, so don't let Jake build it. If Jake built it, it wouldn't be worth a lick."

So of course when Grandma died Jake got the job of buildin' the grave house. That's the way things worked out in her family. No one else wanted to spend that much time in a graveyard, especially not for that sour old woman, but Annie's pa didn't seem to mind.

So her pa Jake set to buildin' that grave house, makin' it big enough not just for Grandma but for all the rest of the family too when they passed on. A grand old grave house just as big as the ones for the most important families down in town, one that would be passed down for generations. But he just plain didn't have the talent for it. Annie's pa built a shaky grave house just like he built a shaky house for his family. Grandma had been right. Nothin' her pa ever made was worth much. Annie hadn't made up her mind yet if that included her. She'd never had the guts to ask Grandma her opinion.

Now, seventy years later, still livin' in this dark and shaky old house, Annie was wonderin' if she'd become her own grandma.

Even though it happened pretty regular, it always came as a sad surprise. She'd get up to use the bathroom in that poor shack of her family home, the responsibility of it all now hers, the beaten wooden floor crackin' loud with each step so she'd feel like the house was about to explode. She'd walk the hallway of gray pine walls, bare now of wallpaper or paint or any other wall coverin' you'd expect of a proper home. At the end of that hall was an old-fashioned bathroom, built with all kinds of crazy corners and slopes that ought'n a been there, like the carpenter was drunk (which he had been, she could be pretty sure), but still a luxury to have one indoors. The hall was fat with pictures, frames a lot finer than the walls they were on, scattered like they got thrown and just stuck there, kids and babies, teenagers, mothers and fathers, aunts, uncles, cousins galore, grands so old they looked more like tree stumps than people, all of the frames full of dust. And each time just before openin' the bathroom door her lantern would pick out the photo of her grandma mounted eye-level, trapped inside the best frame ever, just like she was the queen of Sheba. And each time Annie would forget that was a mirror she was starin' at, and forget that hair full of ice and those eye holes full of wrinkles was her own. Until she blinked, and knew, and started cryin' because it snuck up on her, and she had no idea how she'd gotten so old and lonely inside this mess of boards, this house barely standin' deep in these southwest Virginia woods.

"Applesauce? Why do you cry so, Applesauce?"

She looked up from her plate smeared pretty yellow with egg and found her pa's eyes: big and gray and slow as slugs. "Don't call me that, Pa. Momma says it ain't proper," she said, although in truth she loved the name he'd given her. She just didn't want him to get in more trouble with Momma.

"Never mind your momma." Then he grinned. "Nope. I mean you to mind your momma; just don't worry about what she might say for a half a whisker. Why are you cryin', is what I want to know."

Annie never lied to her pa except maybe oncet, so she just told him, "I don't want to clean up the grave house this mornin'—it's all messed up in there."

He sat down beside her, smellin' of strong soap, tobacco, aftershave, and just under, that forever whiskey stink. She leaned against him, but she'd run out of tears. Her pa always said tears wasn't the kind of water what did the crops any good, so she'd always made it a point not to waste much time cryin'. "You ain't scared o' haints is you?" he whispered.

She looked up at him and saw that he wasn't jokin'. "Not much," she said. "Maybe a little."

"Ain't no haints in there, Applesauce. That's your grandma down in that grave house, and your grandpa Old Charlie, and your baby sister."

"She never had a name, did she?" she asked for the dozenth time.

"I reckon the Lord gave her his own, secret name," he said again, for the dozenth time. But this time he leaned forward and whispered, "I always call her Lilly, but that's my secret, Applesauce. Don't tell your ma. It's probably agin our religion, or some such."

"Oh, I won't," she said, thinkin' that's what she'd call her dead sister from now on, but quiet, in her heart, just like Pa. "Do you think Grandma knows little sister's secret name?"

"I reckon she must. The Lord probably told her when he gave her your sister to babysit."

Annie sat thinkin' quiet about that a little while. One of the things she loved best about her pa was that he was patient enough not to interrupt her when she was thinkin' about important things. Then she said, "They's all kind of twisty dead weeds balled up in that grave house. What if it's got snakes and spiders, too?"

"You can take a stick in there with you and you can move things around slow—we're in no hurry here. I've been checkin' it out every day and I ain't seen a snake yet, but you know what to do if one come along. I just got to take that cow over to Gibson's this mornin'. I'll be helpin' you soon's I get back."

"'Cause cleanin' up the grave house is important."

"Sure is. It's shameful how neglectful we been while your momma was ailin'. We have to show our dead the proper respect if we want them behavin' proper. That way they stay in their little house and keep us good company. You want them to keep us good company, don't you?"

Annie didn't know if she wanted such a thing or not. She couldn't even decide on her favorite color so how could she know what she wanted her dead family folk to do?

"Miz Willis? You in there?"

Annie opened her eyes onto a tangle of dead white weed, her hand clutchin' it with her palsy. She wondered if maybe she'd fallen into the ditch line again—it got so embarrassin' layin' there waitin' for somebody to haul her out. Then she realized it was her own hair spread out over her bed pillow.

"Miz Willis!"

"Who's that callin'?" Her own voice scared her with its brittleness. She twisted her neck and pointed her face toward the door. She could see a big man outlined in the rusty screen.

"Jack Tolliver! I come to do the grave house! Like you wanted, remember?"

She was mixed up for a minute. She didn't want the grave house at all. She was stuck with it. She didn't know what to say, so she said, "I'm not dressed!"

"I'm terrible sorry, Ma'am, but I need for you to show me what to do in there. Some of them old stones been moved around, and broke—I just don't want to do nothin' disrespectful, or mess things up more!"

"Wait a minute!" she cried, "I'm not dressed!"

"Ma'am, I swear I'm not comin' inside. I just needs you to come outside, you hear?"

"I told you I was comin' out, Jack Toliver! You just be patient! I ain't dressed yet!"

"Yes'm," he replied, so soft she could barely hear him.

She couldn't remember where she'd put her housecoat, or her overalls, or anythin' else. She stumbled over her old boots—those had been Pa's, back when he was alive—but she could hardly go outside, in front of a man, with just her boots and her nightgown on. Although she did feel just a ghost of a thrill, to her great surprise, to think there was a man just outside her front door, and she just getting' out of bed. She'd never known men, never been married. Most folk would say she'd never had a real life, locked up inside this old farm, this house, inside her rough old head. She couldn't remember the last time she'd been to town, and company was as rare as a hen's tooth. The thought made her grin. When she was a girl she hated chickens—they got on her nerves.

"Applesauce, you done drawed that chicken with a mouth full of teeth!" Her pa sounded both shocked and tickled. "What's Miz Gibson goin' to think when you bring that picture into school?"

"Pa, I drawed that chicken with teeth 'cause chickens is evil and I hates 'em!"

He crouched down beside her so that his head looked like a big old melon on the edge of the table. He looked serious. "What makes 'em evil, Applesauce?"

"'Cause they squawks all the times and they chases me around the yard."

Then Pa opened his mouth so wide it looked like he was goin' to eat her, and eat the whole rest of the world after, so it scared her, but then he was howlin' loud and slappin' his knee with his eyes shut so tight and the tears leakin' out. It was still kind of scary but she knew that was the way he laughed when he heard a good 'un, so she must a just told a good 'un and it made her feel all growed up and proud.

Then her pa squeezed her nose and ran out the door and she screamed and chased him out the door because that's the way they always did it. Annie stumbled out into the dark yard but her pa was nowhere to be seen. Jack Tolliver was nowhere to be seen neither. No one was anywhere she could see no matter how hard she tried. She looked down at the way she was dressed—just the boots and the nightgown—and thought it was probably a mighty good thing that nobody was there to see her.

She looked around the yard, at the old barn and the chicken coop—that last chicken, Glenda, died at least five year ago, but still, when the wind come up, you'd find little puffs of chicken feather stuck up in every little cranny and snag on the farm. Like special seeds to make new chickens, but Annie wasn't havin' no more of them evil chickens, not if she could help it.

She looked back at the house and was surprised at how purty it looked with the sun just down, like your best memory of the ugliest thing in your life. She hated that old house as much as she hated to be thinkin' the hate, but it wasn't too bad right now. This farm wasn't such a bad place for spendin' your days—she just wished it didn't have to be every last day you had to spend in your life.

She'd always wanted to travel. Maybe to Kansas where the tornadoes lived, but anywhere, really. But who'd be left around to tend to the grave house?

She spun around then, like some windup thing what spring done broke, so's she was dizzy and ready to lose her breakfast, 'cept she didn't think she'd had breakfast that mornin', couldn't remember the last mornin' she'd had a breakfast, not even some nasty egg after that last evil chicken died. But dizzy or hungry she made herself look at the grave house, and staggered out toward it, almost fallin' when she started up the hill, and had to grab onto an old fencepost, so rotten it fell apart in her hand, fillin' the air with little pieces, like she was one of them magicians done a trick.

Mad as spit, she looked down at the pitiful thing. Here she'd stayed all this time because she was the only one left to take care of the grave house—Pa said it had to be her job—but she'd always hated the thing, didn't like to go near it, so when she remembered, she'd hire somebody to tend to it, but that was about it. So why'd she have to stay?

It was a little house, kind of like the family house she'd always lived in, but even smaller. Big enough to stand up inside, swing a pick or sling a spade, haul a headstone in there. The floor was dirt and they was benches all around the inside against the walls, so the family could visit the "dearly departed"—like the preacher called 'em, or the "dead kinfolk," like her pa always said. Sometimes they might have a picnic in there on a hot day. It was shady, and nice, and you brought flowers for the family members what wasn't eatin', 'cause they was too busy bein' dead.

Annie hated the grave house, but she'd always kind of liked them picnics, the shade and the food, just as long as she didn't have to eat no evil chickens, who once they got inside her they might haint her with their squawks and their evilness. Like her pa used to say, "Sometimes you gotta make the best outta a bad sigiation!"

But nobody had stood up in that grave house in a very long time, or sat on them benches, or had no picnics. That grave house was full of weeds, and brambles, and animal houses, and probably snakes, and probably worse, and bushes, and little trees what grew up right through the roof, and dark places, and stinkin' places, and lonely places, and the scariest places in the world. All because Annie didn't take good care. She didn't take care at all. So now when she died, where was she goin' to go? Would they burn her up like some did, or would they just grind her up and feed her piece by piece to the evil chickens?

It was almost like her momma and her pa, her grandma and grandpa Old Charlie, and Baby Sister Lilly, wasn't buried in there at all. How could they be? You couldn't even see their stones no more, you didn't know if they still had stones.

Maybe the only place they was buried now was inside that tiny, rough head of hers, all of 'em waitin' at the picnic, wantin' to be fed.

"Miz Willis? You in there?"

Just like she'd been buried on this farm, in that awful old shaky shack, all her damned life.

"Miz Willis? You in there?"

"I told you I ain't even dressed! What kind of man is it go botherin' a lady what ain't dressed?"

"Now now, Applesauce, don't go bitin' off heads. The man jus tryin' to do a job for the family."

Pa's voice came wet and soft into her ear, heavy with liquor and somethin' stronger. Formaldehyde, maybe, or worst.

Annie looked up at the tin ceilin' of the grave house, the way all the little nail holes in the metal let the sunlight through like they was stars. She didn't like the grave house, for sure didn't like livin' in the grave house, but she did like this part, makin' the best out of a bad sigiation.

"Pa," she said. "You lied to me about that snake. You promised he wouldn't bite me!"

"Oh, Applesauce—I don't think I promised now, did I?"

"Man oughtna make promises he can't keep," Grandma said from somewhere dark, and cold, and nearby. "It's like sayin' you're gonna make somebody a fine grave house, but instead you make them somethin' mean and shaky."

No one said anythin' for a time, then her pa said "Yes'm."

"Miz Willis? You in there?"

This time Annie didn't answer. This time she just laid there quiet with all the others. The old man's face appeared in the doorway. He had a hoe, and a shovel, and some stout clippers to cut through the thick brambles of all her dead white hair. "Why there you is," he said, and picked up an old broken stone, dusted it off, and put it back into place. "There you be."

She wanted to tell him he had it all wrong. She wanted to scream and yell and shake this shaky old house, to pound and claw her shaky old head. She wanted to tell him she wasn't stone, and she wasn't dust, and she wasn't weed, bramble, or bush. She wanted to tell him she wasn't cold. But she knew that would be a lie, and she couldn't lie to the man, not with all of them, her entire family, restin' there, listenin'.

Diorama

The shopping buggy screeched. Jake peeked to see if any birds were caught in the wheels. He knew they weren't but liked to check out even his craziest notions. Maybe he was getting feeble-minded, he didn't know. Sometimes you see the signs in other folks but not in your own self.

He liked to imagine Richmond was inside a big glass case, and he was one of the ant people inside, a critter too small for the high and mighty to notice when they stepped on him. The buildings were cardboard, the details painted or glued on. It wouldn't be hard to make. He could construct a fair to middling Jake with toothpicks, clay, and gray construction paper, bend him some for stooped shoulders as he pushed his jangly buggy around. Those giants wouldn't know the difference.

He couldn't remember a hotter day, but it was Saturday, errand day, so he was out in his dark gray three-piece, wide lapels and wide legs, a shiny blue tie dangling from his neck. The suit had been Daddy's, who wore it better, and once upon a time it fit Jake well. Now the shoulders slipped off if he weren't careful. He used to look like Daddy, but no more.

Folks might think it a crazy thing to wear a suit when it was hot as all get-out, and no breeze to ease your suffering, but he only owned work clothes and this suit, and he didn't want to go into stores wearing grungy overalls, not even into charity shops.

Jake knew the suit needed throwing away, too far gone even for charity. The shoulder seams were popped and frayed, the elbows and knees almost wore through. But at first glance it made a fair impression. Lily, who couldn't see well no more, thought so. From a distance he could be mistaken for stylish. "Lookin' good, m'man!" said a homeless fella camped under a tarp in the alley. "Is it a wedding or a funeral?" said another. He heard that cleverness about once a month.

At least the tie was good, grabbed out of the bin at church. Probably worth more than the suit.

He had more than a few blocks to go before getting back to the cheap residential hotel and the third-floor apartment he shared with Lily. They'd been there four years already and it was home as far as he was concerned, but it never would be for Lily. One of many things he couldn't fix for her. He'd brought her here, but he couldn't take her back. Hell, there was hardly anything left to take her back to.

He took his time. From up there in the clouds it might look like he was standing still. But he couldn't help his wife at all if he stroked out in the street. So he walked slow and took regular breaks. She worried about him out here among the beggars and thieves. But he figured he looked too poor to rob, another elderly man wandering the Richmond streets with no purpose except finding the next meal or a good spot to lie down for the night. He carried Daddy's blackjack just in case, but he doubted he had the strength to use it.

He squinted his eyes against the sun. It made a better way to see. Fields of parking spaces became fields waiting to be plowed. Piles of rubble became stones pulled out of those fields. Abandoned store fronts were places where a hill got cut through to make a road. All the telephone and power poles trees stripped bare but still connected one to the other. Those tall buildings in the distance was a view of the next hazy ridge.

The buggy wasn't heavy, even almost full. More material for the project, although "project" wasn't the word he wanted. Why was it so hard to find the right word? Sometimes there was no good word for a thing, and you had to use whichever one was available. Memory was a good word. He was building a memory.

A box full of dirt. A bag full of fake moss. Some stiff Styrofoam he got from the trash behind a florist shop—the good kind that didn't crumble easy. More of the green paper and tissue he could tear ragged and glue to painted toothpicks for trees. Different shades of green paint in cans and little bottles. It seemed like he could never make enough trees or find enough shades of green to equal the hills he remembered. He could spend a full year just on trees. A couple of little buildings from the model train store he could paint and scuff up to look like houses back home—the big ones the Coxes and the Gibsons lived in at the top of the mountain. He needed a few more for their holler and the one next door. The unimportant buildings— the shacks and barns he and Lily barely remembered—he could cobble up out of match boxes. The funny thing was Lily sometimes said she liked those ones the best.

He had a fresh bag of tiny toy soldiers from the thrift store. Now that Lily couldn't see so well he could cut parts of the soldiers off, melt them some, paint them, and tell her they were Packer Wells, or Emily Williams, or any of their other neighbors from southwest Virginia and she would think she recognized them. Sometimes those were better than the ones he made from toothpicks, clay, and paper, and sometimes not. It depended on who they were meant to be. A little red paint on top of a soldier carved down near nothing created a reasonable image of her dead brother Ben.

He stopped in front of the café with the dirty windows and thought about going inside, but he didn't want to risk his buggy by parking it. He could ask to bring it in, but he was too shy. He rested his face against the glass and watched the folks at their tables, eating their food, or looking at it. It would make a sad photograph. He ate here a couple times before. The food wasn't good, but it was warm and filled you. These folks didn't look too satisfied. An old woman raised her pale head and stared in his direction, but he couldn't tell if she saw him. He moved on, a little embarrassed.

He never saw many people along this stretch, not on a Saturday. Plenty of parking spaces, but not enough businesses open to draw traffic. Plenty of homeless, but most had enough sense to stay out of the sun.

"Hey neighbor, howre you'uns a-doin? Like some squirrel?" Mountain talk.

Jake snapped his head around. The fella was pushed back into the shadows of the doorway. He had one rough-looking hand held out, holding a poke. "Do I know you?"

"I seen you round here is all. Heard you talk once. Sounded like home."

"Southwest corner?"

"Wise County. You want this squirrel or not? There was two. I had my fill."

Jake took the poke out of curiosity. The meat inside looked darker than chicken, and could've been rabbit, but could've been squirrel. There wasn't much. "You got this out the park?" The fella nodded. There were red squirrels in the park, not much bigger, or fatter, than rats. No way he was going to eat this, but he didn't want to insult the man. "Much obliged." He dropped the poke in with his stuff. "You trap this yourself?"

The man scooted a little ways forward. He didn't have much more meat on him than a squirrel. Dirt was ground into his weathered skin. Jake remembered the miners he used to see around as a boy. "Me and the boys. Ain't too hard. Them city squirrels let you get close. We borrow the grill out back of the auto shop after closing, skin them, and grill them up. I always clean the grill real good before I put it back, but I reckon not everybody does."

Jake's eyes grew used to the shadow. He didn't see much there. "Where's all your stuff? I thought you fellers carried everything with you."

"Bastards took near everything after we split up the squirrel. Least they left me something to eat. Didn't have much, but I do miss the blanket. Damn if this concrete ain't hard for sleep."

Jake took off his coat and handed it to him. "Trade for the meat. It might help. As much as I can do right now I'm afraid."

"This is a nice un," the man said, pulling it under him before Jake could change his mind. "You don't need it?"

"The outfit looks fine without, I reckon. And this shows better." Jake grabbed his shiny blue tie and wiggled it with a grin.

Jake once had stuff stole when he left the buggy down in the entry, so he took his time pulling it up each step to the apartment, one hand gripping the railing as best he could, then resting on the landings. There would come a day soon enough he couldn't do this. He barely managed it now. Each time he sat down his arm shook from pain.

He used to take the buggy back to the store it belonged to after every trip out. Not no more. It felt wrong, but he couldn't manage all those extra steps.

Lily didn't call out when he came through the door, so Jake kept things quiet. Sleep ate up more and more of her days. He'd check in on her later, pretending he already knew she was still alive. He emptied the buggy carefully, carrying each load through their tiny living room and into the unused second bedroom. There was a narrow space around the table—two plywood sheets supported by four sawhorses—so he shoved the new supplies into one corner, turned on the overhead light, and shut the door.

Once Jake had the idea, he made a study of dioramas. Back when Lily was feeling better she traveled on the bus with him. The Richmond State Capitol, a medical museum of the Civil War, a miniatures show at the botanical gardens, then further out, and by himself, he visited the American Revolution and Watermen's museums in Yorktown. A tour guide called the dioramas windows into a lost time and place. A sad, but accurate way to look at it.

They peaked in the 1920s, and in recent years museums all over the country dumped them into the garbage, replacing them with video screens. Jake searched the main library for pictures of the lost ones. While there he ran across the work of Joseph Cornell, a shy man living with his mother and crippled brother, making little boxes containing worlds, a man who was considered an artist by other artists. His boxes were filled with ballerinas, birds, and clouds. Jake couldn't say he understood what was in Cornell's boxes, but they seemed to be the man's dreams and memories. Memories especially were small things, Jake thought, the right size for a box you could hold in your hands, and gaze at the miracles waiting on the other side of the glass.

Jake's diorama lacked both frame and glass. You could step right into it. You could be there. That seemed like a miracle as well. Not only was Jake building the thing, but he was also in it.

His idea was to duplicate the place where they'd grown up, married, and lived before coming here, all in this little room. He had no pictures of the holler, just their memories, and their memories didn't always match. He always went with Lily's recollections, even when he knew they were wrong, because he'd done all this for Lily, like he'd done everything else in his life.

At the center was the holler. He couldn't be sure he got the shape right. He never seen it from the air. He crouched down and looked at it from different edges, his eyes an inch above the fake ground, trying to remember what it looked like walking the old clay and rock roadway to the top, then later the paved one that only went part way, then carving away or adding ground as needed. It could never be exact, because memory weren't an exact thing, and he was beginning to lose his.

It was mostly Styrofoam underneath, a few cardboard boxes, covered with modeling clay to hold the shape, a skim of dirt and sand and scraps of artificial turf and moss. He had to keep the weight down. It wouldn't do for the floor to collapse onto the neighbors below.

He plugged the toothpick trees into the clay, hundreds of them, with toothpicks glued into a bundle for the bigger ones. Some painted chunks of foam became boulders. The houses went last. They were supposed to be permanent, though houses never were. The people, the few he put in, were meant to move around, although they tended to congregate at the church, or around Gibson's General down at the mouth of the valley.

Of course, people weren't permanent either, and there were a bunch of dead ones hanging around, like Lily's brother and grandpap, walking down the mountain, visiting kin. Some were dead after Jake and Lily left the holler. A few he told Lily about. A few he didn't.

Jake was the one who made them leave. For once he didn't let Lily do what she wanted. He knew she'd get better care here in the city, and he'd have her with him longer. She went along with it, but he knew she'd never forgive him.

Her daddy's house was in the wrong spot by a mile, but Lily insisted that's where it belonged. She made him move it every few weeks. Jake painted it blue, like it been when she was a girl. He told her that little squiggly of matchsticks and paste was her daddy in a rocking chair. She believed him, though he had to keep reminding her. Seemed like her eyes got worse every day.

On the east side of the ridge the trees were burnt from that fire in '98. That's the way she remembered them, but Jake figured they'd grown back some since then. He used plain toothpicks painted black.

There were a few dozen little houses in this version of the holler, though he knew most were gone, some even before they left. Some got burned, some taken by the state, some just fell. They got letters from relatives and neighbors, but Jake only read her the parts he thought she'd want to hear. Maybe it wasn't the right thing to do, but Jake wasn't always sure what the right thing was.

He'd gotten used to living in the city and thought maybe he preferred it. At least there was work here. He had two janitor jobs. Lily never settled in, said Jake was the only thing from home she had left.

He heard the door open behind him. She leaned against him, and he wrapped his arm around the little of her that was left. "Daddy's house ain't in the right place," she whispered and pointed. He picked up the house, her daddy, and a few trees, moved them a couple of inches over. "Perfect," she said, even though he knew it was still wrong.

"Could you make it winter again?" she asked, and he thought how hard it was to get the seasons right. "It's so hot in this place. I want to remember when it was cool."

"Sure, Sweetheart." The last time Jake made it winter he used coconut shavings and Epsom salt. The coconut attracted mice, who died when they ate the Epsom. He was removing dead bodies from the holler for days, making sure Lily didn't see them. And cleaning up all the salt and coconut took nigh forever. Maybe he could do it like he did last fall, painting a section of trees with yellow, red, and gold, and getting her to look at just that one part.

"I'm going back to sleep. You coming to bed?" She gave him a bony hug.

"I'll be right there, Honey." It wasn't dark out, but he could get up later for supper. Lily ate little, and only when she could.

The light switch had a dimmer, so he could light the holler for morning, midday, maybe a moonlit night in October. He walked over to the window and raised the shade. When sunset began, an orange light passed over the distant buildings and through this window, onto this world which neither of them was likely to see ever again.

Jake reckoned they were lucky to have a landlord who never visited though it meant things in the building seldom got fixed. He didn't know what would happen if the man saw what he'd done to this room.

He hunkered down and pulled out a small cardboard box from under the table. Inside were a few houses he'd taken away either because Lily didn't remember them, or because for some reason she didn't want them in the holler anymore. He knew Lily well enough not to pry.

There was a tiny figure in a bright red dress. She'd been maybe sixteen or seventeen at the time. Seeing Lily in that dress made him know he was going to marry her. He set the figure down among the trees and moved it around, hiding her here and there, remembering the way his breath used to catch every time she surprised him. He put her back into the box and set the box under the table. She was for him after Lily was gone.

He wouldn't be able to afford this apartment after Lily died, not without her social security. Maybe he would find a roommate. Then he'd have to give up this room. But it was just a daydream. He was too shy a man and too set in his ways to ever get himself a roommate. Maybe he could find a small place for hisself. Or maybe he'd live on the streets like them others.

He went into their bedroom and shed his clothes. Lily was restless in sleep, shrinking inside all the sheets and blankets. Always too cold, she said, even when her body soaked through to the mattress. Still, she slept naked except for the socks on her feet and the stocking cap covering her bald head. It made no sense to him, but he reckoned none of it did.

Pill bottles were scattered everywhere, spilling off the side table onto the floor. He used the empty ones to hold small parts. He slipped into bed, and she rolled over to face him. He leaned the side of his head against the scars where they took her breasts. He quieted himself and soon could hear her heartbeat through her thin skin. This was the closest to home he would ever be.

Deep Fracture

When the quake hit, Tom's first thought was to wish he were somewhere other than in Betty's Nackery, among breakable objects with no purpose other than to take up space, searching for a ceramic frog.

He looked over at Walt, who'd been tagging along with him most of the day as he tried to complete Naomi's "To Do" list. One ceramic frog: check, assuming he got it out of the shop intact, a replacement for the one destroyed by the last quake two days ago. Bristol was averaging three a week, 3.5 to 4.0 magnitude range, according to Walt—not common in these old, heavily-worn Appalachians.

Walt had been a geologist for the coal companies over twenty years, and if this kind of thing bothered him he sure didn't show it. He held up a couple of ceramic deer, grinning. "Caught 'em when they fell off the shelf." He looked over at Betty who was cowering under the old kitchen table that served as her checkout stand. He held the deer up, made them dance. "Saved them!" He grinned even wider. Betty looked sick.

Yesterday morning Naomi had demanded, poking at loosened mortar with her thumb, "What if the house comes down? Can't we reinforce the walls somehow?" Her house inspections had become an everyday thing.

"How could we afford that? Maybe they'll just stop."

"The coal companies ought to pick up the tab—all those old mines riddling these hills, no wonder we're having quakes."

Walt had just laughed when Tom had told him about that. "You might break your back falling down an unmarked shaft, but those old mines aren't going to bring your house down. If there's a big'un it'll come along the New Madrid fault through Memphis. Naomi shouldn't be none too concerned about the mines."

This morning when Walt said he wanted to ride along he hadn't seemed quite as jovial. When Tom asked if anything was wrong he'd said a couple of inspectors were late checking in.

The shop trembled for a couple of minutes, although it seemed much longer. Tom had the frog cupped safely between his two palms. Walt put the deer back on a shelf, although he hesitated on the second, as if he were considering an unlikely purchase. He looked around at the broken pieces filling the aisle and shook his head. "Better get the foundation checked, Betty. The store felt a little more slippery than it should have. And I'm seeing some wall cracks I don't like much."

Betty let Tom have the frog for free. She wanted to close early.

His cell phone rang that awful nerve-jangly jazz tune Naomi had chosen as her signature ring ("That way you'll know it's me."). That way, too, he managed to ignore about half her calls.

Walt stared at the phone where it lay on the seat between the two of them. "Not answering it, bud?"

"I'll call her later. She's probably just checking our progress." She was meeting with the drain cleaning company that morning about the disgusting backup in the basement, a problem with the clay line. He would pay whatever had to be paid but he'd never been able to deal with that stench.

Since dawn the sky had looked like saturated cotton and tasted like ice. What appeared to be the arrival of flurries subsided into an extended period of cold, overcast hiding the sun. The last few days the cautious ones stocked up on basic foods, antifreeze, umbrellas, and snow shovels. The incautious ones just drank. The uncertainty was intolerable.

"So, what's next on Naomi's list?" Walt stretched, yawning. "Plaster ducks for the lawn? Maybe a nice stuffed squirrel for the table?"

"Very funny," Tom said, trying to study the tattered list while driving. "Won't this get you in trouble at work? I had to take a vacation day for this."

"Oh, they don't need an old guy like me on a day like today, climbing in and out of those shafts searching for those inspectors, not when the ground's this unstable. I'd just get in the way."

"I've never known you to sit things out before, Walt."

"Well … I've never seen fractures like the ones we've been getting. Deep stuff I can't make sense of. I'm used to having some kind of explanation for things within my area of expertise, narrow as it might be."

"I thought you said Naomi didn't have anything to worry about."

"Oh, she doesn't, I don't think. I guess I'm just getting tired of the job. I should've retired a long time ago—judgment ain't what it used to be. So—what's next on the list?"

"Paint. She wants me to match what we've got in the dining room. The chairs have scraped a line across the plaster."

Walt whistled. "That paint's a good twenty years old, I'll bet. You know you're going to have to repaint the whole thing, don't you? Might as well pick a better color if you ask me, something brighter."

"I don't care, never noticed. I'm just trying to keep her happy. These little repairs—that's what makes her happy. 'Progress,' that's what she calls it. 'It's important we make progress,' she says."

We have this beautiful house, but you won't do a thing to keep it that way. I want things nice for the holidays. That was what she'd said when she gave him the list that morning. Maybe it was true he didn't get to repairs the way he should, but he did have to go into work every day. By the time he got home all he wanted to do was collapse in front of the TV. Especially now these repairs seemed like a waste of time—why couldn't she at least wait until the quakes stopped? There was something a little frenetic about it—it made him anxious just to be a part of it.

All year he'd been looking forward to snow—it was an unusual desire for him. He hated driving in snowy weather. But wouldn't it have a calming effect? Wouldn't it at least make things look better?

"The need for maintenance never ends. Because of that it's doomed to fail," Walt pronounced. "That's why I don't sweat a little bit of shabbiness. Shabby is the basic human condition, if you ask me. Whoa! Watch out!"

Tom slammed on the brakes. A homeless guy struggled to get his grocery cart full of junk out of the way. Tom hadn't seen him at all—it was like the fellow had just popped out of the broken pavement. He recognized him then—everybody called him Freddy. He wandered this part of town at all hours of the day, and people said he slept somewhere in one of the big parking garages. Freddy's hair and beard looked strangely animated, as if gnawing at his raw, swollen face.

"Lines 'n' lines 'n' lines!" Freddy growled.

Tom rolled down the window. "Excuse me?"

"I said you got yer lines 'n' lines all over the damn place!" Freddy shouted, mouth throwing froth. "Lines up there 'n' lines down there, but mostly down there. All a tangle and angry. Them lines is angry!"

The guy wandered off to a crumbling old warehouse next to the road. Traffic was at a dead stop. Tom couldn't get his eyes off that building—an interesting weave of lines wrapped around the corner of the brick wall like the remains of some giant signature. Freddy was poking, babbling to himself. More cracks spread. Masonry and concrete fell away. The ground around the foundation was mounded with debris. The rusty roof sagged, straight lines collapsed into waves, gaps opening in the seams. It was a dangerous situation—the area should have been barricaded.

One wheel of his trembling automobile suddenly slipped into a large hole in the pavement. The right front fender made a scraping sound as he drove out of the cavity. Walt groaned softly beside him. Tom looked over in alarm but Walt just shook his head, made a pained smile. "You need a chiropractor if you're going to drive around this town, I swear."

Ahead of them a line of vehicles rocked slowly along the battered, pitted road. Two city trucks slumped at the edge, workers leaning on picks and shovels. They stared at the disastrous pavement as if unsure what to do. Behind them the highway fence had been patched with plywood and discarded sheet metal.

Tom found the right paint store, parked his car crookedly in the lot. He jumped out holding the little chip of wall board painted the color he needed to match. He felt a little dizzy after the first few steps. It had suddenly gotten very cold. He saw tiny snowflakes like slivers of glass gleaming in the air. The parking lot had obviously been poorly paved. It tilted steeply overall, and the far end appeared badly warped. The lines marking the various spaces were skewed. A good snow would cover all of this. Snow would be a very good thing right now.

Suddenly he realized Walt wasn't with him. He twisted around. There his friend was on hands and knees peering beneath the car. Tom went back and stood over him. "Walt? What's going on?"

Walt backed out with a hand full of gravel. "The whole lot is like this—coming apart into little pieces. This stuff is almost like powder."

"They don't have the funds to keep up the infrastructure. You see this all over these days."

Walt shook his head. "It's like it vibrated apart." He held his head up. "Can you feel that? It's like my teeth are shaking in their sockets."

"Walt—"

"I was here last week, Tom. This lot wasn't like this. I swear it was almost like new."

The faded poster in the front window of the paint store displayed a rainbow of nearly indistinguishable pale paint colors. The clerk's ugly, patchy beard looked as if he'd pulled big hunks out of it, but he seemed to know his paints, identifying Tom's sample as "Mahogany Paradise." Tom was skeptical but took it anyway.

Walt took one look at it. "If you're lucky the next quake'll take the whole wall down, then you won't have to use this."

Outside Tom saw that the snow had increased, but initially it only made the shabbiness of everything a little uglier, as if a highlighter had been used to locate all the cracks. He stumbled and almost dropped the paint, the slick, crooked lines of the parking lot and the tangle of his shoe laces working together to bring him down. Walt grabbed him by the jacket and his left hand landed on a stuccoed concrete post. His palm came away dusty, and several inches of chipped material fell onto the uneven asphalt.

Back in the car Walt seemed troubled; rubbing his hands together as if he couldn't keep himself warm, uncharacteristically quiet. Tom was ready to pull over and ask him what was wrong when Walt spoke up. "Do you know why my daddy left the mines?"

"I'm surprised when anybody works the mines more than a day."

"Oh, he loved the mines. Didn't mind the danger, or the coal dust. He just loved bustin' rock. It was that simple. No, he left because he became convinced that down below the mines, 'somewhat short o' Hell,' is the way he put it, that there was a city down there, one with great towers and highways and magnificent halls, and maybe, well, maybe a UFO, or two, or three."

Tom wasn't sure if he'd heard right. He'd been distracted—the sky appeared to be sinking rapidly, the cold creeping into the interior of the car and scratching at his skin. He began to feel some urgency to get his errands done before it got worse, but slow traffic, crumbling roads, and store facades missing identification were slowing him down. He'd lived in this area all of his life and yet he felt vaguely lost. He still had a replacement lamp shade to get, a new handle for one of the cabinets, a match for a missing knob. "So he believed people lived down there?"

"No—he said he was always dreaming about that city, or seeing things in the shafts that—I don't know—reminded him? And the doorways and windows—they obviously weren't meant for humans. Actually, he said it was like something you might see in an aquarium, like a city for something aquatic, but on land."

"And he got all that from dreams?"

"Not entirely. Like I said, things in the mines reminded him, or sometimes it was like a memory, but not really."

"Walt, no offense, but are you saying your dad left the mines because he was going crazy?"

Walt laughed. "Yeah, maybe I am. He was pretty convinced, and it scared him. I don't believe in any of that Chariot of the Gods or UFO mumbo-jumbo. I'm a scientist, for God's sake. four hundred sixty million years ago the volcanoes spewed enough lava to make these mountains as high as the Alps. When they started to weather they absorbed enough greenhouse gas to cause an ice age, killing off two-thirds the species on the planet. But with their north-south orientation these mountains made a pretty good bridge for some to escape the ice."

"And ..."

"Sorry—I've just been thinking it out. There's a lot of porous limestone under these hills, caves everywhere, most of them unexplored. There's just a lot we don't know—that's all I'm saying."

The jazz music started up again. Reluctantly Tom flipped on his phone. "Hey, Naomi. I saw that you left a message."

"That was a half hour ago."

"Traffic's been crazy. You don't want me answering the phone while I'm driving, do you?"

"The sewer people are still here. They're not having very much luck getting the main line unplugged. They want to run a camera down there."

"Are they sure there's no other way? Maybe they should try some more with that snake rooter thing of theirs. Running a camera is expensive."

"I know it's expensive, but they've been running their machine all morning, over and over, and it's obviously not getting at whatever is blocking the line. They say two hundred dollars minimum—there may be a break in the pipe, or a separation. They say we should have gotten the old clay pipe replaced years ago."

"They always say that."

"So what do we do?"

"Tell them to go ahead. I'll be running in and out of stores the next couple of hours, so I'll probably be unavailable."

They stopped at an older strip mall, junk and surplus stores mostly, to try to get the last few items on the list. Here one store smashed up against the next all along the row, all of it leaning ever so slightly out of true, leaving scattered piles of chips and pebbles from the collisions. The storefronts were so filthy, so mismatched in color, style, and signage; they made Tom think of unsorted boxes of trash.

At least the snow had thickened enough it was beginning to cover all this with a deceptively clean layer of white, and maybe after a time he wouldn't immediately think of the filth, decay, and ruin underneath.

Tom found most of the replacement hardware he needed in a dingy, dirty junk store at one end of the slovenly mall. Walt wasn't much help. As soon as they walked in he became distracted by several crates of "antique architectural remnants" shoved under a battered old table. Moldings, brackets, inscribed metal plates, and various building ornamentation covered in grease, coal dust, and substances unidentifiable. Tom wanted no part of it, but Walt seemed somewhat obsessed.

Walt didn't buy anything, but he was lost in thought when they left. Tom was beginning to feel a little worried for him.

The alley and walk on one side of the junk store were layered in filth spilled over from an intersecting lane. Out of morbid curiosity Tom stepped carefully over the trails of coffee grounds, stained papers, and unidentifiable organic debris and peered around the greasy brick wall into the opening of the lane. It was a long alley bordered by tall walls of windowless mildewed concrete, and at the far end a writhing tangle of what he presumed to be trash consisting mostly of … lines. Strings and tapes and moving tubes of who-could-tell? He stopped Walt from coming around and taking a look himself and ushered him back to the car.

Back on the road the windshield fogged, and the defrosters seemed to be of little help, clearing only a small semicircle of window in front of the steering wheel crowned by a halo of frost. Outside as the day wound down toward sunset the air gradually thickened into a white mist that spread and obscured the more distant buildings, then ate away at the horizon until Tom could see only a few hundred feet ahead of him.

The car suddenly filled with that cacophonous jazz. Naomi again. But a truly serious snowfall felt immanent, and it seemed urgent for him to finish and get home.

"Hey, Tom," Walt said softly. "Do you think you could just take me home now? I've got lots to do before tomorrow and I'm beginning to feel a little poorly."

"Sure, Walt. Sure." Walt never complained about how he felt, ever, so Tom was taking this seriously.

Walt lived in a modest frame house a couple of blocks off the old downtown. When they pulled into the front yard—just a few square yards of dirt and gravel, actually—Walt said, "Come in a minute, will you?"

"Hey, Walt, I'd like to, really. But with this snow, and Naomi freaking out about the sewer, I really oughta get home."

"I know you're in a hurry. But this'll only take a minute of your time. Promise."

Walt led Tom past a mismatched washer and dryer combo sitting out in the side yard, through a small maze of raised dead flowerbeds to a screen door and the crowded porch beyond. Old auto parts, appliance parts, surplus mining equipment, and antique mechanical devices were in remarkable abundance. They padded through the darkened kitchen into another room where Walt flipped on the overhead light.

The object on the dining room table was about six feet long and resembled either a seriously heavy, highly ornate weather vane or a finial from the top of a Victorian tower or cupola. It was engraved along its length with a dense script in a language Tom did not recognize, and a raised design which might have been intended to represent oceanic plant or animal life, or perhaps the internal digestive tract of some long extinct creature of enormous size.

He touched it gingerly. It was hard and shockingly cold. Like touching dry ice. He stepped back—the table legs appeared on the verge of failure, the top sagging significantly. "What's it made of?"

"Haven't a clue. Every test I can do gives, well, unlikely results. Its age I can't even calculate. My equipment's not that good."

"It's so heavy. How did you get it in here?"

"I didn't. My dad found it, with his crew down in the Number 82 shaft. They raised it on the winch, and borrowed one of the big company trucks. Did it late one night. Twenty of them. I thought half of them would die getting it in here. That was a year before my dad quit."

"So is this why your dad got that notion of an underground city?"

"This and a lot of other things he wouldn't say much about. After he died, I tried to talk to some of those guys, the ones that were still left. They didn't tell me a thing."

Tom looked up at his friend. "What's going on, Walt?"

"I'm leaving tomorrow for Colorado. I've got more family out there. I never wanted to leave these mountains, but they've got mountains out there, too. I just wanted you to see this. And I hope you won't think I'm a coward."

"A coward? Why would I ever think that?"

"For leaving," Walt said. "Just for that."

As Tom drove through the empty downtown streets, the snow piled up, covering everything, but not before he noticed that the edges of the old buildings appeared to sag and a white, frothy sort of corrosion on the corners was evident. Hints of twisted and tangled debris peeked over the rooflines.

As his car made the top of a hill, huge chunks of snow were drifting down. In the dim light from the surrounding poles it looked like bits of yellowed insulation. Naomi's jazz sounds started up again and this time he took the call.

She sounded breathless. His chest grew tight. She'd be wanting him to do something about something, and now.

"Why didn't you call me back? I've called you three times!"

Was this possible? He didn't see how. "What's the problem?"

"The sewer line is full of hair, and big long—I don't know—earthworms maybe? Great gobs of them!"

"They're exaggerating."

"I've seen it myself! It's right on their little TV monitor."

"It must be roots. That's always been a problem. You've all mistaken the roots for hair."

His wife didn't answer for some time. Then, "You're ridiculous. I'll just handle it." She hung up.

He dropped the phone back onto the seat beside him. Good, let her handle it. It would be easy enough to put a pre-recorded video into their machine showing any problem they wanted. In a few minutes Naomi would call back to tell him they wanted some huge amount of money to fix the problem. Then he would take over. He would say absolutely no and she would be satisfied that he'd handled it.

It was snowing quite heavily now. He pressed his fingertips against the underside of the windshield, and then jerked them away, feeling burned. But when he examined his fingers he could find no damage; they were just … cold. He eased his fingers back against the glass, and then a palm. He could feel the cold outside through his entire body. It seemed as if he could feel the cold as it spread from miles and deep layers away.

Flakes were multiplying at a dizzying rate. He heard a crack of thunder and in the distance the sky split with a dazzling white light. Unusual in a snowstorm, but not unheard of. He watched as flakes like huge moths touched the glass, rested for a second, then tumbled off. More fragments than flakes, the same color and shade as the sky, as if the sky had fallen out of the sky.

That object on Walt's dining room table—where could it have come from? And the idea that he had lived with it there for all those years after his dad died, without telling anybody? Some things were beyond human understanding. Actually, all things were. There must be a physics beyond the physics we know—it was the only reasonable explanation. Layers upon layers, origins beneath origins. The only way to really make sense of things was through a kind of psychological archaeology.

The snowfall became so heavy Tom stopped the car in the middle of the street. Nothing else was moving—he probably could stay there all night. Maybe he would. Maybe he would just call Naomi and tell her he was going to have to spend the night in the car and he was sorry, so very sorry but she would have to deal with those sewer people herself. In any case she was doing a great job—she should be very proud of herself.

The snow varied in intensity until after another hour or so when it stopped as if the sky had run out of its supply. In fact it stopped so suddenly Tom was vaguely alarmed by the change. He pushed his face up against the inside of the windshield. The streets were empty, and there appeared to be no wind. As far as he knew he might be the last person out in this, out in his car looking out the window, although there was always the chance there were others watching, wedged against their house or apartment or office windows. But even the nearest windows were some distance away. He could see nothing in them.

Some of the roofs here appeared slightly sagged, and some of the vertical lines of the stark architecture somewhat bent, but there hadn't been that much snow. The settling of the snow, and the way it had stuck to corners and onto shallow horizontal ledges, must have created an optical illusion.

The street in front of him and the streets he could see branching off to the sides were a seamless expanse of white, everything looking very much like part of a gigantic skating rink. He was thinking that he could almost see the skaters racing, writing their lines and curls into the white, when the first actual lines began to form.

He thought at first a breeze had come up which was gently sweeping the pavements, skimming off the layers of snow and revealing the lines that separated the concrete and asphalt slabs. But he could detect no breeze in the trees and the snow itself did not appear to be moving generally—it was simply disappearing where the lines were.

Then he saw Freddy, racing down the street across the table of snow pushing his grocery cart in front of him, making such a mess of that clean, seamless snow, churning it, ruining it. Freddy's mouth was open, but Tom couldn't tell if he was saying anything. Freddy kept jerking his head back to look behind him, and that was when Tom saw the rushing, curling dark lines in the snow pursuing him.

And then the huge loops and whirls of tracks made by invisible fingers and tails or whatever might make such marks began to appear, soon covering the street over its entirety, like giant ornate, overlapping signatures in some unknown language. Overwriting Freddy and overwriting Freddy until you could no longer distinguish him in the morass of lines.

Tom seriously doubted this was in fact any sort of writing because it appeared to come from beneath, so they were perhaps cracks as the world shook off its hard coat, but who could know? If so they were unlike any cracks he had ever seen.

If he were a smarter man perhaps he could read them, but for now they were simply his evening coming apart. The lines spread like musical transcription, like a spool of thread thrown from a passing car, like the mysterious lines of force which held the world together.

As the fractures began to deepen, to widen, he noticed that his phone was flashing frantically. In his annoyance with Naomi's ringtone had he turned the ringer off? He picked up the phone. He dialed in for messages and her frantic voice filled his ear. "Why haven't you answered? The lines are coming out of the drain. Did you hear that? The lines are everywhere."

Of course he did not fully understand. It seemed to him now that all year long he'd been looking forward to the snow, and now it was here at last.

Almost a Legend

Jake never looked into the bleachers much—his notion of being a baseball legend-in-the-making was you played to the crowd, you didn't look at the crowd. But sometimes, like today, the crowd acted like a truck load of banty roosters wrecked on a dusty road, hot and tired and spoiling for a fight. So he kept one eye over there when he could, in case they came spilling out onto the field. A whole bunch of folks had money riding on this Coeburn game. It could be a bad day for the Dorchester Cardinals if their new ringer didn't deliver.

Whitey had the ringer behind the mine's commissary, pouring coffee down his gullet, dumping water over his head, rubbing his shoulders, whatever he could do to sober the feller up. The manager paid Whitey extra to drive up to Cincinnati and pick these fellers up, keep 'em straight at least until the game began. But this 'un got away by hisself, came back hell-bent and drunk as a badger, and Whitey could lose that assistant job he was so proud of.

Jake had heard of the ringer when he was coming up, but the man hadn't pitched a major league game in years. Now he was on his way down, and playing with the likes of Jake and the other Dorchester boys. But he'd been almost a legend, not the usual college ball player the coal company'd sneak in for a game or three. But a real player. Just like Jake dreamed of being, but it twere a dream what surely had a price.

Least the ringer was a pitcher, so they wouldn't have to worry none about his hurting hisself out on that jack-leg coal digger Dorchester baseball field. A railroad track run through right field, and the creek winded through one corner of left. A cornfield backed center field, and the broad side of a coal tipple crowded the first base line, shading it so you couldn't always tell where you was running. Least they didn't have to worry about stepping into any holes. Jake had been there in Haysi when Buford Tritt broke his jaw on his own knee cap running into a drainage ditch going after a pop fly.

Worst the ringer might do was bean somebody with a wild pitch. Brushbacks was common, but only a crazy fool wanted a feller hurt bad.

A fist fight broke out in the bleachers just a shade into the second inning. A good 'un too, judging by the way the seats cleared. The umpire, a preacher recruited from the crowd, yelled at the two men to settle down "in the Lord's name." That put a lid on things, but Jake could tell the pot were still boiling. He just hoped the preacher didn't smell a mouse where the ringer was concerned.

Out of habit Jake looked for Mary and his girls. Weren't there of course—Mary'd packed up to stay with her kin down in Rose Hill where things was more genteel. She'd had enough of the smells, the coke ovens making it look like the whole town was on fire, and the coal dust seeping into her drawers and her cabinets and every corner of that little four-room frame house the company provided, and she'd had enough of him too, he reckoned, with all his baseball playing, and that job down in the mine aiming to make her a widow. And his foolish notions about becoming a legend (not that he ever used that word in front of her, or nobody else—that word was private).

"You're a loony for playing a'tall," she said. "Ain't the mines taking enough? And you won't even take them easy up top jobs they'll give you to reward your playing! I swear I married a fool!"

Jake never claimed to be a smart man. His own granny used to say, "the boy don't know 'B' from a bull's foot," but then she'd lean close and whisper, "but he sure gots gumption." Like that was his secret, like he was Captain Marvel or some such.

He reckoned a smart man wouldn't have stayed down in the mines when he could've had an easier, safer job upside in a shop. His supervisor was a true baseball man, and as a star player on the mine's Cardinals team Jake could've took that easier job and been paid well for it too. In fact they'd offered him that job a dozen times.

But Jake Carter had his own ideas. He wanted to be inside, and he told them so. He loved baseball, more than anybody knew. But he also liked being there at the end of a tunnel and picking away at that black wall of coal, shoveling it out and coming right back at it, like he was tearing a hole through the dark. Even though, at six foot six, he had to do it on his knees half the time. Even though his wife kept telling him he'd be a shorter, smaller man at the end for all his trouble (and forty years later he'd tell her she'd been right).

And he liked that feeling of going from digging through the dark to rising up into bright, hallelujah sunshine, like a hero in some fairy tale.

So he told his bosses he'd go somewhere else—Coeburn or Keokee or maybe even Hazard—if they didn't let him go down into the mines no more. Because for Jake, his skills in baseball and his skills down in the mine—weren't nobody could dig more, or longer—were all part of the same plan, his aim to be a legend, at least among the mining towns of southwest Virginia. You never asked a legend how smart he was, but you paid attention when he done something. Maybe he was a fool, but he aimed to be a fool they'd be talking about for a long, long time. He wasn't about to end up like his daddy, dead from working with no one to remember who he was 'cept a couple of sad kids.

And the crowd sure was paying attention during that game against the Coeburn Blues. The Blues was up two runs going into the third inning. But Jake was hitting about every pitch—if he ever gotta hold a good 'un the Cardinals would have a fighting chance. Mostly what was stopping him was the usual bullcrap. He'd hit one into the left field creek and Big John Kelly on the Blues would just run over, dip his hand into the edge of the water and bring up a dripping ball right quick. Or he'd drive one into the centerfield corn and Frank Green would run in and right out again waving the ball in the air and hollering, "I found it! I found it!" Like hell. Players caught on real quick in the Appalachian League. Anytime they played in Dorchester they'd have those extry balls stashed in their shirts for when they needed 'em. It was hard to mind too much 'cause so many players did it. It just meant you had to hit harder—knocking them balls over the creek and the cornfield so everybody knew you hit a homer.

The ringer took the pitching spot top of the next inning, and Jake felt a little shamed what with that preacher umping and all. Course the preacher probly knew—everybody else did. The fellow limped out to the mound without looking at the crowd (guess this was just a paycheck for him), even though there was scattered cheers, some folks standing. So he got his applause, though not as much as the Cardinals shortstop Little Jim Gibson when he went into the stands at the end of that inning to pull the rotten tooth out of a man what was suffering.

Course they always put the ringers in the newer uniforms, soze you'd have eight men in baggy uniforms, all different shades of gray since they were made in different years, and this one guy gussied up in an outfit that was cleaner than the rest. Yeah, he fit right in.

He looked slicker than horse snot, but when he threw that first ball he let go too late, the ball hit the ground before it got to the plate, and he about fell flat on his face. The manager looked 'bout to throw a conniption, but then the next pitch just kind of floated by slow as molasses, and Hobart Sage got all twisted up trying to swing at it, fanning air.

The ringer done fine for three innings, in control, not smoking it past them, but placing the ball just right soze none of them Coeburn hot shots could get any wood on it. He gave the Dorchester power hitters a chance to catch up, and Jake, he was more than ready, bringing the Cardinals two homers—one so high and deep into the cornfield that centerfielder would have been crazy to try a ball switch, and another that went straight down the first base line, catching one edge of the coal tipple in a shower of splinters before the outfield players lost it in the afternoon mist and the smoke that settled down from the coke ovens. The preacher coulda called it foul—nobody had any idear where it went to—but he closed his eyes and raised his hand like he was praying afore yelling "Fair ball!"

Soze the Cardinals had their chance—Jake was sure they was going to win it—with his own superior performance taking him a ways toward his goal. They was scouts in the bleachers from the big leagues—they usually was these days—but he'd never go up. He didn't want to. He knew that for sure now. He'd known other fellers from the hollers who went up to Cincinnati and New York and some of them other big clubs, but they most always came back. Most of the coal camp boys just never felt comfortable no place else. All Jake wanted was to be remembered, maybe just a clipping in some fan's scrap book. No more than that. He'd been thinking that way for a time, but watching that ringer out there that day, well that made him sure of it. He didn't want to be no legend. Hell, almost a legend was plenty good enough. And he could be that staying right here. No way was he going to end up like the ringers, living in some crappy place, still hawngree for the cheers, and sneaking down to the camps for a few bucks now and then.

Jake was watching the ringer close now, 'cause he was beginning to look pretty shaky, moping along, staring at the catcher kinda rattle-brained, and these shadows as black as a mule's rear end was starting to creep into his face. Jake had heard his granny say somebody'd looked "like Death warmed over" a hunderd times, but he'd never actually seen it for hisself.

The Blues started getting a piece of the ball now and again, and in the seventh that Beattie Bowman, who'd played with a lot of coal camp clubs but never been that much of a hitter, he batted one high up into the smoke still hanging over right field. Lefty Williams went after it with his head thrown back, but got tangled up in them railroad tracks and went down hard on the steel. The crack his arm made was loud enough to pull a groan out of the crowd. C.D. Walker skipped back from second base, but he was like a dancer on them long feet of his, prancing over the screaming Lefty and those ties and rails like a little girl in her ballet slippers. When the ball slapped into his glove half the fans came to their feet and cheered.

That was the last good time the Dorchester boosters had that day, unfortunately. The next four at-bat had balls delivered to them just like they was the pitcher's young-uns, and if Jake hadn't been watching the ringer so closely he'd swear the old codger had snuck another drink or three. He were staggering under the weight of his own head and sweating like a whore in church.

The Blues got three runs out of them four, and good fielding on the part of the Cardinals was the only thing that stopped them that inning.

By that time of course the Dorchester crowd was screaming for blood. They was yelling for the ringer's head, and hell, he probly woulda handed it over iffen he could pry it off his neck. Problem was the crowd didn't know what to call him. Oh, they knew he used to be famous—he was a big leaguer after all—that's why they'd cheered him at first. They just didn't know who. He'd been announced as A.B. Collins. ABC. Everybody knew that was made-up. So they just generally booed and cussed.

Jake never could figure out why the manager kept the ringer in for that eighth inning, pretty much guaranteeing a Cardinal loss. Maybe because he'd spent so much on the ringer already he didn't want to give up on him. Or maybe he'd bet on the Blues. Worse things had happened since Jake started playing. Whatever it was, the Cardinals went down in the eighth quick as a buzzard on a gut wagon.

Them loyal fans didn't even wait until the end of the game. It was like the bleachers exploded. The preacher waved his arms around and shouted about all the prophets and saints trying to calm those good church-going people down. Didn't do nary a bit of good. Punches and kicks was thrown, along with a goodly amount of the company's property, tools and whatever weren't nailed down. All the players (both sides), being athletes, was gone by the time those fans got out on the field.

As for the ringer, well Jake Carter threw that completely tuckered individual over his shoulder and carried him off the field full-speed, jumping over broken seats and upended equipment, dodging big men swinging rakes and sticks, ducking more than a few thrown fists, even a boot or two, not stopping until he reached the camp infirmary. Professional courtesy, was the way he explained it later to his teammates. Some of them was probly sore about his little bit of charity — after all, it being a big game, and some of them known to gamble a time or three. Or four. But nobody said nothing.

It was probly the most heroic feat the almost legendary Jake Carter ever did on a ball field, but it was never mentioned again, at least as far as he knew. As great as it was, it had nothing to do with baseball.

Cattiwampus

Imember me a lot from those old days. I member the fog on
the mountain come morning, hangin' round the top of the
ridge like hit twere heaven up there. And I member how the
pine smelled as the day heated up, so strong the way it carried
ever other smell on hits back: the perfume of the mountain mint,
the beans bubblin' on the stove. But mostly I member the
changes, and how things been changin' ever since.

The day we finally figured everthing all out I member how
Anna cried like she tweren't never gonna stop. I reached round
and found her little milk jar, give hit to her. She sucked that
nipple for all hit was worth, but there was just some sugar water
in there. She dropped that jar and commenced cryin' again.

"You keep that up and that cattywampus'll get us all three!"
Jimmy used to spit when he talked. Hit made him look crazy
mean.

"Shut yer face," I said. "You're just makin' things worse."

Jimmy stopped. He used to listen 'cause I was older, even
though I'm just a girl. And because I been to school one day and
he ain't been none. I told him a day don't mean nothing but if

he'd shut up then I reckon I didn't care. I don't know who he listens to now. Maybe he even got some schooling. I hope so.

I figure I was eight almost a year then, so's almost nine. 'Bout this time of year. We didn't have no calendar—still don't—but I member when I had my last birthday the light was like this and the trees was like this and I felt just this way, like something new was 'bout to happen. Not bad, not good, just new. We didn't have no house that year. We went down that cave with Ma the Christmas day before then, with nothing but the clothes we had on and what she could stuff into a couple of tater sacks. Ma said tweren't no time for nothing else. Least she membered to bring us our coats and a quilt or two.

Jimmy and Anna didn't see none of the fight that day we left the house—I pushed 'em into the back room with me once hit started. I didn't see much myself—didn't want to—just a peek through the door ever once in a while to see iffen we needed to get out the house.

Before Grandma died she used to say Ma and Pa "fights like cats n' dogs," but I never seen a cat fight back like Ma, not just snappin' and clawin' but jumpin' in with all four feet, howlin' like some kind of demon from the bible. Ma was Grandma's daughter—she never knew her own Pa—and everbody always said Grandma was the one she done took after. I don't know hit twere true or not, but Miz Lambkin down the church said Grandma was one of them witchy women, and never even lived in a house til Pa married Ma and they took her in.

I never much liked Grandma, and Jimmy and Anna wouldn't go near her. She always smelled like our old cat Daisy right after she dropped a litter. And she had them narrer eyes with them bruised grapes inside. I know hit ain't nice to bother on a person's appearance, but the worst thing was she never had a nice thing to say 'bout nobody, but 'specially 'bout the menfolk. She only talked to me 'cause I was a girl.

But like I said I never saw nothing that Christmas day, and I'll keep sayin' that 'til I'm an old woman like Grandma got to be, with hair growed off my chin. But what I heard—after they'd been punchin' and throwin' things round 'bout a hour or so—was this loud howly whine like a child dyin', or a woman's scream while her soul got ripped out. Then something hit the wall and made the whole house shake.

That cry tweren't exactly something I never heard before. I'd heard something like hit a few times off in the woods when Pa and I was outside alone, and once in the middle of the night that sound woke me up and run the ice right through me. But those times that sound twere a long ways off, and more like a cryin' baby sound, or a little child done lost her way. Pa said, "might be that wampus cat, what folks in these parts call cattiwampus," but he'd been drinkin' like usual, and I never paid much mind to what he said when he was drinkin'.

After everthing come out, of course, I heard that cattiwampus cryin' all the time. All three of us did. I reckon you can get used to 'bout anything.

But that day at the house the sound was a hunderd times louder than ever before, so close, and though I didn't knowed what all it meant, I knowed hit meant bad, so I picked up Anna and grabbed Jimmy by the arm and we skedaddled out of that house.

My Pa tweren't no saint—I knowed that very well. He drank too much and sometimes when he drank a whole lot he'd hit Ma, and once he chucked a split log at me. But he never hit Jimmy, or Anna, and he was always so sorry afterwards about anything he'd done. Course that didn't make him right as rain, but I reckon he still didn't deserve what he got.

Not that I could say fer sure exactly what he got. Of course now I got a pretty good idear. Like I said, I never seen much, but after that first crash in the wall there twere a few more, hard enough to pop some shingles off the roof. And Ma screamed at us through the winder not to come inside, 'cept her voice was high and full of something like rain so's I could hardly understand her, but I knowed I better not budge. A while later she come outside lookin' like she'd just washed up, but you could still see the dried red streaks in her black hair and on her clothes. And that's when she took us down the cave.

That cave tweren't so bad. And I missed hit awful when we moved on. You could build a fire under that little hole that went all the way through the ground so things stayed warm but not too smoky. And we'd all huddle together and eat the food Ma would bring back from trips in the woods, and she'd tell us stories about animals and people and people what acted like they was animals, and hit was pretty nice.

I don't know why we ever left that cave—Ma just said hit tweren't a good place to hide no more. And after that she moved us around in the woods or down in some root cellar or maybe even just a pile a wood with a little space inside, while she went huntin' for food or for whatever we needed.

I member that day we twere just sittin' between two big old logs, been there for hours waitin' for her. We was all hungry, but Anna the only one complainin'. Jimmy and me, we'd learnt that complainin' didn't help none so we didn't do that much anymore.

Now with all them high ridges and the way the tall trees and boulders bigger'n churches make them shadows, the sun dies early in them woods. And hit starts to get cold pretty quick. I member Anna started to shiver like a wet kitty and me and Jimmy pulled her into one of the quilts with us. Wasn't much left of that quilt after it got hauled around, but least hit was something to cover us with and hold some of our own heat inside.

All of a sudden we could hear them huntin' dogs up and down the ridge. They twere after something—you can hear that in they howls sure enough. We made ourselves stay down with just our eyes and the tops of our little heads peekin' out like bumps on a log—we wanted to be ready in case we had to move.

Something came to crash about a hunderd feet away, snappin' the brush and poundin' through the trunks. Something black and shiny like oil, and all bendy like hit got no backbone. Hit was in and out of the trees like they tweren't nothing, and when hit slowed down, which was hardly at all, I could see that as fast as hit was there was still something wrong: legs bent two diff'rent ways, arms all twisted, and a body like hit got folded the wrong way and somebody done a poor job puttin' everthing back.

Now I must've knowed things I didn't realize yet, because right away I was thinkin' two arms and not four legs, but when Anna perked up and said "Mama" the light bulb went on, then I seed the long black hair down hits back and I knowed that thing was Ma.

But before I could figure no more on hit them dogs come through the trees like the dog dam done broke, and some of 'em went after her and some of 'em went sniffin' over to them logs where we kids was hidden.

I can't say for sure them dogs would a hurt us, but they got all mean and snarly and Baby Anna started bawlin'. Maybe they still knowed some things we didn't yet. But I reckon that was the last time they knowed anything, 'cause quicker than spit a black streak done smeared the air in front of us, and one of 'em's head went gone, the rest floppin' like a fish on the grass. And then another one fell, and just kept fallin', 'cause that poor thing was like some bloody soup what forgot soup can't stand. The rest got throwed here and yonder, or ran away.

We never seen what happened to the men, them hunters what had been behind them. But they just never got there, and I tweren't 'bout to go look for 'em.

Ma must a knowed we'd finally seen her for what she was, because later when she come back to us with some old chicken meat to cook she still showed some signs—her legs was still kinda crooked, but with each step they'd straighten up just a tad more. And her clothes was all torn, not nough to be indecent, but almost. Them muddy blood stains looked like she'd fell in the Powell, down by that bend near the Watkin's place where the bank's all red clay. And she still had some of them black furry spots on her arms, what slowly disappeared like her skin was eatin' 'em.

I didn't care to say nothing, but Jimmy he had all kinds of questions. Ma just shushed him, said she'd talk about hit later, though she never did, not really. After that she'd just act like we already knowed everthing, and tell us to go hide 'cause she had some huntin' to do and she didn't want us to see when she made her change. When Jimmy got all uppity she just snarled, I mean really snarled, and told 'im hit twere private, kind of like when a body went to the bathroom. Hit tweren't something for others to see.

I didn't unnerstand that part too well. Not then. Course now I knowed exactly how she felt.

She and Jimmy had their troubles a lot after that. Course Jimmy had always been high strung and mouthy, but I think 'cause her changes twere somehow wimmen's stuff hit made hit harder for him to take. Besides, she'd done killed his pa. I knowed he twere Pa to all of us, but I'm thinkin' Jimmy took hit harder than us girls. Anna hardly knowed Pa, and I reckon I knowed 'im too well. Wasn't like Jimmy done nothing wrong, but he just got all up into Ma's nerves.

Then when he got older, and I got older, he started his fillin' out, and started to look like a man, just like I started to look like a woman. And Ma, she twere lookin' at us both different, at me like maybe she could stop huntin' soon, at him like, well, like he don't belong.

So after one right nasty fight when she done scratched him up something awful Jimmy done took off and we ain't seen him since. More power to 'im, I say. Course it meant Ma could spend more time just watchin' me. Which she did, day after day, watchin' me and watchin' me.

Like she was waitin' for something to happen. Which hit did. And I been doin' the huntin' and the fishin' and the chasin' and the bein' chased ever since.

Last fall Ma done got real sick. Course she'd been sick for years—this kind of life be hard on anybody. But this time hit twere a lot worst, and the things with her twisted old body, well, hit ain't the kind of thing a person likes to share in public.

Anna and me put her out of her misery. I'd a done the job by myself, but Anna wouldn't take no for an answer.

Me, I never got myself married, never been with no kind of man at all. Wouldn't want one, like I am. And for certain wouldn't want kids. I don't worry 'bout hit none neither, I just get on with getting' on.

Cept sometimes this time of year I see the fog up high and I smell me them pine and perfumy flower smells, and I think 'bout the way hit all was once upon a time. I think about Jimmy, and what would I do iffen I seen him some day on t'other end of a rifle? And I watch Anna, like Ma used to watch me, 'cept I'm hopin' for a differnt outcome. And iffen I get that differnt outcome I'm gonna send her away, just like Jimmy.

And, my sweet, beautiful little sister, this time I ain't takin' no for an answer.

Bingo Thompson's Flying Cat

Paul and Ralph were sitting on Ralph's ma's front porch swing like they did every Saturday night, figuring on what they might do to entertain themselves. Ralph was feeling a little cross because Paul kept trying to set the pace on the swing. Paul liked it fast and Ralph liked it slow, especially on a weekend. Some things were meant to go fast—like cars and horses and leopards out in the jungle chasing down their supper—but there was just no call for a fast porch swing.

"Slow 'er down, Paul. I ain't telling you again."

"I like 'er fast. Makes me feel like I'm going places."

"You already ruint it. We're starting to shimmy sideways again."

"I like it when it shimmies sideways. Makes me feel like I'm riding one of the rides down at that carnival what come through last summer."

"Well you ain't riding no carnival ride. You're on a porch swing and porch swings are supposed to swing up and down not all crookedy!" Ralph slammed both feet down. His end stopped short. The swing shook for a second then stopped altogether.

"Well, you're in a mood," Paul said. "You should learn to relax like me."

"You're always relaxed 'cause you ain't got no job."

"Well that was pretty uncalled for—you know I got chronic pain."

"Chronic pain my lily white …"

"That's not where the pain is located, Ralph." Then, when Ralph didn't reply, "I'm just sayin'."

Paul tried to start the swing back up but Ralph still had his legs locked. Another evening spoilt unless they could come up with something. "Bingo Thompson got him a cat what got wings.

"No he ain't."

"Ralph, you ain't been up there in a while. For all you know Bingo's got hisself an entire zoo. He could have some lions, and bears, and some of them convict horses …"

"Convict horses?"

"Uh huh, they got them stripe-eds on 'em."

"You mean ze-bras."

"I don't know if they is all females or not. They just got them stripe-eds is all I know. Other than that I reckon they's naked."

"Now that might be worth seein'."

"Oh he ain't got none, Ralph. I was just saying he might, for all you know. I was just spec-ulatin'. No, all Bingo's got is a cat what's got wings."

"I know he ain't got a cat with wings 'cause there's no such a thing."

"Now there you go unbelievin' again. I bet you don't even believe in the Easter Donkey." Ralph just stared at him. "I'm just sayin'."

Against Ralph's better judgment, they drove his old pickup up the ridge to see Bingo Thompson's cat. "Tain't got nothing better to do," was Paul's reasoning.

Last Saturday they drove around the county chucking rocks at cows. Ralph guessed Paul had a point. Paul wanted to drive, but Ralph said he'd rather put honey in his drawers and lay down on an ant hill. Paul said he oughta try it sometime instead of puttin' it down and Ralph said it was best if they didn't talk the rest of the trip.

Bingo's house was out a gravel road that ran up over the ridge through some trees, then over an old creek bed with rocks the size of raccoons(dodging about half of them), then up a gulley and around a big pile of old tires. "Ralph, this here is what they call 'secluded.' You reckon old Bingo is some kind of secluded millionaire or something?"

"No, I'm thinking he just don't like drop in company."

Finally they pulled up into Bingo's front yard. They didn't think he'd mind—he had five other cars there already, none with tires. There was all kinds of rusty machinery, and tools, and waist-high piles of branches, and an axe or two like an invitation to a chopping party. Up on the porch the screen door hung from a single hinge, leaning like an old man sleeping in church.

Bingo came out of the house. Followed by seventy or eighty cats.

"What'd I tell you, Ralph? Eccentric. I mean, that many dogs I could see, but kitty cats? Ralph, you think that makes old Bingo a cat lady?"

Ralph ignored the observation. "I'm not getting out of the truck until he corrals some of those kitties. That much static electricity could fry a man."

"Ah, Ralph. He's got some real cute 'uns in there!" Paul opened the door and stepped down into the yard, slamming the door shut behind him. Ralph watched as Paul took a few steps toward the house. "Bingo!" He raised his hand. "Bingo!" He turned back toward Ralph and grinned.

He's going to ask me if I noticed his little joke and I swear I'm going to punch him, Ralph thought.

Then Ralph saw a change in that wriggling, mewling sea of cats, the kind of change that you might see out on the ocean, on a windy day with a darkening sky and the clouds are rolling in. One part of that ocean commences to rising, and it draws up all that nearby water with it, and before you can say "fix-them-eggs-to-go-thank-you-very-much" you have this giant wave heading your way.

Now instead of ocean, think of cats, and you'll pretty much understand what Paul spied heading his way. Paul turned and came scrabbling back toward the pickup, his face white as a dumpling. Ralph thought about leaving Paul to his own devices, but then opened the door just enough to let him in, and they both had to push out a mess of legs, paws, and claws before he could get it closed again.

"Ah, Ralph, that was bad. I'd been a bunch of cat toys for sure if you hadn't let me in."

"Just siding with the human in the deal is all. What say we go now? We've had our Saturday excitement, I reckon."

But he was interrupted by a tapping on the driver's side window. Bingo Thompson was standing there grinning, holding up the ugliest cat Ralph had ever seen. The only reason he knew it was a cat was them catty eyes, and that downturned mouth that said despite all appearances Ralph was the ugly one. But around them eyes and that mouth hung a storm cloud of fur the filthy color of a puddle at the bottom of a strip mine. And there were these pointy places that came out from the cloud like trapped lightning bolts. Long bits of dead stem and twig sticking out of those big mats made Ralph figure that cat was probably half vegetable. He rolled down the window, but only about halfway.

"I reckon this is who you come to see." Bingo spit the words past his huge grin. "I shooed them others—they won't bother you none. They're jealous of Daisy here, what with her being famous and all. Come on out of there and I'll show you what she can do."

"Careful, it might be a trick," Paul said out loud, probably thinking he was whispering.

"Come on, I'll protect you," Bingo said, still grinning. Ralph was beginning to wonder if the man had some kind of affliction.

Ralph and Paul slipped out of the truck, watching for any signs of a kitty flood. Bingo put Daisy down on the ground, but the cat just sat there, looking all peevish and put-upon. For the first time since their arrival, Bingo frowned, and it wasn't a pretty sight. "Sometimes Daisy thinks she's too good to perform for folks. Well, 'round this house we all do our share." Bingo nudged the cat with his square-toed boot. The cat gave him one final, resentful look, then waddled across the yard. Once the cat got going the big fur mats on its sides came loose and started flapping. The grin came back onto Bingo's face. "I reckon if Daisy lost a little weight she'd be able to take off with them wings."

Paul and Ralph watched as the mound of fur turned around and came back, sides still flapping, stopping at Bingo's boots to hack up a little gift before waddling on.

"Bingo, you trimmed that cat lately, or brushed it out?" Ralph asked.

Bingo snorted. "She weren't born with no scissors and no brush—I figure she don't need 'em now."

"Babies weren't born with diapers, but I hate to think about life without 'em."

There was this ungodly screeching, and all three looked around at the cat, who'd got herself tangled in all those branches. She was hung up with those big flaps of matted fur and stem acting like a noose, her eyes like popcorn.

Ralph had to admit that sometimes Paul came through in an emergency. But maybe not this time. Paul ran over, grabbed one of them axes off the ground, and started chopping all around the cat's head. In fact there was such a flurry what with idiot chopping and cat screeching Ralph couldn't tell exactly what was going on.

"Daisy!" Now there was a shotgun in Bingo's hands as he ran toward that developing disaster. Against his better judgment Ralph followed and almost ran into his backside when he stopped abruptly.

Ralph had heard about shocked silences before but he'd never actually been in that vicinity. He wasn't exactly sure what had happened, but in the middle of it Daisy was sitting there between the three of them, looking a whole lot skinnier.

And at the end of it Bingo was picking her up, examining her upside, down, and sideways. "You done amputated her wings," he said sadly, and Ralph saw that he still had the shotgun in one hand, and it was lifting.

"Wait!" Ralph cried. He went scrabbling around among them, picking up clumps of fur. "See, Bingo?" He stuck two handfuls of filthy mats in the frowning man's face, "Weren't no wings. Just fur, full of twigs and stems and crap like that, but no skin, no blood. Not a scratch on her."

Bingo just stared at him. Then he said, "I want you two boys to shave her."

"What?"

"I want to make sure she ain't got no cuts nor scratches, and the only way I knowed to do that is to shave all that fur off. And I reckon that's a job for you boys."

In short order Bingo supplied Ralph and Paul with a bowl of water, some rags, and a very nice men's cordless electric shaver.

"That your personal shaver, Bingo?" Paul asked.

"It is. What of it?"

"Just askin'."

Ralph thought it appropriate what with Paul having saved the cat from a horrible choking death that Paul be the one holding Daisy during the delicate shaving operation. Daisy responded by being pretty enthusiastic about the whole deal. At the end of it Paul was the one looking liked he'd tangled with a dull axe, as Daisy walked around naked, wrinkled, and confused.

"See, Bingo?" Ralph tried his best to sound reassuring. "No cuts or scratches—least not on Daisy. But no wings, either, I reckon. Looks like Daisy here was just a regular old …"

But at that moment the wrinkles along Daisy's sides began to swell. Paul, Ralph, and Bingo fell back in awe and just a little disgust, what with this new stink coming off the cat as two little naked, never used wings that had been hidden under all that matted fur popped out of its pale hide. Ralph thought Daisy looked an awful lot like a chicken fresh plucked and ready for the oven.

Apparently that's what her cat brothers and sisters thought too, because here they came out from under the porch where they'd been hiding, chasing Daisy up over the ridge with Bingo following, waving his shotgun and threatening them with all manner of dire consequences if they didn't settle down.

Paul and Ralph seized the opportunity to climb into the pickup and make their escape. But Paul, who'd never learned the value of keeping his mouth shut, just had to turn to Ralph and observe, "Lot more interesting than last Saturday, huh?"

Ralph stared at him for a long time.

"Just sayin'."

Crawldaddies

Thirty years after his mother had taken him out of Rayburn Twist, Josh discovered that getting back in hadn't gotten any easier. If anything it was more difficult now that the new highway bypassed that forgotten little appendage of the state boundaries. With but a small population to answer to and no businesses to speak of, the state of Virginia had apparently decided to stop maintaining the two remaining access roads. One was taken out by a slide impossible to repair—half a mountain collapsed into a dying lake and no place to adequately support a bridge. The other was mostly gravel and clay with occasional craquelure patches of ancient asphalt.

You might be able to travel it on horseback, but, not having a horse, Josh was making the journey up from the highway on foot carrying a loaded backpack. Arlene had dropped him off at a wide spot in the road.

"What if you get hurt? Do you really think they'll have doctors up there?"

"I've got first aid supplies, and I'll be careful. People are always getting hurt; I imagine the locals have ways to take care of them. Even if it's just a mountain witch woman with some nursing skills. At least I've had all my shots." He tried to grin, but it didn't help. Arlene was mad, and scared. Josh had made sure his affairs were in order, his life insurance substantial and paid up. But that was not the sort of thing to bring up now.

"You think the locals would lift a finger to help you? A stranger? An outsider?"

"I was born there, Honey."

"You left when you were five."

"Well, I'll make sure they know I'm family right away. It'll help."

She gave him that familiar look that said I love you, but right now it's more like I'm saddled with you. He kissed her and said, "Tell Trace I love him, every day I'm gone."

He knew it wouldn't help things to say more, so he opened the door of the old station wagon and stepped out onto the gravel curb. The whole car rattled when he slammed it shut. When she got home she'd find money in an envelope and a note telling her to get the car fixed up, or buy a new one if she preferred. A woman by herself with a toddler needed a reliable car.

Josh knew she might take the cash and the note as some kind of goodbye, a confirmation of her fear that he had no intention of returning. He did intend to return, after finding out all he needed to know—he just wanted to make sure they were taken care of just in case. But nothing he could do or say would ever reassure her. That had always been one of the truths of their marriage.

Another truth was that whatever it was in him that repelled other women—some untraceable scent, some hormone vaguely sensed, some hidden anatomy or geometry or psychology—

somehow attracted her. He'd never been entirely sure if that was a good thing for either of them.

Descending the embankment from the highway to the traces of old road below was made easier by a well-used series of makeshift steps dug out of the ground and lined with flat stones. Clearly some of the locals had jobs or family somewhere off the mountain.

Trees shielded much of the way from whoever might happen to gaze down from the road. Josh soon found himself by a small creek that ran alongside the old broken road as it wound its way higher up into the hollow between two steep ridges. Compulsively he kept looking down into the water, but had no idea what he might be searching for.

Small creatures scuttled along the bottom of the stream where it curved slightly, partly sheltered by the bank. "Crawldaddies," he whispered.

Nothing he had seen until that moment had triggered any memories. He'd only been five, after all, his world constrained to patches of bright color, lines of dramatic movement, the occasional mostly-forgotten game or song, the stronger flavors of food, the scents of the adults who carried him. But "crawldaddies," the word evoking both a strange delight and a stranger terror, echoed clearly through the years.

Until her death the previous year his mother had still talked about how that had been his "baby word" for crawdads, the name these mountain people used for crayfish, those smaller relatives of the lobster who lived in the fresh running waters that didn't freeze to the bottom. His mother thought they were disgusting because they didn't care whether the plants and small animals they ate were alive or dead. Now he thought of them as dark and ugly but good with lemon juice.

Before she died they'd talked about his need to come here, to know what he'd come from. Her own memories were failing her, and she'd never been much help filling in the details of his distant past, "We all best just move on" being her standard answer. But even through the fuzziness it was obvious the idea made her anxious; she thought the whole notion was bad business. "Why'd you want to go there?" she asked from her bed, pushing her head up to look directly at him, even though it was an obvious strain. "Nothing to see there, specially now. We left all that to find something worth seeing."

"It's where Dad grew up, and I hardly know a thing about him. Even looking at his picture I can't really remember him. And frankly, Mom, you haven't been much help over the years."

"Not much to tell," she rasped. "He grew up there, and he stayed there. That place is pretty much all he was. I wanted better for you." She started crying.

"I'm sorry, Mom. I know you did the right thing for us. I have a life—I'm not sure what I would have had there."

"If you go." She lay back down with a deep sigh. "It's your daddy's hometown, but you won't be seeing him there. You'll want to feel some—disappointment—over that, but don't allow yourself to give in to it. He'd only make a mess of things. Believe me."

"You mean he's still alive?"

She blinked, shrugged. It was the last time they talked.

So Josh knew next to nothing else about the place. What research he'd done in books and on the internet told him nothing about the people, but a little of the local geology. As in much of the region, beneath a few feet of rich earth was a recurring sequence of beds including coal, sandstone, shale and clay, and marine limestone. In many spots the limestone directly underlay the coal. The deep shaft coal mine, Clyburn, just on the other side of the ridge, had given out early when the difficult landscape had made it too expensive to mine further.

The remains of a couple of the old coke ovens were apparently still there, the tipple, the ruins of the company store with advertising still hanging on part of a free-standing wall. Some hiker had posted photos on the internet.

Then there was some information about the uniqueness of "the twist" itself. A diagram showed how several lines of strata had been pushed up and turned into something resembling the warped corner of a tissue, the folds turning and growing tighter as they entered the twist. Reference was made to the huge volcanic forces required to create such a phenomenon, and its inherent instability. Mountain streams had percolated through the porous limestone layer creating a random series of caverns and tunnels. Even though the whole thing was encased in millennia of dirt and rock debris the nature of the twist was still evident in aerial photographs.

In the midst of all that lay Rayburn Twist where Josh was born and his father had lived, and perhaps still did.

As Josh got further up the old mountain road he found fragments of old houses deserted and torn down, pieces of wall left standing or blown apart by growing trees.

So far he'd seen no attempts to preserve anything. Halfway up the mountain he stopped to rest at an abandoned house by what had become no more than a path with occasional asphalt flagstones. He sat in the doorless doorway for benefit of the shade, but not trusting the roof enough to venture in farther. He ate an orange and a protein bar, washing it down with a bottle of water. He liked oranges and wondered if he'd be able to buy any in the Twist. Probably no bottled water, but he'd keep the empty bottle and borrow someone's tap, and pray that he didn't poison himself. More protein bars were unlikely—he'd try to stretch the supply he had.

Before he left he did a quick check inside. One large room and a small bathroom—that was it. He watched his step. He could see the bare dirt cellar through gaping holes in the floor, and he kept looking up to make sure insects, snakes, or roof beams weren't about to fall on him. The little house had been stripped—no cabinets or fixtures, no doors, no pipes, and all the copper wiring yanked out. There was a small rusted child's wagon twisted up in the middle of the floor. It looked like it had been run over a few dozen times.

At first the long dark streaks looked like tire marks, as if a motorcycle had driven around the walls like in a circus act. But by the time he'd left he'd decided they were some combination of scraping and rubbing, almost as if something large had been trapped here, or a group of such things, and had struggled to get out again.

Now and again the creek wandered back into view. Dark came early to these shadowed ridges, and he had no desire to travel the path at night. But there was something so compelling about the proximity of the stream he just couldn't keep himself away, and he wandered off the path again.

The stream here ran narrow, constricted by the large rocks on either side, but it ran deep. Moss and plants and layers of dead specimens of each caked the banks. Beneath all that was leaf mold several inches thick. He looked down into the clear waters. But not completely clear. Here and there a trail of fog, or light smoke, marbled the stream. Still, he could see most of the bottom, and the scuttling creatures there, so like rough bark or broken rock suddenly given legs. He went down on his knees and then to his side to get a better view. The crawdads ignored him, going about their business.

The water smelled vaguely of metal, or maybe some chemical. But deeper than that—and it surprised him that he could actually perceive layers of smell—was something old and long dead, bathed in the waters. So much for trusting the water supply. But Josh didn't think it was dangerous. Just different, perhaps, from what he was used to.

His eyes kept straying back to the crawdads. They were certainly ugly brutes, festooned with an unsortable battery of legs, and pincers, and miscellaneous appendages whose purposes he could not begin to fathom. He used to draw them when he was a kid, using crayon and pencil stubs or whatever he could get his chubby little hands on. It disturbed his mom, who didn't understand how he could have remembered them so clearly, and who thought they were horrendous looking (which is what he liked most about them—they were bold, they had presence, they were scary).

But what seemed to disturb his mother most was how he drew the crawdads. Instead of segmented legs and pincers he gave them a forearm, biceps, elbow, and shoulder. Human arms, big, inflated arms for the pincers, little ones for the antennae. He'd bend the arms in ways human arms weren't normally bent. Sometimes he would add little tattoos to the arms: an anchor, a boat with sails. He would paint the crawdads different colors: forest green, pale yellow, blood red. And when his researches taught him all about swimmerets, those small appendages along the edges of the thorax, he drew those like long, wiggling fingers.

Crawdads liked it dark, cool, and isolated during the day. Josh had understood that very well. Sometimes he'd lie under his bed all afternoon, and wouldn't come out even when his mother called him. Sometimes he would sneak out of his room during the middle of the night and steal a piece of cake out of the fridge or a banana off the counter. Sometimes he'd even take something that tasted bad, like a piece of raw fish or a spoiled dish of vegetables he discovered at the back of the fridge, because crawdads couldn't always be picky—they ate what they found. He'd tear the food into tiny little pieces with his fingers and stuff it into his mouth.

During the long summer afternoons he would hide under the covers and try to sleep, imagine that his skin was molting. He would grow to many times his size in his dreams and he would destroy his room.

He passed no one else on the trail, no one was out working, or even lazing about, no voices echoing down the valley. No more houses, either, not even abandoned ones. Now and then something would rustle through the brush alongside the trail, animals of some kind, although whatever wildlife was native to the place was staying out of his way. Maybe because he was a stranger.

He reached Rayburn Twist, near the top of the mountain, around sunset. If there used to be a paved road through the town there wasn't one now. A wider passage of compressed clay and traces of wheel ruts with weeds growing out of them. He didn't see any cars, or signs of their recent passage. No one said hello, but he saw several women perched up on the weathered gray porches, staring down at him with somber, broken faces. He waved, but they didn't wave back.

Josh thought maybe it would be better to find some place more official than a private residence. If not a mayor's office (he couldn't imagine there was one), at least a store. At a store they might talk to him—even here a store owner might want to encourage business.

A couple of more houses with women on the porches. One old lady waved and he waved back. He was beginning to wonder if this was a town of all women when he saw an old man in a rocker sitting on the ground outside his house, a shotgun across his lap. The man looked stuffed, except for the rocking, and Josh didn't try for his attention, turned his head and kept walking.

A little girl peered at him from beside a tree. Her face was as pale as something out of a cave, her eyes gray in her dirty face. "Is there a store?" he asked, smiling broadly. She didn't smile back but she pointed.

The battered old building looked like all the others except for "Store" painted in faded black letters beside the front door. Three men standing at the counter turned to look at him. On the wall behind them a lot of shelves displayed very few goods—a few cans, some boxes, a few bags. Most of it looked aged and out of date. On the counter itself, however, were some fairly fresh-looking bags of meal and beans.

"My name's Josh Morgan. I lived here a long time ago, with my mother—"

"Emmett Morgan's boy." One of them stepped forward and studied Josh. His face was a series of flaps of skin, as if it no longer fit his skull. He raised an arm that looked too long and too thin for his body. "You look like him, or the way he was before."

One of the other men chuckled. "He means before he got old. I'm Andrew, Josh. We're cousins."

The third man laughed then. "Hell, Andrew. We're all cousins up here." And then all three of them laughed.

"My father, so he's alive? He's living here somewhere?"

They stopped laughing then. "Don't live here, but he checks in from time to time," Andrew said. "He checks in."

Josh was taken into one of the houses where he met dozens of people, all introducing themselves as cousin this-or-that, or aunt this-or-that. Most of them were elderly, his mother's age and older. The women looked sad even when they smiled. All the men seemed to have that same skin condition—which was too much of it, finally, as if they'd lost a large amount of weight very fast.

"So, I reckon you'll be seeing your daddy while you're here?" one of the women asked, which caused the rest of them to quiet their talking for a time.

"If he's around," Josh replied. "If not, maybe some of you could tell me something about him, and about the rest of the family too, if you would. My mother never told me much."

"Your ma never should have taken you out of the Twist in the first place, especially with you being a son in the family." The others tried to shush the woman. "'Specially when you ain't reached your majority yet."

"Majority? I'm thirty-five years old."

"Think you're an old codger do ye?" one of the old men chuckled. "Well maybe out there. But up here, you're just a naup." A little girl giggled, and Josh realized then some younger people were in the room. He looked around and saw them hiding behind the older women and back against the walls, little kids and teenagers with sullen, red and pock-marked faces. He saw, too, the pale young girl who had first pointed the store out to him. They nodded at each other.

There was a meal at some point, and another round of introductions, and a sweet drink home-brewed from roots and berries that made him sleepy. But he was already tired, having hiked most of the day to get up there. He didn't even remember going to bed.

When Josh got up the next morning there was no sign of anyone else in the house. He searched the rooms that were open, knocked on those doors that were locked, but there was no answer. He figured they'd all gone out to jobs and chores. A couple of the women in the house were quite old, but he supposed up here everybody was expected to work. They had a lot of mouths to feed.

He stepped outside. The air was warm, but there was a taste of fall. Smoke hung over the trees up the rise ahead of him, at the top of the Twist.

The pale young girl from the day before suddenly appeared at the edge of those trees, and waved.

"Hey there!" he cried. "You must be Cousin Something-or-other." The girl just smiled and waved some more. "Is that smoke I see?"

She looked back up the hill in the direction of the smoke. Then she turned around and motioned him to follow her. She kept her distance, but she stopped periodically to make sure she didn't get too far ahead of him. Finally they cleared the trees, and the hill continued a few more feet, ending in two great lips of stone poised as if speaking to the sky from the top of the mountain. The creek bubbled out of there, and steam floated above it.

"So this is where the creek starts?" But she had run ahead again, and was pointing at something at the top, mounds of smooth clay by the stone lips.

He walked up to her, and she backed away. He looked down.

They were the ends of enormous clay tubes, or maybe smokestacks, maybe chimneys, that went down into the water as far as he could see. Water filled them, but if he looked closely, and God knows he didn't want to, he could see that dark shapes swam just beneath the surface in each one. Around the edges were large pellets of mud, like bricks, that had been worked and smoothed. And several bits of shattered armored plate, like thin flat sections of bone, worn and scratched and frayed along the edges.

Something seemed to move inside him, as if a rib or a muscle had slipped free. It wasn't painful, but it felt dreadful just the same.

That night there was another huge supper. And more of that sweet root drink, which he was beginning to see as some blend of dessert and liquor. It left him soft and sleepy and barely able to move.

He didn't even notice the old people leave. Suddenly it was just him with the younger ones—the sullen teenagers; the anxious-looking twenty-somethings; that shy, pale girl whom he'd come to think of as his only friend in this strange homeland. There were even a few babies in the mix, squalling and fussing in the arms of the older children.

Andrew appeared in front of him. "You're oldest of these, I reckon, so you're in charge of these youngins, but not for very long, I 'spect. Visiting day, you see. Won't be long now."

When Andrew left, the pale girl looked over at Josh, but not smiling. Josh tried to get to his feet but he couldn't quite manage it. "Visiting day? Did he say visiting day?"

He heard the rumble. The whole house shook. Some of the smaller kids fell onto the vibrating floor. Josh thought of how much he missed Arlene.

A dozen or so came in, but they more than filled the room. Some of the little kids were crying "Crawldaddies! Crawldaddies!" and squealing with delight.

He kept thinking how scared his own son Trace would have been, and how much he missed him.

And they did have human arms, or what might have once been human arms, too many of them, and they walked on them, and some of the arms did have faded tattoos. They moved as if they had broken backs, their heads hanging down as they crawled over the furniture and gathered their children up in their enormous daddy arms. "Crawldaddies! Crawldaddies!" the children cried, and even Josh found himself whispering it as he felt the changes beginning inside, as his own father held him up in his powerful backwards Daddy arms.

Lookie Loo

Jackson had moved back to Monroe County a year after retirement, three years after the divorce. Without the divorce he probably would've worked until he dropped, making Sheila a pretty comfortable widow there in Ann Arbor. She hated Tennessee. How could anybody hate Tennessee?

Jackson stood behind a purple avalanche of Catawba rhododendron like some kind of peeper and watched as the three large men in their roomy homespun coveralls cleared a lot of rotted logs and tangled deadfall. He'd been following them as they worked odd jobs all over the Smokies: clearing trails, cutting firewood, moving furniture, putting up barns. Folks just told them what to do and they did it.

He didn't know yet what their story was, but he was pretty sure they had one. Since he'd moved back here he'd been taking notes on eccentrics: that fortune teller living on the old Poor Farm, that granny woman who cured pretty much everything, that fellow in Gatlinburg who could talk out of his belly. Someday he'd make a book out of these stories, *Strange Tales of the Smokies* or some such. He wouldn't be putting the locals down—it would just show how interesting folks around here could be. He'd finally have something to say about the world.

Jackson didn't know if he was a great writer or not, although he daydreamed about being known someday as the Henry David Thoreau of Tennessee, who understood living in these hills and appreciated the mysteries they surely contained. In Walden, Thoreau said, "The mass of men lead lives of quiet desperation." Around here people got desperate and didn't have anybody to tell it to. Oliver Wendell Holmes talked about people "that never sing, but die with all their music in them." That surely was these people. That surely was him.

He'd first seen the brothers two weeks ago shambling between the trunks in a dense stand of trees, like apes with their too-long arms, faces a dark shaggy blur, and in the shadows with those baggy coveralls they looked like a family of Big Foot, or Cave Yellers as they called them in Kentucky. And wouldn't it be a hoot to include those monsters in his book?

Those coveralls must have been uncomfortable, it being mid-July and steamy. But they worked as if their lives depended on it, picking berries and seeds out of the bushes and trees and dropping them into their sacks. Jackson could tell there was something wrong with these fellows—something physical or nervous or both. Every once in a while one of them would jerk his head back and forth in a seizure-like motion, and he'd turn his head and open one eye wide as if trying to see something better. They all three looked agitated and impatient, but about what?

Then another fellow would be moving his shoulders funny, so they looked tremendously swollen, ready to burst. He would leap up on a log or a big stone, teetering, waiting to fall or jump again, until he'd calmed himself down, and then he just closed his eyes as if he were taking a nap in that awkward position.

190 / Steve Rasnic Tem

It appeared that whoever'd made the coveralls had kept running out of cloth in one direction or other so different fabrics and colors had to be added on. These men had odd, swollen shapes, and the coveralls had been built around them. So they weren't pretty outfits, but they were tailored.

All three men resembled one another with the same kind of rough face, carved from flesh and bone by a sculptor who really wasn't all that talented, who didn't have a very sure hand. One was smaller than the others—Jackson named him "Junior." The biggest one looked like a "Bubba" to him, so that's what he called him. And the one that kept turning his head around and looking sideways, one eye a little bigger than the other, he called "Walleye."

There surely were strange things in Monroe County: maybe some version of Big Foot, and that Lost Sea attraction that was supposed to be the largest underground lake in North America, and the ghosts of all those displaced Cherokees, and the tales about big birds that walked away like men, and the mountain witches and the UFOs and maybe once or twice a hitchhiking Elvis had been seen out on Highway 411. But these fellows had real potential. There wasn't a thing normal about them.

So he followed them around from job to job, taking notes and not a few pictures, keeping his distance but still close enough to observe their habits, just waiting for them to slip up and betray their secrets.

That very morning he'd followed them to the rough shack where they lived. He parked his beat-up Datsun on an old logging road and used his binoculars to spy right through their open front door. At one point he saw an old woman's hideously-scarred naked back. She wore this silly hat loaded with feathers, as if she were getting ready to go out to some high-class society do, but she'd forgotten to put on her blouse.

This afternoon, peeking at them from behind these big purple flowers like some kind of low-life voyeur, he thought there was something different about them, an increased nervousness maybe, as if they knew they were being watched. Every once in a while the smaller one, Junior, would jerk his head up and twist around, staring as if he'd heard something. Jackson stood perfectly still, wondering what excuse he could make if they caught him.

Walleye, whose mismatched eyes made him look surprised or suspicious, kept messing with the zipper on his coveralls and shrugging, adjusting their fit. The zipper came down a bit, and something dark and ragged sprang out before Walleye tucked it back in.

"What you doin' here?" the deep scratch of a voice asked behind him. Jackson turned around. Bubba stood there, and Jackson realized the binoculars and the distance had been flattering. The fellow was far uglier close up. "Trespasser," came out with a spit, scraped up from inside the big man's chest.

Jackson made himself smaller, the way you were supposed to do if you ever ran into an angry bear. But it was hard to look away. It looked as if Bubba had tried to shave both his face and his scalp, and the hair had resisted, or he'd just been clumsy, because he had little nicks and scars everywhere, and the remaining stubble was too tough, each whisker too thick, like heavy-gauge wire, and there were all these protrusions that looked like tubing that had been severed at the surface of his skin, but the roots went deep into his face, as thick as straw, as if he'd been in an explosion, or the bad end of a hurricane had driven these broken stalks into his flesh.

"I got lost." Jackson couldn't think of anything else. "I was hiking."

"Hik-ing?" Bubba's mouth tried out the word as if he'd never heard of such a thing. "No pack?" The fellow stank badly. Jackson had a foul taste in his mouth from breathing the air between them. It wasn't much like any body odor he'd encountered before, a little like dirty feet mixed with kids' crayons, and maybe some greasy French fries in the blend. He'd smelled something like it before, around his daddy's old chicken coops and near the bird cages at the pet store.

"Didn't think I'd be out that long."

Bubba raised his heavily gloved hand and pointed at the binoculars hanging from Jackson's neck. "Bird watchin', I reckon."

Jackson patted the binoculars. "Yeah. You got me there. Kind of a hobby, but I bet it seems goofy to you."

Bubba didn't look happy. He pulled his yellowish lips back to expose a large row of teeth that made a beak-like edge. "Some kind of lookie loo, ain't you?" he said, and the air whistled sharply through his teeth. That's what folks around there called fellows who stared too much. Peeping Toms. But the way Bubba said it, that whistly "lookie-loo," made it sound like some kind of rare and despised bird.

"I honestly wasn't trying to eavesdrop." Jackson knew immediately how lame that sounded, since it was exactly what he'd been trying to do. He felt seriously in trouble now. People down here were territorial; they'd had too much taken away from them.

"Don't worry none." The big man grabbed him by the arm. "Me and my brothers, we'll be giving you a ride."

Jackson was afraid to ask where they were taking him. They weren't headed back toward town, but farther up the mountain. The Smokies had some of the highest peaks in the Appalachians, but Jackson had never been one for heights. He was jammed between Junior in the passenger seat and Walleye behind the wheel. The smell was nearly overwhelming. Beyond what he had smelled before was this older, underlying stink like old and moldy cardboard.

Bubba was in the back of the pickup, standing in the bed, not holding on to anything. He had his arms outstretched as if flying, and the way the truck bounced when it hit some of the ruts, maybe some of the time he was.

The truck screeched to a stop so abruptly Bubba went flying over the hood, but still somehow landed on his feet. Nobody showed any concern. They were near the top of the mountain, at a small clearing bordered by tall trees, mostly white pines, and some of them a hundred fifty feet high, maybe close to two hundred. Junior grabbed Jackson by the arm and dragged him into the center of the clearing. The brothers started chanting this high-pitched, loony singsong, "lookie-loo, lookie-loo, lookie-loo."

They stood around him, stretching, jumping up and down, looking increasingly excited about what was about to happen. They started making soft little scraping sounds way down in their throats, which after a few seconds became screeches and calls. One by one they shrugged out of their coveralls, great masses of oily black feathers popping out and spreading as their constrictive clothing slipped farther down their bodies. Finally the garments lay in rough pools beside them, and they stretched their muscles and fluttered, their immense black wings spreading until the shadows of them darkened much of the open ground between the trees.

Junior took off, whooping, climbing high and then swooping down, one edge of his wing tracing Jackson's left cheek and ripping it open. Walleye's turn was next. He kept low beneath the trees, his broad wings creating a wind that initially felt soothing against Jackson's overheated face, but then froze him in terror as the hard wings beat against the sides of his head and drove him onto the ground.

Finally Bubba dived in and lifted Jackson as if he weighed nothing, climbing parallel with the tallest tree to reach the top in a rapid ascent that stole Jackson's wind away. Breathless, Jackson viewed the mountain in a way he'd never seen before, the Ocoee Series of peaks spread out before him, ancient results of that collision of the great tectonic plates, and he was thinking what a perfect way that was to begin his book, which might now include the true story of the legendary Madisonville Tennessee bird men, when Bubba let him go.

The boys' mother was looking down at Jackson when he woke up. This was the old woman he'd seen a few days ago, topless and with the scarred back. That feathered hat he'd thought she'd been wearing had actually been her head, covered with a thick layer of feathers that started around the eyes and flowed down around that jutting jaw and made a soft and luxurious, Renaissance-like collar around the neck.

The feathers had been partially removed from her torso, scarred and hacked at like the brothers' faces. Quills were thicker, tougher than hair, and would be a lot more troublesome to remove. You couldn't do it without a lot of scarring, a lot of pain. But she'd kept much of her plumage, so he supposed she'd stayed at home and let her boys forage for her. In her case the scarring was apparently decorative, or maybe tribal.

Forage. He'd been foraged. The bird watcher had the tables turned on him. Lookie-loo. She strutted around him, her head jerking back and forth. She made a soft and dry scraping noise deep down in her throat. She stank of birds and what birds ate.

He'd been in enormous amounts of pain. He'd passed out, and come back numb, then passed out from the pain again.

Now he was riding a returning wave of pain—he could feel it rising from deep within him.

He told her, "The mass of men lead lives of quiet desperation. They never sing, but die with all their music still in them." He was delirious, but determined to have his say in the end. He had no idea if she understood him.

Her boys had joined her at the dinner table. He giggled, thinking it was a kind of Thanksgiving. They'd left their coveralls behind, and now preened in all their feathered glory.

Once he'd seen a bird eat a frog. You couldn't call it cruel because it was an animal. The bird had picked the frog up and dropped it several times, played with it to soften it up. The frog was still alive, but then the bird attacked it with its beak.

Powell Mountain Cedar Grove

1.
Up at five:
planting red cedar with Grandad,
grassy slope, sun,
limestone outcrop with ocean algae tracks.
Lunch of cornbread and goat's milk in a pail.
Black locust and cedar, fifty feet high.
Grandad says, "Trees won't ever be that tall again."
He points four ridges away: stripped mountain;
mine acid killed the pine, grasses,
killed the watershed and buried Uncle Ralph's farm
under sand and gravel from a farm he'd never seen,
two farms in one grave.
Deep in the shaded grove,
tulip poplar and red oak
drive out the cedar.
Grandad says cedars come first, take the sun.
Poplars need shade, and soon take over.
But they grow so big they darken their own
seedlings, die out.

Beech and hemlock grow last to fill the forest.
New ground animals, plants come.
Used to, a town moved when they lost
the water, or the land changed.
Planted the rest of the day,
listening to brown thrasher song,
waxwings in good fencepost wood,
woodpeckers nesting in knotholes
softened by fungus.
Bess Bugs get under the bark.
Catbirds in the oak
eat their weight in bugs every day.
Rabbit for dinner. The grove loses heat.
We make our bedroll.

2.
Wake staring at naked locust root,
swellings full of bacteria left when the roots die,
nitrogen for growing cedar,
flowers, horns, cattle.
Early morning sun fires each cell in the bark,
fills it with light. In the blue-green leaves
cells weave sun and carbon into webs of sugar,
spiny twigs, snow-white flowers.
Caterpillars eat leaves,
float away on wings of light.
Beetles eat these,
deer mouse devours beetle, to fox,
sun passed on tongues mouth to mouth,
woven into bones.
A rest during ground-clearing,
Grandad and I watch a gang of men
burning grasses down the valley.

They work for Mr. Sexton.
Big breakfast of sausage, rice, potatoes.
Grass covers acres, each blade shines.
Cool, silent, dry, yet hot enough
to roast a man if he falls.
The sun will burst from him, too,
burning inside and out.
In dark, loose clothes,
shadowed behind the flames, the men
covered in black hair,
huge jaws and teeth.
Their food moves the fire
through their bodies. Sun drains
from hair, jawbone, incisors,
and through their spines, the fire
leaping into their brain stems,
into the seed, bursting, blooming
into two swollen halves, white, glowing flower:
Hiroshima, the Taj Mahal.

Redbud Winter

"Our life is March weather, savage and serene in one hour."
— Ralph Waldo Emerson

Ted took his late wife's station wagon out of the garage thinking he'd drive it to his daughter's house in Norton. It was what, an hour's drive? These days he drove little, but surely he could manage an hour's drive.

It wasn't like him. He wasn't the spontaneous type. But even a quiet life will sometimes generate disturbances.

That morning he was sitting in his dining room, sipping tea, when he gazed out the window and saw his redbud tree in full bloom, magenta blossoms exploding everywhere, directly from the bark on the trunk and limbs. An outrageous display of optimism. *Too early*, he thought. *Winter will come back and put an end to you*. Southwest Virginia had four or five of these mini winters in March and April, each named after some tree vulnerable to a late freeze after the beginning of spring. He'd looked out this window many times since his diagnosis, and never seen anything quite so hopeful, and yet so doomed.

He thought of Janet, his mercurial daughter, up there in the mountains with the boyfriend and Ted's granddaughter Abby.

He hadn't seen them in months, and that wasn't right. He imagined she would get a kick out of seeing her mother's old car running. He tried calling again. She wasn't picking up, but even if she wasn't home, he wanted to climb the watch tower on High Knob one last time for its spectacular view.

He hadn't left the house in weeks. He didn't see the point. He hadn't driven the car in the two years since his wife died, but it started with only a few moments' hesitation. This surprised him. That flimsy garage was so cold. Once he had the vehicle out in the sunlight it distressed him how dirty it was. He went back into the garage and got the hose, attached it to the outdoor faucet, and turned it on. He expected leaks and felt inordinately pleased not to find any. But the pressure was low, and it took forever to wash the car. It would be a late start, but he was determined to go. Once Ted decided something he never reversed himself.

The station wagon moved and turned and stopped and did all those minimal activities one expects a vehicle to do, albeit with a certain amount of noise. Ted didn't know cars, so he didn't understand what any of the noises meant. But the car was in better shape than he was. His driving was shaky. He was six months away from his license renewal, and maybe he should just let it go. There comes a time when you have to stop driving, stop doing everything. His hands trembled on the wheel.

Still, the prospect of the trip pleased him. The previous weekend saw the first real thaw of the new year, with the four-month-old ice caking the ground north of the house breaking and beginning to run.

In fact, everything was running this weekend. The melt and leaves out of the gutters, the last of the snowpack from the shaded paths, and his heart, racing with the anticipation of seeing family again.

It was a foggy morning. During long stretches he couldn't see the edges of the road. He should have waited and done this another day, but he wasn't about to turn back now. A few minutes out of town, the tires making a pleasant splashing noise on pavement dark with layers of leaf rot, he smelled it for the first time. The scent of death, clear and palpable, an unmistakable presence in his nose and lungs.

He drove on for a short distance with this stench, wondering if it might be due to the general thawing, the smell of winter's decay trapped under snow torn open by the greenness just now breaking through the rot. The beginning of Spring could be an adequate explanation for this disturbing perception. New things had a stink on them.

Or it might be him. What was it his doctor said that last visit? "Make the most of your time." He wondered if Janet and Abby would notice. He should have asked more questions. He should have used more deodorant.

He pulled to the side of the road to wait for some specific event, a heart attack, or a brain aneurysm, a dramatic occurrence which did not come. He got out of the car and lifted the hood. He had no idea what he was looking for, maybe a dead possum or a mouse cooking on top of the engine, poor thing. But he saw nothing so obvious. It might be a mechanical issue, but he knew nothing about mechanical issues. He understood the insides of a car no better than the mysterious workings within his own body.

People driving by waved hello and Ted waved hello back. Some of them he recognized. Several he'd been sure died some time back. But it was years since he last socialized, and that had been with Catherine. She had many friends. He'd never been good at making friends.

When the last vehicle passed, and he saw no others coming, he lifted his arms one at a time and smelled his armpits. She had always hated that. She said it was uncivilized, something a hillbilly would do. She was sensitive about the whole hillbilly thing, living in Appalachia. She said people in other parts of the country thought Southerners were ignorant, and Ted had a responsibility not to prove them right.

He breathed into his cupped hands and smelled nothing more than this morning's bacon and eggs. He could hear Catherine fussing at him. He wasn't supposed to eat bacon.

So, no unusual odor was detectable, unless he was simply used to it. But that death smell, who could get used to such a thing? Once he'd driven by a slaughterhouse and the scent was vaguely reminiscent of that. Blood in the air.

His doctor never mentioned a smell. But doctors don't tell you everything when you're old. They don't want to upset you if there is nothing they can do.

The fog lifted around the time he reached Norton. The trees and roads were dripping. In some spots it was cold enough for the drips to re-freeze, leaving the trees rimed and the pavement glassy. He slowed down. He wasn't the driver he used to be, not that he'd ever been much of a driver.

He was no longer aware of the stench. Whatever it was had burned off. Now he was feeling uncharacteristically positive. He rolled down the window to listen to birdsong: black-throated blue warblers and scarlet tanagers in the spruce, fir, and sugar maples. Dense thickets of rhododendron lined the road rising toward the knob. They didn't always keep the ditch lines trimmed, but that was a problem all over this part of Virginia. All that mowing and removal cost money these poor counties didn't have. But it was a good environment for wildlife. He saw a white-tailed deer on the slope above him, and for a moment what might have been a red fox.

Janet's house was off the side of the mountain on the way to the recreation area. Ted felt a sense of vertigo as he turned off the road and the station wagon descended the driveway. Something in the suspension groaned. Was that normal? He wasn't sure the old car could make the steep trip back up to the road. But Will was a mechanic, and knew everything about cars, according to Janet. But what if they weren't home? He should have talked to her before coming. Already this felt like a disaster.

The front yard had five cars in it, three in different states of disassembly. The other two appeared drivable. The gravel and dirt drive ran beside the house, ending in a drop-off which terrified him. The house looked smaller than he remembered, and shabbier.

He stopped a few feet short of the end of the driveway and pulled the emergency brake. The engine made a rattling sound but kept running. Steam started pouring out of the front end. Ted began coughing. He didn't realize he'd been holding his breath. He felt so incompetent he thought he might cry.

"I didn't know you was coming. She didn't bother to tell me."

Ted didn't hear Will come up to the car. How was that possible? Janet's boyfriend was a big man, and now he filled the driver's side window, leaning in with those massive forearms. Both were tattooed with thick black stripes, like bracers. His long blond hair completed his resemblance to Marvel's Thor. Ted had never mentioned it—he didn't know how the man felt about comic books.

"It's a surprise. I tried calling first, but no one picked up."

"Phone's broke, Your daughter dropped it again. Was she always this clumsy? Now Abby's taking after her."

Ted gritted his teeth, insulted. He wanted to say something. He'd wanted to say something to this fellow many times, but

Janet insisted it was best he didn't. He knew it was a bad idea for a father to involve himself in his adult children's relationships, but when the insults shifted to his grandchild what was he supposed to do?

Will must have been working on his cars, because he had black grease on his white T-shirt, his forearms, the backs of his hands. Ted wanted to tell him to be careful about touching his upholstery—Will was further into his car than seemed necessary and Ted could smell the beer on his breath—but he kept his tongue. Will reached in and turned off the ignition. "You're wasting gas."

"Dad, I didn't know you were coming." Janet appeared behind her boyfriend, who moved out of the way. Still, she held back, her arms folded across her stomach. She looked thin. She'd always had problems keeping up her weight. It had been a major topic of conversation between Ted and Catherine since Janet's junior high days.

What was wrong with her mouth? Was that a split lip? She reached up and played with the hair falling across her forehead. Will put his hand on her shoulder and she flinched.

She had small black spots on her arms. She noticed Ted looking and pulled her arms behind her back. "I was about to make us some sandwiches. Come inside. Abby will be thrilled you're here." Ted kept squeezing the steering wheel. It was like he couldn't let go.

Will didn't look happy. "I can't stay too long," Ted said. "I don't see well late in the day. And my driving skills are rusty. I'm getting old, sweetheart."

"Oh, Dad. You're not that old."

The pair exchanged looks again, and Will had his dirty hand on the small of her back, pushing her toward the house. She turned around suddenly, wiggling away from his touch. "Dad? Are you okay?" Ted kept sitting there, unable to let go of the steering wheel. "Dad?" She leaned through the window and put the back of her hand on his forehead. "You're hot. Have you been sick?"

He wasn't ready to talk about it. "I'm fine. Fine. This car. I think I pushed it too hard. There was smoke coming out of the hood."

"Will can look at it after lunch. Let's get you inside." She opened the car door and unbuckled his seat belt for him. He swung his feet out and she helped him up, supporting him as they negotiated through the weeds and past rusted car parts into the house. Will walked a few feet away. Ted glanced at her left hand on his arm. One of the fingers looked a little crooked.

Abby met them at the door. She burst into tears and clung to him. "I'm fine, sweetheart. I'm fine." But he had no idea, really, why she was crying. Abby didn't look like Janet or anyone on his side of the family. He'd never met Abby's father. All Janet would say about the man was, "you wouldn't have liked him."

They helped him to the couch, with Abby sitting beside him holding his hand. Janet brought him a glass of ice water which felt far too cold, but he downed it anyway. He slumped back onto the couch still clutching the cold, empty glass, holding it away from his body.

"Grandpa. Are you sick?"

He smiled at Abby. "No, no, I don't think so. I got a little confused for a second. I must've been thinking about math."

"I don't like math."

"Nobody does, Sweetheart. But it helps when you're balancing your checkbook. Are you doing okay?"

"I'm fine," she said softly. He noticed she was wearing terry cloth wristbands on both wrists. It seemed odd. He looked around for Will but didn't see him.

Janet came back in and took his glass. "Dad, have you been sick?"

"No, not really. A little congestion. I'm fine."

"Then what was all that about? The only time you say you're fine is when you're not fine." He thought about Abby sitting next to him. Was she understanding this?

"Well, I might be going senile, but I can't remember for sure."

"Dad."

"I just smelled something, and I was trying to figure out what it was. I guess it was nothing."

Will yelled from the kitchen, "Might be the air conditioner. It stinks if you haven't used it in a while." So, he'd been listening.

"I don't think I had it on." Of course not. It was March.

"I'll flush out the radiator—I've seen radiators so bad they were like swamp in a can! When's the last time you flushed it?"

Ted barely understood what Will was talking about. Back when he drove regularly he took the car into a garage, told the mechanic to perform whatever regular maintenance needed to be performed, and paid no attention when the man recounted the work he'd done. "I have no idea," he said.

He saw Janet looking at Abby, who readjusted her wrist bands. "Lunch will be ready soon." She left and Ted glanced around the room.

The house initially appeared more orderly than he would have expected, especially on a day when he dropped in unannounced. Janet had never been a meticulous housekeeper, worse once she had a child at home. The pictures were perfectly straight on the walls, including a formal photo of Catherine taken a year before her death. The magazines on the end tables were aligned with all their edges straight. The books on the tall narrow bookshelf by the door appeared to be arranged by size and color. Everything looked dusted and polished, including the baseboards, an area Ted always had trouble with since it had become too painful to get down on his knees.

But the coffee table had been pushed into one corner, covered with various auto parts. A crudely lettered sign lying on top said DO NOT TOUCH! The TV sat in another corner, an obvious crack running across the screen. By the door frame leading into the kitchen there was a fist-sized hole in the wall. At the other end of the living room another door led to a hallway and the bedrooms. It was off its top hinge and leaned against the wall.

He heard murmuring and rock music blared from the radio in the kitchen. Then Will's voice rose above the music. "Why is he here?"

Should he go in there and say something? He couldn't hear Janet's response, just the high-pitched nature of it. He felt Abby stirring beside him, but he was hesitant to do anything. He'd always believed in minding his own business, although Janet's choices often brought him pain.

The radio was suddenly louder, but Ted could still hear Will's voice above the din. "I don't care what your friends say." Then something else, followed by a clear "Try me."

Ted waited for signs of a physical struggle. Then he would surely intervene. Abby got up and scurried down the hall toward her room. Ted believed he'd somehow failed her, but he didn't know what he should have done.

Janet appeared in the doorway, smiling tightly. "Lunch is ready."

It was an uncomfortable meal. Abby ate half her tuna sandwich and prodded her orange slices with her fork as if she couldn't quite decide what they were.

"Abby, you love oranges," Janet said. "Aren't you feeling well?"

Abby mumbled, "May I be excused?"

Will intervened. "Not until you eat every bite. I pay good money for groceries, along with everything else in this house."

Janet glanced at Ted, obviously embarrassed. He didn't know what to say but was fairly sure he shouldn't say anything.

"I'll work on your car after lunch," Will said without looking at him. "Probably needs a new hose and a tune-up. I'll get you back on the road so you won't have to waste any more time here."

"Oh, it's not—"

"Shouldn't take long." Will got up abruptly and left the table. "Make sure she eats every bit," he said without looking back.

Over the next hour Ted and Janet and his granddaughter sat in the living room attempting to make conversation while Will banged around on the station wagon, his work punctuated with curses and yells. At one point Ted looked at his daughter and said, "I do appreciate Will looking at the car." Janet nodded, red-faced, and Ted felt like an idiot. Abby left the room without saying anything. Ted wanted to follow her but did not.

Ted and his daughter sat in awkward silence until Will stuck his head in the door. "Come out and start it for me." Janet started to get up. "Not you! Your dad!" Ted struggled off the couch and followed him outside.

He sat behind the wheel while Will rambled on about hoses, belts, the caked grease around the oil cap, and something about the wagon's crap carburetor. Now and then Will slapped one of the fenders for emphasis. Ted could see the man was working toward some kind of explosion but was at a loss as to how to prevent it. What could he say?

He remembered asking Janet after she first started dating Will, "Is he a good guy? Does he treat you and Abby right?"

"You've never liked any of my boyfriends" had been her reply.

"Give her some gas!" Will shouted from the front of the car. Ted gingerly pressed his foot on the gas pedal, released it, and pressed it again, not sure if he was doing it right. He kept glancing at the shifter, making sure the car was still in Park. Will was shouting, but Ted couldn't make out the words because of the revving engine noise.

Will slammed the hood down and stared at Ted through the windshield. He looked demented. Maybe he wasn't. Maybe it was the angle, the circumstance, or the terrible smell filling the car. Ted wasn't aware of making the decision, but he watched his hand slip the gear shift into Drive.

The station wagon lurched forward. For a split-second Ted could see the fear in Will's eyes, and a spot of blood on his lip. Ted wondered how the blood got there. Did Will bite his tongue, or his lip? Then Will slid beneath the front of the car, and there was a roughness as the car rolled over him, followed by an abrupt tilt and the vehicle was roaring down the hillside, through bushes and small trees, the windshield shattering and debris falling into the car. Ted stared at his right foot, wedged against the gas pedal, and he couldn't make himself remove it.

There was a sudden stop as something interrupted the station wagon's rapid descent. A log, or a rock. The engine was still roaring, the tires spinning, and there was that terrible stench.

With unnatural calm Ted gazed out the driver's side window. He was near another house, a woman struggling to reach him, but there was an older man in overalls holding her back. They looked terrified, of him, or of the crashing car, maybe both. Certainly, there was every reason to fear him, every reason for the man to keep his wife away. Ted had made a serious mistake. What did he actually know about this man he had just killed? Why hadn't he asked a few questions before committing to this terrible thing?

When the car struggled loose of its obstruction and hurtled on Ted felt relieved. He could see more trees and rocks ahead of him, and a steepening of his descent. He understood it was essential that he did not survive.

Old Crow

Sleek and dark as the forest night, the crow glided over the Appalachian ridges corrugating southwest Virginia. Wallens, Powell, Cumberland. Those were their human names, but for Old Crow they were Home.

He flew early each morning, before the mountain witch got up, because he didn't want to remind her he had the freedom of the skies, and she did not. She'd tried when she was younger, but on her best days her long skirts barely cleared the ground. Now she'd lost even that. She couldn't keep the right words straight in her mind.

During the first hour after sunrise, the crow chased a rabbit and tormented a stray kitten. He meant them no real harm, and after a few minutes tired of the play. Having lived too long, over a hundred years now, games quickly bored him, as did most everything else. He still felt grateful and loyal because of the witch's gift, but he couldn't remember the last time his long life gave him pleasure.

During the second hour he paid his respects at a crow funeral, of which he'd seen many during his time in the world.

They'd gathered around the body and in the surrounding trees, hundreds of them, because it was late summer and more than the usual few families were on the move, to gaze at the broken fledgling on the path. According to rumor a farmer's hunting dog was the cause. The alarm over the danger went out hours ago. But now they watched without noise, and after the appropriate time departed in silence but for the sound of all those flapping wings.

Old Crow felt grateful to be included in the rituals of his kind. In their black eyes he was no longer one of them. He was an outcast, barely tolerated because of his differences, but they still sometimes allowed him in. A century spent with the witch woman, Emer, made him something more than crow, although he hadn't the language to say what.

On his way back to her he spotted an acquaintance, the scrub-jay, far below, hopping and bobbing his blue head about the forest floor. Old Crow dropped out of the sky, rustling his tail feathers as he landed in front of him.

"You can't have my food!" Scrub-Jay scolded.

"I don't want your food."

"Well, you can't have it! It's not here!" But Old Crow had already seen him shove acorns, worms, and seeds under a nearby pile of leaves and bark. Scrub-Jay made several such caches in the area, no doubt a few more than he remembered.

"The woman feeds me well. And I'm quite capable of scavenging for myself." To demonstrate, the crow hopped onto a log, pulled a stiff twig into his beak, and used it to fish a grub out of a deep fissure in the wood. Showing off, he then flipped the grub over to Scrub-Jay, who trapped it beneath a talon.

"Mine now!" the scrub-jay squawked.

Old Crow jumped from the log and fluffed his glistening black mantle. "Enjoy the fruits of my labor."

"There's a possum nearby. We can share."

The crow was genuinely surprised by the offer. "No thank you."

"He's dead now."

The crow knew the possum when he was alive, not that it made any difference. Once dead, friends were food, unless, perhaps, they were crows. But more than once he'd fed on the eggs and nestlings of crows.

"I mean *completely* dead."

"I *know*," Old Crow said sharply. "I know the dead very well. My kind invented death, haven't you heard?" He wasn't sure if this was true. There were stories. But he wanted to say a bold thing and so he did.

"I just thought. Well, the gossip is your woman isn't doing so well. You might need to find another one to live with."

"You shouldn't listen to gossip. Where did you hear this?"

"Around. Just around. They say she wanders."

"She has always wandered. It's how she finds what she needs for her spells and cures."

"They say she writes on trees. They say she speaks to herself."

"When she casts a spell she *is* speaking to herself. Who else would she be speaking to? And she has always written on trees. She has always made her signs."

What Old Crow didn't say was writing on trees kept Emer from getting lost. She once knew the woods as well as she knew the many lines marking her own face, but now the simplest journey could be the cause of endless confusion. She marked the trees between her cabin and the nearest store so many times they were losing their bark. But no one needed to know this.

Three blackbirds landed nearby. The scrub-jay went into a panic, jerking its head in a series of sharp turns. "You can't have my food! You can't have my food!"

The blackbirds tried to talk at once, running around and flapping their wings. Old Crow stared at them. He'd been known to eat a blackbird or three when he thought it necessary.

Emer had fallen in the woods. One of the blackbirds suggested that now she was dead she might make a good meal.

Without a word Old Crow took flight.

The crow first met the woman when he was young and eager to try out everything in his surroundings, no matter the risk. He'd settled down in the middle of the highway to dine on some carrion, an unfortunate squirrel who thought she could outrun the humans' automobiles. In those days, the crow was short enough to duck beneath their metal bellies. He only had to avoid their tires.

He soon became aware of the woman watching him from the side of the road. She looked no better than roadkill herself with her ragged clothes and dirty flesh, but beneath the grime he could see the youthfulness in her face and the sharpness in her eyes. She carried a large sack for gathering treasures — castoffs and trash and roots and seeds — detritus which only the smartest of granny women appreciated their hidden value. "Clever Crow" she called him back then. "Clever Crow," she whispered until in a trance he hopped over, and she added him to the collection in her sack.

He considered himself lucky she didn't eat him or take him apart for some esoteric project or other. Instead, he became her constant companion, surprising since she lived alone and did not enjoy the company of others. Depending on her mood, if uninvited strangers ventured near her cabin she might send them away with stings and rashes and running sores.

But the mountain folk owed her much and hired her often for tonics and charms to protect themselves, spells for the sick and lovelorn. But she would not guarantee spells of attraction and sold them only when she needed food or money. Sometimes she would sell a farmer a special scarecrow, and the crow spread the word those fields were not to be touched.

No one liked or fully trusted her. To these people Emer was the outcast crow. But he stuck with her, and over time Clever Crow became Old Crow as she rewarded him with a long life for his loyalty, replacing his deteriorating parts as needed using spit and cobwebs and singsong words spoken barely above a whisper. As her powers grew, so did his.

He found her sprawled off the path among the phlox, bearberry, and creeping juniper. She'd lost her way again, became tangled in the undergrowth and went down. She sometimes forgot there was food in the cabin and went off foraging on her own. He should have been there.

She was poorly dressed for the cool morning weather. She wore her thin silver nightgown and she'd forgotten her hat and shawl. She lay motionless, staring at the sky, her long gray hair twisted and stiff with briars and sticky weeds.

"Old woman, are you dead?" It came out harsher than he intended, but most things did. His voice had no music in it.

"I don't ... know. Am I?" Her eyes did not move when she answered him. Her voice was flat and sounded as if it came from a distant place.

"Get up. You cannot lie here."

"I don't know how."

He had no strength to give her, but he possessed serious power to annoy. He plucked at her shoulders and pecked at her legs until she rolled onto one side, then pulling at her sleeves made her get up on one knee. Further torments drove her to her feet, swinging her arms to swat him.

He floated up and made two barrel rolls overhead to remind her any attempt to catch him would be wasted effort.

"Who are you? Are you my husband?" He was alarmed by the tears on her face. In all those years he never saw her cry. If she were ever married it was before he knew her.

"I'm Old Crow. You used to call me Clever. Do you remember?" The idea of being her husband amused him. What was he to her anyway? She never gave it a word. The crow had always been a bachelor, but he loved the females.

"And my name? What is mine?"

She misplaced many things in the past few years, but this was the first time she lost her name. "Your name is Emer. You have told me it is Irish, but I don't know what that means. You are my oldest friend."

During the next few months, the crow stayed closer to the cabin and discouraged the woman from venturing out. She had plenty of food stored away, but if necessary he could kill a small rabbit or squirrel and drag it inside and leverage it with a stick into the fire. Like most crows, he was good with tools, but all these years in her company made him—what was the word she used?—her *engineer*.

But some days, if she were determined, he could not stop her from going out, either to the small country store, or the cabin of some acquaintance, or some favorite source for bulbs, seeds, or roots. For she was a granny woman, a witch, and although he was special, he was mostly a crow. He always followed her, flying between trees and bushes, perching on the edges of roofs or cliffs along her route, waiting while she completed whatever business she had, and then followed her back, cawing his signals, waking her up, reminding her of the safest way home.

Old Crow did the best he could, but he knew his assistance was not adequate. Some mornings she put her clothing on backwards. Other days she had difficulty dressing at all. He could pick the proper clothes for her and pull her sleeves in the right direction, and sometimes turn a blouse around using talons and beak if she hadn't put her arms in yet, but he couldn't button her up and she tended to fight him over zippers.

She fell asleep most afternoons and he used these breaks to fly, gliding through the air making observations, patrolling for predators, and chasing them away with his harsh warning cries. Once freed from Emer duty, he was available to search for the sights which buoyed him, a lovely spider's web perhaps or a wasp colony's elaborate multichambered nest. These were not treasures to bring home or cache in a secret collection like a gathering of shiny stones or buttons or bits of jewelry. They were valuable primarily as memories, and he filled his aging crow brain with as many of them as possible. Isn't that what wise creatures do, before their inevitable end?

Fall soared into winter, and winter meant not letting the flames in the fireplace go out no matter what. Old Crow couldn't count on Emer remembering how to restart the fire or even wanting to. On freezing afternoons, she slept more, waking up only to take a bit of food from his beak or to accuse him of carrying unwelcome messages out of her troubled dreams.

Eventually the seasons circled to spring again and the rising warmth encouraged her to talk, but what she said often made little sense.

"How are you feeling today?" the crow asked, perched on her mountain of quilts.

"I am dead, sorry bird. Please don't try to wake me."

"You're not dead, Emer, but you have been sleeping for quite a long time."

"Can't you smell me, stupid bird? I stink. I am dead."

"You just haven't been able to wash yourself, old woman, and that's beyond my powers to help. Let me find a nurse somewhere in the hollers, or another granny woman to perform the chores I cannot."

"I am hot and then I'm cold and then I'm hot again."

"See? The dead feel neither cold nor heat."

"What is your name again?"

"You once called me Clever Crow and then Old Crow. These have been my only names."

"Well, shut up Old Crow or whatever your name is and let the dead lie in their well-earned peace." She was silent for a time, but then added, "Just don't leave me by myself."

They had been through this charade a few times before. Periodically over the years Emer decided she was finished. She was dead, and all indications appeared to be this was a fact. She had no pulse. She had no breath. Her skin became discolored, her lips blue. The locals took her to a funeral home, and she'd lie there a few hours, but then in the middle of the night she would forget, or change her mind, climb off the mortician's table and leave. Each time it became Old Crow's job to find them a new place to live where she could start all over under a different last name.

She did this for decades. Sometimes the locals put up a gravestone, anyway, waiting for her body to return. Emer's big secret was she had graves all over the Appalachians, each under a different last name.

But not this time. This was clear in Old Crow's brain. There was no getting up this time, no changing her mind and climbing off the table. As spring sailed into summer Emer ate less and less, until it seemed she was living on air alone, and maybe the smells wafting through the cabin windows. She got out of bed only to go to the bathroom, but he wondered why she bothered since there was so little waste produced.

She slept entire days and most of every night. She became reduced to a speech of single words like wind, and dream, and empty, and crow.

For months, the crow wondered what he would do once his granny woman died. Could he organize a crow funeral, or would that have insulted her? Could he get the other crows in these mountains to come?

Could he stay in her cabin forever? This seemed unlikely, unless her reputation was such no one would want to trespass even after her death. It had been decades upon decades since he'd lived in the wild on his own. Could he do it again?

Old Crow began to notice his own changes. He had always had such sharp vision, able to spot a hint of food on the ground even when flying high in the air. But lately the world was always at dusk, his vision reduced, a time to find a roost and avoid the owls.

Before he met the woman the crow roosted with other crows in the same group of trees near water. There they shuffled and squawked, moving down through the branches as more crows arrived, exchanging gossip before settling down to sleep. Since moving in with the old woman he grabbed sleep whenever he could. She gave him so much to do there was little time for slumber.

Now he could barely keep his eyes open in the middle of the day. He barely noticed when his tail feathers began to fall out. He could still fly, but badly. He kept bumping into things. When his wings started falling apart, breaking down into cobwebs and bits of bark and leaf and yellowed witch's spit, Old Crow knew his flying days were over. As Emer died, he was losing everything she gave him.

On their last day he hardly noticed when she climbed out of bed. He realized what was happening when she shuffled out the cabin door. He crept slowly behind her, losing feathers and talons, a withered eyeball, along the way.

Halfway through the yard she stopped, her limbs stiffening. She raised her arms toward the sky, and they froze. Old Crow dragged himself up her hardening skin with beak and broken claws, desiccated feathers, and fracturing bones, until in the crook of a branch he was able to rest.

He wondered if they would gather, all his dark crow kin. He wondered if they would grant him their minimal respect.

A Jack Tale

One time there was a retired librarian named Jakob who told stories to children in the southwest Virginia schools. He especially loved telling them Jack Tales. "One time there was a boy named Jack," he generally began, and told them of the time Jack went to seek his fortune, or the time he got the silver sword, or the tale of Jack and the Northwest Wind, and of course Jack and the Beanstalk (Jakob knew six different versions). In these tales Jack was variously a fool, a clever boy, a liar, and a trickster.

"And that's how Jack got rid of all them rats. He's still doing it and doing it well as far as I know, at least he was the last time I saw him."

It was the last day of school and the last day of stories. Jakob was tired, old, and wondered if he'd ever tell another.

"I wish I was like Jack," said a tall girl in pigtails.

Jakob smiled. "Me too, child."

"Did you ever have adventures? I mean when you were younger?"

Jakob lost his smile. "No, I guess I never did."

The next morning Jakob filled his backpack with fruit, sandwiches, pocketknife, a favorite book, and a jar of drinking water. He locked up his house where he lived alone, went down to the road, and stuck out his thumb. He had bad arthritis, so he was counting on rides to get him wherever he needed to go.

Eventually a rusty Ford pickup stopped. The driver, a thin stranger with a long white beard, opened the door. "I'll take you as far as you're going, Jakob. I'll take you all the way to the end."

How did he know my name? He started to ask the stranger his name, but he hesitated. Jakob pondered all this as the man drove up and down every road in the country, stopping now and then because "I got business here." The skinny fellow would run into somebody's house then back out like a thief. Oftentimes wails and crying chased him out the door.

Jakob, already bored with this adventure, drank some water and ate most of his sandwiches. Night fell and the driver pulled over. The dark sparked with lightning bugs. Jakob grabbed the water jar, stepped outside, and poured it out.

"Don't do that Jakob. You'll get thirsty later."

"I want to catch a few." By the time he got back he had several dozen making the jar glow yellow. He dropped in an apple slice so the bugs wouldn't dry out.

Driving around the next morning they came across an abandoned coal mine. "Stop the truck. I've never been inside a mine." Jakob slipped on his backpack and limped toward the entrance.

"Don't go down that hole. You'll regret it just like your daddy!" the old man shouted.

Jakob went inside, guided by the sunlight streaming through the opening. He shuffled closer to the darkness, seeking a taste of whatever his daddy went through. Soon he was enveloped in the pitchiest of pitch blacks, able to see nothing at all. He got so scared he didn't know if he was standing, sitting, or lying down.

"I need you to come closer," a familiar voice said from the dark.

Jakob knew no good would come from saying the man's name. "I'm not doing that."

"Obey me, boy. I need the company."

"If I trade will you let me go?" He pulled the jar of lightning bugs from his pack and held it out. He heard a sliding noise and two black-encrusted hands grabbed the jar and raised it high. Jakob hadn't seen that face in years.

"Good enough. Turn around, take eight steps forward and turn left. Then you'll see the light."

Jakob watched the jar's yellow glow fade until the mine swallowed it entirely.

He didn't say what happened and the bearded driver didn't ask. After another half day running up and down the narrowest of roads, stopping twice so the driver could "conduct business," they came to the biggest cornfield Jakob had ever seen. "I'd like to stop here," Jakob said.

"Jakob don't go into that cornfield. You'll be sorry you did." But again, Jakob ignored him and walked into the corn the moment they stopped.

Soon enough Jakob was sorry he did. He didn't know which direction he was going, and the blowing corn silk made him itch. Crows pecked at his jacket and britches like he was a scarecrow no good at his job.

"Stop right there!" A farmer with a shotgun stood in front of him. A pig, tied to a rope around the farmer's waist, snuffled the dirt at Jakob's feet.

"I mean no harm," Jakob said. "I'm lost."

"Maybe and maybe not, but I could use the company." The farmer pointed his gun at the porch a few yards behind him.

Jakob led the way and they both sat down. The pig curled around Jakob's feet like a dog.

"So, Thomas Oliver, you reckon he's telling the truth?" the farmer said to the pig. He smiled at Jakob. "He seems to like you."

"You gave your pig a fancy human name." Jakob knew little about pets. He'd never had one. He always wondered if it would be like having a child, which he also never had.

"What else would I call him? You're staying for supper. I'll cook Tommy here up until he's nice and tender."

"What? He's your pet!"

"You must not be a farmer. Farmers don't keep pets, less it's a dog, or a cat or twelve. I've been keeping him around to have somebody to talk to. I get bored. But now I've got you."

"If you give me Thomas," Jakob said, "I'll trade you for something to better fill your time."

He pulled the book out of his pack, *One Thousand and One Nights*, gold lettering on shiny red leather. The farmer took it reverently. He began reading, carefully turning the pages. Without looking up he said, "Deal. Take the pig."

The pig dug his feet into the dirt and screamed like a frightened child. Jakob picked him up and whispered, "You don't want to get eaten, do you Tommy?" He stuffed the pig into his pack. The pig was so heavy Jakob staggered through the corn to the road. There he collapsed. The pickup was nowhere to be seen.

Jakob laid the pig on the ground and covered him with his jacket. They fell asleep spooning.

A loud noise woke him. It was morning twilight, everything gray and a few degrees less than real. The bearded man was there in his pickup, revving the engine. "Best hurry. We got business," he said.

Thomas was gone. Jakob's backpack was empty, the pig having eaten the rest of his food. He turned and saw a little boy wearing his jacket and nothing else, running into the cornfield. Jakob figured he wasn't cut out for either mining or fatherhood.

Wordlessly Jakob climbed into the cab. The ancient driver looked even skinnier and paler than before. He was missing more of his teeth, and some of his skin. A few miles down the road he said, "You're awfully quiet. You got no new stories for me?"

"Sir, I'm all storied out if you don't mind." Jakob realized then he'd never told this fellow he was a storyteller.

They drove all day, and around sunset they arrived at the town where Jakob had lived his entire life. But the man drove past his house and past the other houses, stopping at the cemetery on the far end of town where Jakob's father was buried, along with everyone else he could remember from all the years before.

"Why are we here?" he asked.

"I told you we got business."

Jakob stared at the driver. The old fellow smiled and there were no teeth and not even a mouth, just a raw open hole. "I'll trade you," Jakob said. "That's what I'll do. I'm good at making trades."

The man laughed from some place so far away it took a while to reach his mouth. "You ain't got nothing left. That pack of yours is empty."

"But I have stories to keep you company. Jack tales and tales of his brother Tom and tales of his other brother Will. And now quite a few about myself."

"You said you were all out."

"There's a whole orchard of tales out there. I just have to reach up and pull one down. I won't know what I have until I hold it in my hand."

That's how Jakob became old Death's companion, visiting folks and taking folks and leaving their loved ones burdened with sorrow.

He's still doing it to this day and doing it well as far as I know.

The Return

Joel hadn't been back to his hometown in over forty years, not since his parents' funeral. His health was so poor the last couple of years, he knew this was his last chance. It wasn't a trip he wanted to make, but he believed it was a journey whose time had come.

Nothing on the map seemed familiar, not even the names of nearby towns. The topography of Southwest Virginia appeared threatening. Had there really been so many ridges, so many winding roads? It seemed unlikely any of those features would have drastically changed over the years, so the difficulty must lie within his aging memory. He might be better off ignoring his recollections completely.

He'd read that the geology of the region consisted of folded sedimentary rocks from the Paleozoic age, limestone, dolomite, shale, and sandstone. Sinkholes riddled the karst terrain, many of them leading into the hundreds of caves lurking beneath the surface. He didn't know any of this when he was a child. But hadn't someone warned him to be careful where he stepped?

As a boy he'd isolated himself much of the time. Painfully shy, he relied on his books and comics for company. After graduation he lost contact with the few he might have called friends. A few years after his parents' deaths the house he grew up in burned to the ground. There was nothing in that town left for him, and yet he still felt compelled to return.

If Celeste were alive she would have traveled with him. She would have made things so much easier. Throughout their marriage she'd been his go-between with the outside world. They'd made plans to come a few times, but something always came up. "Don't wait until it's too late," she said. "These memories won't last forever." She understood him all too well.

Joel took a direct flight into Knoxville, Tennessee. A two-hour drive in a rental car carried him across the Virginia state line and into a wide green valley between forested ridges. The Woodland Indians camped here before the white men invaded. His grandfather took him arrowhead hunting a few times, and once to a cave on private land full of their bones. This angered his mother and the trips with grandad stopped.

There was now a better road, but it bypassed the old highway going through town. A small, weathered sign showed him the way. Another, barely readable sign indicated the area was a bird sanctuary. He recalled the large flocks of birds which filled the trees around town. The clamor they made sometimes frightened him. He'd been a fearful child. His father used to say he didn't know what to do with him.

The winding road skirted a pond and followed the complicated curves of a low-lying ridge, the lane narrowing until he wasn't sure what he'd do if he met a vehicle coming from the opposite direction.

But he confronted no such vehicle. Joel encountered no cars at all. But he remembered it was always a sleepy town. Now that the mines were gone, and so many people moved away, he imagined it was practically comatose.

It occurred to him he hadn't checked for hotels. There had been two on the edges of town when he lived here, decades ago, but the chance of them still being in business seemed remote. How could he have missed such a basic aspect of trip planning? He felt like a child again, helpless without Celeste to watch out for him.

The radio played a constant stream of bluegrass music. He wasn't used to the genre, but it was so different from the things he usually listened to it was almost charming. During the two plus hours he'd been listening there had been no interruptions for news, ads, or announcements of any kind. Changing the channel delivered static. Apparently this was the only choice the locals had.

So far nothing he'd seen on this trip was at all familiar to him. He gazed at the passing landscape, looking in vain for something to trigger another memory. Certainly, he grew up surrounded by neighbors, relatives, classmates, their houses, their businesses. An entire community. He hadn't spent *all* his time in his room. But this world had nothing to do with him. He'd never had a good memory for faces, and names often eluded him. But this was worse. He had only the vaguest ideas about his own parents. He couldn't remember the last time he looked at their photographs. And his beloved grandfather — was he tall, or fleshy? Did he have a beard? Joel vaguely recalled the sweet smell of tobacco, but had that been on some other old man's clothes?

Celeste was ten years gone, and she too, he had to admit, had become a bit less real, no longer a vivid part of his now. And the now was important — that's where we all lived. He had an abundance of photographs, of course, in almost every room: Celeste at various ages, in the blue Mexican dress she'd worn on their wedding day, a closeup of the marigold she'd pinned in her hair, dancing at a party, lying in bed reading, and standing in the park she'd loved so much, smiling so broadly at the camera, the same spot where he scattered her ashes.

All these images folded one into the other until they were all the same. Joel could no longer hear her voice in his head, or remember the smell of her hair, or the particular way she felt when he held her in his arms. They were no longer a part of his experience of the day, of any day.

The ditches along the roadside had been allowed to fill with weeds. It felt negligent and dangerous. He drove slowly, afraid of what might wander into the path of the car.

Coming out of a long bend in the road he came upon a beautifully preserved antebellum home. He knew there were houses like this when he was a boy, but he couldn't remember any in such good condition. There were columns out front, and a second story porch above the main porch. Filigreed brackets ornamented every corner of those porches as well as the eaves. The house looked freshly painted. Flower beds flanked the sidewalk leading up to the steps, and rose bushes hid much of the stone foundation. A small sign by the front gate promised ROOMS. He pulled off the road into a narrow parking area.

The small woman behind the screen door tilted her head. "Can I help you?"

"You have rooms available?"

"Sometimes. Come inside and let me have a good look at you." She wore an old-fashioned dress with a lace collar and a print of tiny yellow flowers on a field of cream. With her pale, papery skin, and white hair she almost disappeared into the pastel patterned wallpaper behind her. But her eyes, like dead coals resting in cloudy water, held his attention. "I taught you in school, didn't I? You were in my sixth-grade history class. Jack, or Joe, something like that."

"Joel. I grew up here, but I think I'm too old to have been one of your students."

"Nonsense. I'm not always good with names, but I know my faces. And I'm always happy to rent to a former student."

In which case Joel wasn't about to argue with her. "I'm not sure how long I'll be staying."

"Stay as long as you like. People aren't lining up to rent here. Not since they moved the county seat."

"This isn't the county seat anymore?"

"Not for over twenty years. They decommissioned the courthouse, tore it down and sold the parts to one of those architectural antique companies. There's not much left of downtown I'm afraid. I take it you've lost touch?"

"I have." It felt more than a metaphor.

"Most of Main Street is empty. We don't have a newspaper anymore, a hospital, or a school. The sun's setting fast on this old town. You should have come back sooner."

She showed him around the house. The dining and living rooms were from another era, full of antiques. The kitchen looked as if it had been last updated sometime in the Fifties.

"Lock your bedroom door. Folks around here tend to sleepwalk."

"You have other renters?"

"No. You're the first in a long time. Supper's at sunset if you're around. Breakfast at six a.m. You're on your own in between." A white cat came bounding down the stairs. It halted, frozen, when it saw Joel. "Do you like to bird watch?"

"I suppose. Sometimes."

"Birds are the only things worth looking at around here." She pulled out a drawer in a sideboard and handed him a pair of binoculars. "This will help."

After settling into his room Joel came back downstairs thinking he'd drive into town and see for himself the changes the woman talked about.

"Hello!" he called out. "Missus?" But he'd never gotten her name. He wandered downstairs looking for her but found no indication of her presence. Out of curiosity he opened the refrigerator. It was empty. He checked the cabinets. They were empty as well. Perhaps she'd gone grocery shopping? He wasn't hungry in any case. He might skip dinner if he got busy in town.

He got into the car and continued down the road. He assumed he would reach part of the town that way. If not, he could always double back.

He needn't have worried. Almost immediately he was within the town limits. Block after block of tidy little homes. White and blue were the predominant colors. This sense of perfection was spoiled now and again by a weed-filled lot, and areas where the woods took over. Tall plants and brush now filled many of the old gardens.

He had to veer away from low-lying branches, and sections where weeds and saplings grew across parts of the roadbed. Had the town given up on road maintenance?

He kept hearing the distant sound of chainsaws, but he never saw the workers using them. The sounds seemed to descend from the sky, so they may have come from miles away.

He drove up a hill with boarded buildings on either side. Suspended over the top of the hill was a single dead caution light. Joel remembered it well. It had been the only traffic light in the town, meant to warn drivers about the cross street beyond the peak of the hill. Perhaps the warning was no longer needed?

He turned right at the dead light and parked. The courthouse used to be on that corner. A few large foundation stones marked the spot. He got out of the car and looked around. There was a used furniture store across the street. It was hard to tell if it was out of business or simply poorly kept. Dust filled the windows, and the interior looked shabby. But cosmetics might not dissuade customers from looking for a bargain. He was sure the building used to house the post office. Marks on the brick indicated the lettering had been removed. He remembered as a teenager going to the post office to pick up his magazine subscriptions, the books from his mail order book club.

He began walking down the hill into the short block they'd called downtown. A pair of boarded-up law offices. An empty drugstore. He didn't remember this building exactly, but he recalled sitting at an old-fashioned soda counter and browsing the paperback racks. This could have been that place. He pressed his face against the glass. A square window resolved out of the dimness in the back, a dirty PHARMACY sign. A man in a white coat leaned over the small counter, waiting for his order. The sky brightened behind Joel, glazing the window yellow, and the man was gone.

Next door was an empty lot, scraped down to a broken concrete slab littered with cans and rags. He thought there might have been a clothing store here, or was it a hardware? Two more empty stores, their windows plastered with browning newspaper. One of them might have been the old Five and Dime, but he had no idea which one.

A tall man wrapped in swaths of gray stepped out of one of the boarded entries then disappeared. No doubt some trick of the light played on Joel's aging eyes. It was unnerving to see the town empty, with no evidence of human habitation, so maybe his nerves created a presence or two.

Their family doctor had his office in a building on this block. The building was no longer there. His grandfather died in that doctor's waiting room one hot July afternoon.

Where was everyone? It wasn't even three o'clock yet. Despite its problems, this had been a good place to grow up. He could find no justice in its abandonment.

He heard the children running down the sidewalk. He used to do this with his friends, excited that classes had ended for the day, they'd raced each other to the drugstore, or the tiny newsstand attached to the barber shop, eager for a treat, or one of the new comic books. He moved closer to the wall lest they trample him. He was brittle now, frail. That was the biggest change in his life. He had to be on his guard against falls. The right collision with a gang of eager youngsters could break him.

When he turned his head he saw it was a small dust devil carrying pebbles and grit. But what made those clomping sounds, those thrilled children's voices echoing down the walkway?

Joel hadn't thought of this street in years, or these businesses, these houses, this town. He doubted he remembered it accurately, and there were holes. But now it was crucial that he remember, that he recover every lost detail.

He allowed his fractured memories to lead him down the street and into the now-empty lots, where he prodded the rubble for clues as to what once stood at that location, to mostly empty store fronts, where he pressed his forehead against the cool shop windows, his eyes searching the shadows for either goods or occupants. Sometimes there was movement, a shift in the light, the silhouettes of forms coming and going, but nothing definitive, and nothing confirming he'd lost his senses.

Finally, he arrived beneath the grove of ancient Hickory trees on the edge of town, then wading through the tall grass he made his way to the narrow, winding creek. Everything seemed impossibly hushed. Even the shining water tumbling over the dark stones apparently felt the need to keep its voice down.

Shadows drifted and fell apart like smoke. He remembered fishing in this creek when he was a boy. He couldn't remember ever catching anything. They stocked the big stream on the other side of town with trout, but not this small branch. No one else ever fished here. That was why he preferred it.

He wondered if they still stocked the streams in the county. If anyone fished. If they bothered anymore. Everything has its time. Everything eventually dies.

He heard distant chainsaws again. He looked up. Birds were circling overhead. No. They'd made a circle, but now were motionless, frozen, suspended in midair. He never knew birds could do such a thing.

It occurred to him there were many more insects here than he was accustomed to. They filled the air, and they were crawling all over his clothes. Had one gotten into his ear? That might explain the mysterious sound of chainsaws.

He had a moment which he experienced on every trip he'd taken as an adult, a nagging suspicion he'd forgotten something important at home. Had he turned off the stove? Did he lock the back door? He couldn't remember if he'd requested a mail hold or not. Did he tell anyone where he was going? He had no memory of those last few days before getting on the plane. He was usually so careful, obsessively so. He couldn't remember packing.

Joel returned to his lodgings just before sunset, but no dinner was evident. He went searching for her again and found no one. No matter. He was exhausted and had no appetite. He lay in bed gazing out the window until it was dark. During the night, a new assortment of bugs came out, the big moths and the lightning bugs like sparks fallen from the stars.

Joel woke up to a morning muted in both color and sound. He turned on the lights in his bedroom, but they did nothing to increase the ambient illumination. He dressed quickly, eager to get out of this silent mausoleum. The wallpaper lining the stairwell had turned sepia. He noticed some peeling. Everything revealed itself to be much shabbier than when he moved in the day before. The downstairs furniture was scarred. A gray dust had settled into the wounds. He didn't bother to call for the landlady. He was convinced she was either dead or missing. He would find other accommodations before nightfall.

When you grow up in a place you never imagine it going away. People don't last, but it seemed to him a town should.

He drove out to the cemetery to visit his parents' graves. It was a small distance out of town, but up a steep rise which the car struggled to negotiate. He remembered as a child going with them to pick out the three plots.

The cemetery wasn't fenced so he walked right in. To his surprise his parents' graves had been well taken care of. No weeds and the grass well-trimmed. The empty space by his mother's was meant for him. The flowers in the two vases were dead but appeared to be recent additions. He went to the small office at the back of the graves to thank whoever was in charge, but the door was locked. No hours were posted.

He could hear the rain before he felt its distinct drops, on grass, on headstones, on tree leaves, on the small building's roof. He could feel it before he saw the small spots of gray, like fingers touching his shirt, his skin, before it became a rapid flutter, and then a painful scouring of his flesh. He ran to the car and got in. Even with the wipers on he couldn't see past the windshield. On the other side of the glass pale figures writhed as if suffering. He waited until it stopped, then rolled down the window to gaze at the mist rolling off the grass.

After the rain, the worms came out, fleeing the saturated ground, rising like pink, boneless fingers eager for a touch. He must have known many of those buried here, but for the life of him he couldn't remember any names. Did they ever imagine they would someday be gone and how much of their lives did they spend trying to avoid that realization?

If he gazed in a certain unfocused way between the mist and the narrow trees and the gray tombstones he could sometimes make out their faces staring at him with resignation, disappointed they no longer mattered in the world.

On the way back through town he tried to find the spot where their house had been, but as hard as he tried he couldn't remember the address. He drove back and forth through the neighborhoods for hours with no luck.

The next morning a scream woke him up. Of terror or bereavement Joel couldn't quite decide. He thought the voice had been female, but it might have been male. He should find out whose it was and offer help, but he had no idea where to begin such a search.

Some of the wallpaper in his bedroom had fallen off and curled into loose rolls lining the baseboards. The dried yellow paste on their undersides looked like patches of disease. The downstairs area had furthered its progression into brown. Two side tables lay collapsed due to their rotted legs.

He wasn't sure whether it was Friday or Saturday. Perhaps it wasn't even the weekend.

In the early morning light he could almost hear the sigh as the fog flowed down the mountain hollows into the flatlands below. He decided he would walk that day, but instead of going into town he turned onto a narrow gravel lane which pointed toward the distant hills. The area was farmland, but the fields were dried up and dead, the plots marked by small, ragged farmhouses missing both doors and windows.

An awful stench drifted through the air. Deeply unpleasant, and in certain pockets it was intolerable. In those moments he picked up the pace and tried to ignore it. Farm country was rife with unseemly aromas, but this stink was unfamiliar to him.

Joel thought he saw a man walking through a distant stretch of amber-colored grass. He started walking in that direction, calling out a strained *hello*. But the closer he got, the more distant the man became. He had to give up and returned to the gravel road.

He came to an apple orchard. The trees sagged with heavy, bright red apples. He hadn't eaten in a couple of days, so he thought he should be eager to eat one, but he was not. He didn't feel hungry at all. He should eat something anyway, at least to nourish his body. He walked into the trees and reached for an especially beautiful apple, but couldn't make himself pick it.

Joel thought he saw a woman high in the next tree. He walked around the trunk, looking up to get a better view. He saw part of her back, an arm, a portion of one leg, but he could never quite apprehend her face. "Hello, do you need help?" he asked. She said nothing. He tried repeatedly, rephrasing the question each time. But she refused to speak to him, even when he was as polite and apologetic as possible. He gave up and moved on.

Most of the fog lifted by mid-morning, leaving dew on the grass and brightening the bark of the trees. The sun rose higher and by lunch it looked glorious, inviting anyone living to come out and enjoy the day. He was eager to witness this. He remembered the town and its surroundings as always an unusually sunny place. But he saw no one, and supposed the downtown area was as empty as it had been since he arrived. He couldn't figure it out. Someone must live here, more than a few since many of the lawns in town were mowed and the bushes trimmed. And someone had taken care of the gravesites in the cemetery.

The next morning Joel woke up with no memory of the walk back to the woman's lodging house, or what he might have done with himself the previous evening. There was a sourness in the air, and he thought maybe it was him, because he'd neglected to take a shower since he'd been here. Not on purpose—he simply forgot. He slipped into his bathrobe and walked down the hall to the bathroom.

He looked at himself in the mirror. The glass was hazy, and appeared as if it hadn't had a good cleaning in years. But there were clear areas, and in those areas his face was pale, unhealthy, and the skin had a broken, crepey appearance, which he thought was new, although he might be mistaken.

There was no shower, just a tub. He bent down and stuck the cracked black rubber stopper into the green-stained drain, then turned the faucet handle. A hollow sucking sound erupted accompanied by a rattle in the pipe, but no water. Then a long-legged black spider crawled out of the spout, over the handle, and back into the wall through a narrow gap. He tried the sink faucet with no better luck. At some point he would have to figure out how to wash.

After getting into the last of his clean clothes Joel started down the staircase, pausing halfway because of all the cracking sounds. He looked down. Several of the treads had split. The ones below him looked rotted. He stepped carefully onto the more solid-looking bits for the rest of the way down. Downstairs the walls were painted with mold. When he got back he would retrieve his luggage and find somewhere else to sleep.

He drove in town for a while taking the long way around the back, then through the alleys, and the narrow streets of the outlying neighborhoods. He saw no one, not even a cat or a dog. Areas were impassable because of downed trees or bushes growing through the pavement. The sidewalks were practically destroyed. Some houses had burned. A few leaned so badly a moderate wind might knock them flat. He saw none he would have considered intact.

He chanced upon a familiar backroad he remembered led out to his grandfather's farm. It wound upwards into the ridges and through a series of wide valleys. He passed several abandoned farmhouses. In some their walls had fallen inwards making them resemble crushed skulls. A few barns had been left partially disassembled. He remembered there used to be a market for gray barnwood. Many landowners sold their old outbuildings to feed the demand.

Joel found no signs of people, but birds were now plentiful, roosting on telephone lines, filling the branches of trees, soaring overhead in great flights of migration. Their overlapping wings made Escher-like patterns in the sky. But they made no sound, which he found bitterly disappointing. He would have given anything to hear a disruption in the dead silence, even if it were a scream.

The sun was high overhead yet provided no warmth. This didn't make much sense in summer, but was it still summer? He couldn't remember the name of the month when he had flown in. It would be on his return ticket. He had a return ticket, although he had no idea where it was.

He gave up looking for his grandfather's farm. He may have passed it without recognition, or it wasn't on this road at all. On his way back into town he found a high place overlooking downtown. He parked and grabbed the binoculars off the back seat.

He used them to take in the distant views: the side of a cliff, hay bales arranged artfully in an empty field, old farmhouses with peeling paint. He still looked for signs of human life. It was impossible he was the only one. But there was nothing, or worse than nothing, as among those brief glimpses of beauty he could see plentiful evidence of extensive loss and decay.

We are slight, he thought, *and temporary.*

Joel drove back to that once lovely antebellum home to pick up his luggage and find someplace safer, or at least more intact, to sleep. He wondered if he should leave money on the kitchen table for the lady in case she ever returned. He hadn't yet paid her anything and he owed her *something*.

The question was moot. He couldn't find the place. He drove from one end of town to the other and beyond, trying every road, sometimes driving at a crawl to make sure he didn't miss it, and found no indication of its existence.

Joel couldn't think of anything logical to explain this omission, or what a next reasonable step might be. He went back through town and parked near the Hickory grove at the end. He was uneasy about the prospect of sleeping in any of these abandoned buildings, and it would be too uncomfortable sleeping in the car. But it was warm. He would stretch out beneath these trees and think about what he could do tomorrow about his situation. His search for the woman's house would be more successful with a rested pair of eyes. If all else failed he had his wallet with him. He could drive to Knoxville tomorrow and find an actual, normal hotel. He could stay there until he got a new plane ticket home.

He was alone beneath the trees and the moon, the scatter of stars from one end of the darkness to the other. He knew there were things which once made him happy, but he could not remember what they were. He remembered there was pleasure, when he was young, in simply being alive, but he could not remember any of the particulars. He remembered wanting to be married. He couldn't remember if he ever asked her, and he couldn't remember her name or whatever happened to her. A wife would have made all this much easier. But if he had learned anything during his lifetime it was that we all face death alone, trapped inside that secret self which can never be shared.

He could hear a distant storm, a crackle of electricity like a chainsaw inside his head. Lightning filled the air above the trees. He felt the hairs on his arms stand up and knew how incredibly lucky he was to be surrounded by such a terrible beauty.

He awakened as the sun peeked above the distant hills. He knew he had much walking to do. Why hadn't he rented a car? He was too old to be doing so much walking. He raised his head to look around. There was a road, and fields of rubble on either side, and nothing else. The world was perfectly quiet. He remembered he'd wanted to visit his hometown one last time before he died. He couldn't remember how he'd lost that opportunity.

He could remember nothing else and knew that what he could remember only yesterday had faded away. The morning came up all silver, and he was aware that something new was about to begin.

Acknowledgments

"The Cabinet Child," originally appeared in *Phantom*, ed. Paul Tremblay & Sean Wallace 2008

"Smoke In a Bottle" originally appeared in *Appalachian Winter Hauntings*, ed. Michael Knost & Mark Justice, 2009

"Willie the Philologist" originally appeared in *Now & Then*, vol. 26, no. 2

"The Bible Salesman" is original to this volume

"Old Men On Porches" originally appeared in *Spectres in Coal Dust*, ed. Michael Knost, 2010

"Nightcrawlers" originally appeared in *Weirdbook*

"Sundown in Duffield" originally appeared in *Nightmare Abbey* No. 4, 2023

"Saved" is original to this volume

"Scarecrows" originally appeared online in the *Tough* crime blogazine

"Miranda Jo's Girl" originally appeared in *Appalachian Undead*, ed. Eugene Johnson, 2012

"Mr. Belano's Visit" originally appeared in *Legends of the Mountain State* 4, ed. Michael Knost, 2010

"The Passing," originally appeared in *Mountain Magic*, ed. Brian Hatcher, 2010

A slightly different version of "La Mariée" appeared in *Art From Art*, ed. Stephen Soucy, 2011

"The Grave House" originally appeared in *Strange Tales* V, ed. Rosalie Parker, 2015

"Diorama" is original to this volume

"Deep Fracture" originally appeared in *Madness of Cthulhu* Volume 2, ed. S.T. Joshi, 2015

"Almost a Legend" originally appeared in *Hills of Fire: Bareknuckle Yarns of Appalachia*, ed. Frank Larnerd, 2012

"Cattiwampus" originally appeared in *The Devil's Coattails*, ed. Jason Brock & William Nolan, 2011

"Bingo Thompson's Flying Cat" originally appeared in *Stories from the Hearth*, ed. Brian Hatcher, 2011

"Crawldaddies" originally appeared in *Searchers After Horror*, ed. ST Joshi, 2014

"Lookie loo" originally appeared in *Turn Down the Lights*, ed. Richard Chizmar, 2013

"Powell Mountain Cedar Grove" originally appeared in *Mountain Thought Review*

"Redbud Winter" is original to this volume

"Old Crow" originally appeared in *Feisty Felines and Other Fantastical Familiars*, eds. Kevin J. Anderson and Allyson Longueira, 2024

"A Jack Tale" is original to this volume

"The Return" originally appeared in *Nightmare Abbey* #5

Meet the Author

Steve Rasnic Tem was born in Lee County Virginia in the heart of Appalachia. He is the author of over 500 published short stories and is a past winner of the Bram Stoker, International Horror Guild, British Fantasy, and World Fantasy Awards. His story collections include *City Fishing*, *The Far Side of the Lake*, *In Concert* (with wife Melanie Tem), *Ugly Behavior* (crime), *Celestial Inventories* (contemporary fantasy), and *Figures Unseen*, his Selected Stories. His novels include *Excavation*, *The Book of Days*, *Daughters*, *The Man in the Ceiling* (with Melanie Tem), *Deadfall Hotel*, Blood Kin, and the recent *Ubo*.

Steve Rasnic Tem's short fiction has been compared to the work of Franz Kafka, Dino Buzzati, Ray Bradbury, and Raymond Carver, but to quote Joe R. Lansdale: "Steve Rasnic Tem is a school of writing unto himself." In 2024 he received the Lifetime Achievement Award from the Horror Writers Association.

NOVELS

Blood Kin
Deadfall Hotel
Excavation
The Book of Days
The Mask Shop of Doctor Black
Ubo

WITH MELANIE TEM

Beautiful Stranger
Daughters
In Concert

The Man on the Ceiling
Yours to Tell: Dialogues on the Art & Practice of Writing

COLLECTIONS

Absences: Charlie Goode's Ghosts
Celestial Inventories
City Fishing
Decoded Mirrors: Three Tales After Lovecraft
Everything Is Fine Now
Fairytales
Figures Unseen
Here with the Shadows
Out of The Dark
Rough Justice
Scarecrows: Appalachian Tales
Thanatrauma
The Far Side of the Lake
The Harvest Child and Other Fantasies
The Hydrocephalic Ward (poems)
The Night Doctor and Other Tales
Twember
Ugly Behavior

Curious about other Crossroad Press books? Stop by our
website: http://crossroadpress.com
We offer quality writing
in digital, audio, and print formats.

Subscribe to our newsletter on the website homepage and
receive a free eBook.

www.ingramcontent.com/pod-product-compliance
Lightning Source LLC
Chambersburg PA
CBHW030251200626
46816CB00002BA/593